Peril for Your Thoughts

Freida,

Enjoy!!

Also by Kari Lee Townsend

Kicking the Habit

The Fortune Teller Mysteries
Tempest in the Tea Leaves
Corpse in the Crystal Ball
Trouble in the Tarot

Writing as Kari Lee Harmon
Naughty or Nice
Project Produce
Destiny Wears Spurs
Sleeping in the Middle

Peril for Your Thoughts

Kari Lee Townsend

This is a work of fiction. Names, characters, organizations, places, events, and incidents are either products of the author's imagination or are used fictitiously.

Originally published as a Kindle Serial, August 2013

Published by Thomas & Mercer, Seattle

www.apub.com

ISBN-13: 9781477849903
ISBN-10: 1477849904

Cover design by Inkd Inc

Library of Congress Control Number: 2013913998

Printed in the United States of America

This book is dedicated to my best friend
and critique partner, Barbara Witek. There is NO way
I could have ventured into the land of serials without you.
Thank you so much for going through this journey with me.
I wouldn't want to do this with anyone else.
Love you.

Episode 1

Chapter 1

"Kalliope, why won't you listen to your mama and go out with the nice Greek boy?" Ophelia Ballas boomed through the speaker on my cell phone. This was the fifth time she'd called today, and my patience was wearing thin.

"You're killing me, Ma," I responded loudly so she could hear me. I was working in the loft above Full Disclosure, my best friend Jazlyn Alvarez's boutique, as I put the final touches on my latest design.

"You're killing *me*," she ranted two decibels higher. "How am I supposed to have grandbabies if you won't date? And he's Greek, for goodness sake. Do you know how hard it is to find a nice Greek boy who isn't related to us in this town?"

Clearview, Connecticut, was a quaint small town with plenty of amenities and close enough to New York City to suit me perfectly. I didn't need or want a man. I sighed and then said, "He's *half* Greek, and you know why I don't date." I turned the manikin around and pinned another piece of black lace to the red satin nightie, readjusting it three times before I let go.

"It's just a phase. You'll grow out of it," was her response. The same response she always used.

"You've been saying that for the past twenty-eight years. I don't like germs, and I don't like to be touched. That's not a phase; that's a condition. One not exactly conducive to romance," I pointed out, turning the manikin around again and again to check out my handiwork.

I had learned to live with my little quirks and was coming to accept that marriage and children were not in my future. That's why I poured all of my fantasies into my lingerie designs, much to the horror of my family. They couldn't understand why a nice girl like me didn't design something respectable like wedding dresses. Yet most of my cousins and several of my aunts secretly commissioned me for a Kalli Original.

It didn't help that Jaz was a hot-blooded South American, with her supermodel mother's looks and her banker father's head for business. She had dated half the men in town. To say my family thought she was a bad influence would be putting it mildly. But I didn't care. I adored Jaz, and I loved what I did for a living.

"Condition smition. No one in our family has that," my mother broke into my thoughts. "I'm telling you it's just a phase."

"I'm adopted, Ma," I said wearily. "Remember?"

"You're mine, and that's what matters. Besides, you're all I've got. *Remember*?"

And just like that the same old guilt stabbed through me. My parents were the only Ballas members who couldn't conceive. As their only child, they were desperate to "fix" me and marry me off to the first available Greek boy they could find. Since Detective Nikos Stevens had moved to town, they'd been on a mission. I hadn't met him yet, but I'd heard he was only half Greek.

Apparently that was Greek enough.

"What's that? You're breaking up, Ma. Bad connection. I gotta go. I'll call you tomorrow."

I backed up and reached to the side to shut off my phone before my head exploded from the headache she'd given me, and then I lost my footing. Arms wind-milling, I stumbled back, hit the railing, and watched my feet flip over my head in a back somersault.

As if in slow motion, I felt weightless, sort of like flying. Cool air rushed past me as gravity took over and I fell one story down, landing flat on my back with a whoosh in the center of the store below. My head hit hard, and I felt like something popped internally. A high-pitched ringing clogged my ears, stars danced before my eyes, and I couldn't breathe... then everything faded to tunnel vision as the world around me went black.

"Kalli! Oh my God, Kalli! Talk to me, honey. Can you hear me?" echoed someone in the distance.

Expensive perfume that smelled like exotic flowers on a tropical island drifted to my nose. My lips parted, and I finally sucked in a much needed breath of fresh spring air blowing in from the open windows. Where was I? A car's horn honked from somewhere outside, sounding much closer as the ringing in my ears faded a bit. Oh, yeah. I was in Jaz's clothing shop. The metallic taste of blood coated my tongue from where I'd bitten it seconds ago.

I felt someone grab my hand and heard, *Oh, I knew I shouldn't have let her work up there. She's not the most graceful person. Her mother's gonna kill me.*

"I can hear you, you know," I said with my eyes still closed. "And don't worry about her." I slowly blinked my eyes open to find Jaz kneeling over me, her thick mass of honey-brown curls cascading down the front of her flowy designer dress more suited for a cocktail party than work as she held my hand. I cringed, and she immediately let go, backing up a step.

"Sorry," she mumbled, averting her amber eyes, but then her exotic features puckered into a frown. "What are you talking about? Don't worry about whom?"

"My mother." I discreetly fished the hand sanitizer out of my crisp cotton suit pocket, admittedly more suited for an office job, and poured some into my palm then rubbed my hands together. She was party central, and I was practical. She had the flair and the head for business, while I had the creativity and the common sense. So vastly different from one another, yet somehow together we complemented each other perfectly.

"Your mother?" Jaz blinked at me for a moment, looking at me in the oddest way, but then she shrugged. "Are you hurt?"

I thought about her question. Was I hurt? Oddly, no. I had a whopper of a headache, but that could still be from talking to my mother. Except, I felt different. Tingly. I ran through concussion symptoms in my head three times, but I didn't think that was it.

"I'm not sure," I said as I carefully rolled to my feet. I ran a hand over my head and discovered my normal chignon had fallen loose. Sliding my fingers through my long hair, I lifted the ends to inspect the golden-blond strands, but didn't see or feel any blood. Just a large lump on the back of my skull. "Nothing's broken," I said after testing my limbs.

"Maybe you should go to the doctor."

I was already shaking my head. "No way. You know how I feel about doctors. I'm fine, seriously." Jaz knew me too well. I was a bit of a hypochondriac, but doctors gave me more anxiety than worrying about my health. I preferred a more homeopathic approach.

She stared into my eyes, studying them closely as hers filled with worry and fear. "Pupils look normal and eyes as green as ever. I don't think you have a concussion, but you are so lucky you didn't hit any furniture. I'm just shocked you didn't break your neck . . . or worse." She closed her eyes and shuddered for a moment, then snapped them open with reprimand and anger now blazing within. "Are you crazy? You are not the most graceful person, you know."

"So you've said," I muttered.

She arched a brow as though she didn't remember, but then shrugged that off and sighed. "What the hell happened, anyway?"

"My mother." I held up my hands.

Jaz scowled. "Enough said. And you said not to worry about her. Ha!" She paused, the fire leaving her as quickly as it had appeared. She bit her full bottom lip and then blurted, "So, um, since you seem to miraculously be okay, are we still on for tonight?" She pouted her lips and fluttered her lashes in a way she had spent years perfecting.

"Wait, how long was I out?" I asked, still trying to process what had just happened to me.

"Only for a minute. So, what do you say?"

"I guess," I grudgingly responded, realizing nothing had changed. So much for things being different.

"Great." She clapped her hands then did a little dance—graceful being her middle name, I thought with envy. "Oh, chica, wait until you meet your blind date. You're gonna love him."

Envy shmenvy, I thought as my mother would say, my wistful smile evaporating instantly. "Don't get excited. I'm not going to *anything* him. I only agreed to this double date so you wouldn't have to meet your online date alone," I hollered after her.

"Technicalities," she called back as she salsa-ed her way through the clothing racks to the front of the store and flipped the sign to CLOSED.

Later that night, Jaz was running late as usual, so she'd asked me to go ahead and get us a table. I had agreed to her double date as a thank you for displaying my designs in her boutique. If it wasn't for her connections, I never would have gotten discovered by Interludes. To think that my spring collection would be available next year in such a high-end store in New York City was a dream come true.

I owed her. I just never imagined a double date would be the favor she would choose, especially knowing how I felt about dating. At least she had agreed to a small restaurant on the outskirts of town, run by a woman I'd gone to high school with. My family was Greek, aka they owned half the eating establishments in Clearview. We chose to go to Rosalita's Place, a small Mexican restaurant with great margaritas. I had a feeling I'd be having more than a few before the night was over.

After putting our names in for a table, I stepped outside in the cool evening air to wait for Jaz and catch my breath. Crowded places tended to get to me. Springtime in Connecticut was chilly, but dropping temperatures felt good. Nerves had set in big time, which was ridiculous because this wasn't even a *real* date. This was just someone I could spend one simple evening with and then walk away, no strings attached and no feelings hurt.

Jaz had made me go for a bit more flair than my normal practical attire, insisting I had to help her make a good impression on Darrin, the online guy she'd been chatting with for way too short a time, if you asked me. She barely knew the guy. I'd agreed to a sexy green silk number from her store, which was way too short and low cut for my tastes, but then I insisted on leaving my hair up. I felt more in control that way. Besides, a hair could fall into my food, and that just wouldn't do. I shivered simply thinking about it. Eating out gave me anxiety, so I only ate at places where I knew the kitchen was clean.

"Calm down, Ma. It's just dinner." A tall man with thick, wavy, coffee-colored hair, olive skin, and what looked like a heavily whiskered face even after a close shave came to a stop before me as he talked into his cell phone.

I didn't mean to eavesdrop, but it was kind of hard not to since he stood so close. Besides, the way he said "ma" had me riveted. He raised his eyes, and the most piercing blue I'd ever seen locked onto mine. I choked on a breath mint, then looked away, feeling like a fool.

I just hadn't expected that striking color is all. He began to pace, his earthy cologne caressing me in ways that made me most uncomfortable. I saw him look at his watch out of the corner of my eye while I pretended to inspect a hang nail and tried not to squirm. The guy didn't have a clue about personal space, something I was a stickler about.

"Just stop, okay?"

I blinked at him, startled, until I realized he was still on the phone and not talking to me.

"We've had this conversation over and over," he went on. "I'm thirty. I think I can handle my love life on my own. I have to go now...yes...no...good-bye, Ma." He shut his cell phone off completely and slipped it into the pocket of his gray sport coat. Parting the lapels, he loosened the tie over his baby blue dress shirt then dropped his large hands to his jean-clad hips. His eyes met mine once more, and I couldn't help notice how thick and long his lashes were. What on earth was wrong with me?

I smiled uncomfortably.

"Mothers," he muttered.

"Crazy species," I responded.

"They should have a warning label that says proceed with caution." He grunted.

"That says it all." I rolled my eyes.

We both laughed, and I relaxed for the first time that day.

His smile dimmed, and his jaw hardened a bit as though he was clenching his teeth. "More like *she* says it all. Over and over and over. She's relentless." He stared off like he was speaking to himself.

"For what it's worth, I feel your pain," I said gently, bringing his gaze back to my own. "Mine won't take no for an answer even when I already have a date."

"Mine, too." He nodded. "It doesn't matter how far I move, she finds a way to interfere with my life."

"You're preaching to the choir, mister." I held a hand over my heart.

"Amen to that." He smiled a genuine smile this time that softened his chiseled features in a most appealing way.

"Well, I'd better not keep my date waiting. Don't want to make a bad first impression."

"Something tells me you'll do just fine." I gave him a genuine smile back, and he lingered as though he didn't want to leave.

Standing up straight and inhaling a deep breath, he finally said, "Well, thank you for that. It helps. And good luck to you. Is your date inside?"

"You know, I'm not sure. I suppose I should check," I forced the words out, sounding less than excited to my own ears. "Don't want to make a bad first impression, either," I added, swinging my fist through the air in a non-verbal *yay* that I so didn't feel.

"Something tells me you'll do *more* than just fine." He winked as he opened the door and held it. "After you."

"Thanks." I stood, thinking here was a man I wouldn't mind sharing a conversation with over dinner, but I knew it wouldn't work out. It never did.

I walked inside the southwestern-themed room and headed to my empty table, feeling suddenly nervous again. I couldn't believe I was still the only one there. One thing was for sure, Jaz was in big trouble. I planned to clue her into that the second I saw her. In the meantime, I sat down and watched the attractive nice man I'd just met stop and speak to the hostess. It dawned on me that I'd never even gotten his name.

Seconds later, Jaz walked in, looking as fabulous as ever in a dazzling red number that should have been illegal. A huge smile spread across her face, and she marched right up to . . . to *him*. My shoulders slumped a bit as she hugged him hard. He must be her online date. A small twinge of jealousy pinged through me. Not so much because she got to go out with *him*, but because she could date at all. Once guys found out about my "quirks," they lost interest pretty quickly.

End of romance.

I'd learned not to set myself up for that kind of disappointment any more. This time was no exception. I pasted a bright smile on my face when I realized they were headed my way, deep in conversation. When they reached my table, the man's eyes met mine once more and then sprang wide with pleasant surprise and curiosity.

Jaz bit her bottom lip like she had earlier, which usually meant she was up to something—not a good sign—and then she went for it. "Kalliope Ballas, meet your blind date, Detective Nikos Stevens."

His curiosity turned to shock followed closely by disbelief. My smile faded as my jaw unhinged. Jaz wasn't just in big trouble...she was a dead woman. No wonder my mother had stopped calling the shop. My blind date wasn't someone I could spend one simple evening with to pay off a debt and then walk away. Oh, no. That would be way too easy. This wasn't just any date...

This was my mother's *nice Greek boy*!

Chapter 2

Two hours and two margaritas later, I was ready to call it a night as I sat across from Nik. He sat next to Jaz's big blond Nordic God, Darrin, who had arrived shortly after she'd delivered her bombshell. I could tell by the look in her eyes she'd known the detective was the "Nik" my mother had been trying to fix me up with. I'd ordered a drink immediately, and awkwardness had set in. Meanwhile, her Darling Darrin was going on and on about himself. Nik, on the other hand, wasn't any happier than I was to realize I was the *nice Greek girl* his "ma" had been trying to fix him up with since she'd found out he was moving to Clearview.

I should have had a clue.

Greeks weren't anything if not thorough. She'd done her homework and had found out which Greek women were of age and single. Since he was only half Greek, most of my cousins had said no. But since my parents were as desperate as she seemed to be, they'd been in cahoots ever since.

Neither one of us wanted anything to do with having two Greek families to deal with, not to mention we weren't ready to settle down. Only one problem. It didn't matter what we wanted. When Greek mamas got involved, weddings were being planned from the get-go.

"No offense, Kalli," Nik said, "but I just arrived in Clearview. I only said yes to Jaz because she seemed nice enough, and she offered to show me around town. I really need to focus on my career. You know how it is."

"No offense, Detective, but I hardly remember asking you to focus on me," I pointed out. "And I only said yes because I owed Jaz a favor. You're really not my type." I smirked. "You know how it is." It frustrated me that I let him get to me. That normally never happened. I liked being in control. There was just something about him that unsettled me.

He narrowed his eyes. "Good to know. And just so *you* know, you're not exactly my type, either."

"Fabulous." I wiped off the outside of my water glass where the waiter had touched it to refill, and then I rearranged my napkin three times before I took a sip.

"I'm surprised you didn't bring your own glass, too." He smirked back at me, and then those unnerving blue eyes of his studied me intently.

I cleared my throat. "I always carry my own silverware. You have no idea what sort of sanitation device they use in places like these."

"It's called a dishwasher. Last time I checked they kill 99% of bacteria. Most likely cleaner than the inside of your purse."

"Ah, yes," I held up my finger, "but they don't kill the bacteria on the waiter's hands, now do they? And you obviously don't know me. You could eat out of my purse it's that clean."

"The scary thing is I actually believe it." He snorted, then sighed as his leg bumped into mine beneath the table.

I looked down and frowned at my purse when I heard, *I'm usually always the perfect gentleman. What is it about you that brings out the worst side of me?*

My eyes whipped up to his and I gaped at him, shocked that he would ask me that. "Excuse me?"

"Never mind." He turned to focus on Darrin, and I did the same.

Normally I didn't care what people thought of me or my quirks, and it made me so angry that it actually mattered to me what he thought. I repeat...Jaz was so dead when this night was over. I tried to give her "the look" so she would know I was more than ready to go, but she clung to every word that came out of Dingleburg Darrin's mouth.

"And then I traveled to Europe and closed a forty-million-dollar deal all before lunch. It was a good week." A smug look seemed permanently plastered to his handsome yet annoying face.

Nik's leg bumped mine beneath the table once more, but no matter how much I discreetly squirmed, there was no room to move away.

That is such bullshit.

"Well, that was rude." I looked away from Darrin and shot Nik a surprised look. He was a lot more vocal than earlier, like he suddenly had no filters.

"What?" He scratched his head, his brows puckering together as he stared at me.

"I hear ya, man," Darrin said to Nik. "Those bean burritos will do you in every time. Word of advice. That's not cool in front of the ladies." He snorted, laughing at himself. There was nothing appealing about him except for his admittedly amazing body and looks, but I knew Jaz. That was all she cared about. Same as me, she had no interest in getting serious. Yet unlike me, she was more than ready to be seriously seduced.

"But I—" Nik started to say with a slightly flushed face.

"I can't believe you live such an exciting life," Jaz purred to Darrin, cutting Nik off and drawing my attention back to their conversation as she played him like a violin.

"It's no big deal. Maybe I'll take you some time if you want," he purred back to her, and she gave him a look that said, *Yeah, baby, I most definitely want!*

Take her where, to the shed? Because you're obviously a tool. International businessman my ass; you're a car salesman. I saw your slip-up on eRomance.com Why don't you take Little Miss Designer instead? Maybe she can design you a new life. Then again, you're probably not her type either.

I gasped, completely stunned as I focused on Nik and didn't even try to hide how appalled I was. "*You're* the tool," I said to him, then hissed, "What are you doing?"

"What are you talking about?" Nik asked, looking at me warily. "What did I do this time?"

"You know what you said, and so does everyone else." If he didn't care, then I didn't either. I didn't even try to lower my voice this time. I might not like Darrin, but I wasn't about to ruin things for Jaz if that's what made her happy. "I just can't believe Darrin is being so gracious."

Darrin gave him a look of sympathy. "Sorry, man. Some of us have a way with the ladies, and some of us don't. Better luck next time."

Jaz shot me a look as though I were the one ruining things for her. "You'll have to excuse her, gentlemen. She took a bit of a spill this morning."

I sent her a questioning look back.

Her expression changed to one of worry and concern as she studied my pupils again. "Honey, are you sure you're feeling okay. I still think you should have gone to the doctor. You're, um, not quite yourself."

"I'm fine," I said, confusion knitting my brow. I crossed my arms and stared at Nik. "Just know that I'm watching you."

"You do that," he responded, staring right back at me. *Mothers aren't the only crazy species around here.*

"Aha!" I pointed at him. "See what I mean?"

Jaz glanced at Nik and then back to me, shaking her head no and looking more confused than ever.

I stared at his mouth when it suddenly hit me. I'd heard him speak, but his lips hadn't moved even a smidgen. "I think I, um, was mistaken," I said as my breathing picked up and my heartbeat started pounding in my chest.

"You were saying?" he asked with that damned eyebrow of his arched sky-high as we reached for our water glasses at the same time and our hands touched. *You might look like an angel on the outside, sweetheart, but you sure are one odd woman on the inside.*

Before, it had sounded like he'd muttered, but now it sounded like he had raised his voice and was speaking right next to my ear. I jerked my hand back.

He frowned. *Now, what the hell did I—*

I jerked my leg away from his until we weren't touching at all, and the voice in my head stopped.

As much as it would kill me, I had to know. I reached out and grabbed his hand with mine.

His eyebrows crept all the way to his hairline, but he didn't say a word, yet I heard, *Oh yeah, someone has been watching one too many episodes of the Looney Tunes.* He gently pulled his hand away from mine, and the voice stopped once again.

"Sorry," I said, whipping out my hand sanitizer and scrubbing my hands, which didn't help my case any, judging by his expression. "You're right, Jaz. I'm not myself today. In fact, I think I'm going to be sick." I bolted to the bathroom with Jaz hot on my heels.

Nothing had changed? Ha! Apparently everything had changed, because somehow, someway I was hearing voices in my head, but I *wasn't* crazy. Oh, no no no. Crazy was treatable, and that would be too easy. What I had was much worse.

I could read people's minds.

"Thanks for giving me a ride home," I said to Nik.

Jaz had cornered me in the bathroom, refusing to let me drive home. I'd explained what had happened, and she'd been ready to call 911, but I convinced her it was just the margaritas after a head injury talking. She'd finally capitulated, but only if I agreed to let Nik drive me home. She had plans with Darrin. She swore she wasn't in on my mother's scheming; however, she *did* think Detective Dreamy was exactly what I needed. And I let *her* know exactly what I thought of that.

She so owed me!

"No problem," Nik said, glancing at me with a frown as I hugged the door, not chancing a random touch. After gaining way too much information from Jaz when she'd held my hand in the restroom—information that I'd yet to recover from—I hadn't said a word since getting in the car.

I had always thought if I could just read people's minds, my life would be so much easier. Not so. Reading people's minds was scary, giving TMI—too much information—a whole new meaning. I'd heard of dog whisperers, cat whisperers, horse whisperers, and even ghost whisperers. What did that make me... a people whisperer?

"What was that?" Nik asked.

"What was what?"

"I thought you said something."

Oh, God, had I? I couldn't be sure. It was all so confusing. "No, yes, maybe... I don't know, did I?"

"Kalli, it's okay. Really." He took a deep breath and glanced at me with a smile. "I think we got off on the wrong foot. Hi, I'm Nik Stevens."

"Kalli Ballas," I responded, still a bit wary.

"Did I tell you I'm half Greek? I hear you're Greek by association. That's Greek enough for both our families, apparently." We laughed, and his voice lowered an octave to a husky soft tone. "Look, our mamas have made us a bit crazy. You're not alone, okay? Not to mention, you took one hell of a spill from what I hear. Are you sure you don't want me to take you to the hospital?"

"I'm sure." I smiled at him and meant it this time. The stranger I'd met outside the restaurant was back, and once again, I relaxed. "Thank you for not making me feel like a freak. I've had enough of that in my life."

"Nobody's perfect," he said quietly. "Believe it or not, we all have our quirks." He shot me a wink.

Oh, boy. Not good. Nikos the argumentative, sarcastic, smug Greek I could deal with, but Nik the sweet, sympathetic, gorgeous nice guy was way too dangerous to be around. Time to change the subject. "So, tell me, is Darrin a decent guy? I mean, you didn't find anything bad on his profile, did you?"

Nikos and Nik disappeared as Detective Stevens took over, sending me a sharp look. "How did you know I checked out his profile?"

Crap. He hadn't said that out loud. I'd read his mind. I would have to pay closer attention to what information I revealed in the future. "You're a cop, and knowing Jaz, I assumed she asked you to check him out before she agreed to the date. I don't know. Something about him seems off. I just want to make sure she'll be okay alone with him."

He relaxed a bit, but his features were still guarded and unreadable. "You assumed right. Jaz did ask me to check out his dating page. Nothing too invasive, just look it over. Far as I can tell, he seems okay. Other than lying about what he does for a living. He's a car salesman, not an international businessman. He's harmless, just a total player."

"Exactly how Jaz likes them. She likes to meet them, love them, and leave them. Why do you think she had to move on to men from out of town?"

"Interesting. That would explain why she's not the most popular person in town with the ladies, yet the men seem to love her."

"Exactly. Except some of them don't know how to let go. That's why I don't date."

"Really? Again, interesting."

"Okay, so it's not the only reason, but it's reason enough. Relationships cause complications, and lately, my life has gotten complicated enough."

He glanced at me as we pulled up to the house Jaz and I shared and said, "You are just one big mystery, Miss Ballas."

"The power of a woman, Mr. Stevens. Gotta keep the other half guessing." I winked at him this time. Why not end the evening on a playful note. It wasn't like I would have to see him on a regular basis, so what was the harm? Our town was small, but it wasn't that small. If I could avoid running into him, we would be just fine. "Wait a minute. You don't have to pull into the driveway."

"Actually, I do."

"Seriously, I can get out by the curb."

He ignored me and pulled in anyway, then climbed out of the car.

I scrambled after him. "Wait. You really don't have to walk me to the door." Oh, God, please don't tell me he expected a good-night kiss. He had to know I was fooling. This wasn't a real date. Besides, he'd seen enough tonight to let him know kissing was *not* an option.

"Again, I do."

I walked beside him, fishing in my purse for my keys. The quicker I got this over with, the better. I practically tore the doorknob off in my haste to jam the key in the lock. The door finally swung open, and Miss Priss stuck her head out, purred at me, took one look at the detective, and then stuck her nose in the air as she walked away.

"I missed you, too, Prissy," I said to her retreating back, welcoming the feel of something normal. She was a beautiful calico cat, and her name was Priscilla, but everyone insisted on calling her Miss Priss because it fit her to a tee. "Well, Detective, it was nice meeting you. I hope everything goes well for you in fitting into this town. And I apologize ahead of time for anything my family might put you through."

"Please call me Nik. It was nice meeting you, too, Kalli. And don't worry about your family. I've had enough practice to know exactly how to deal with them." He smiled, but made no move to walk back to his car.

A loud whining noise sounded from the door to the other half of the house. When I'd gotten my big break with the store in New York, I'd stopped working in my parents' restaurant, moved out of their house, and moved in with Jaz. She owned a big old colonial house with a huge fenced-in backyard on Picture Perfect Drive—a dead end road just off of Main Street.

She'd had carpenters split the house into two halves, insisting she didn't need that much space. I couldn't afford to rent the other half by myself yet, and I was determined not to take charity from anyone, so I paid to live with her. So far the other half had remained vacant. She insisted she hadn't met anyone nice enough to rent it to yet.

I had been away in New York City for the past week, meeting the people at Interludes and firming up plans for my spring line. Everyone had been there except my PR representative, whom I would be meeting with for dinner right here in Clearview. I had gotten home late last night, excited yet exhausted. By the time I had left this morning for Full Disclosure, I hadn't noticed a thing.

Someone had obviously changed her mind and moved in. By the sounds of it, they had a dog. A rather large dog. Why hadn't Jaz told me? My insides knotted, and I suspected that was why. Cats I could handle. They were self-sufficient and as clean as me. Dogs...not so much. Her mission was to help me come out of my shell. Was this part of her plan? I swallowed hard.

"Wh-What's that?" I asked.

"That's Wolfgang," he answered.

"What's a wolfgang?"

"Not what...who." Nik grinned like a schoolboy and pulled out a set of keys from his sport coat and then proceeded to unlock the door.

My jaw hit the floor.

A humongous St. Bernard leapt out the door, stood on his hind legs, and slammed his front paws onto the detective's broad shoulders, standing nearly as tall as his six-foot-something frame. The canine's enormous tongue tried to reach every inch of the detective's face, slobber flying everywhere, and the detective just laughed.

Laughed!

I convulsed and gagged, trying not to vomit. That was all it took for "Wolfgang" to notice me. His eyes grew huge and focused on me. I didn't have to be a dog whisperer to know his thoughts: *Fresh meat.*

He dropped down on all four paws and lunged.

I screamed.

Prissy appeared out of nowhere and hissed, her hair standing straight on end.

Detective Stevens grabbed the dog's collar and yanked. "Heel, Wolfgang."

The dog stopped immediately and sat, though his tailed thumped rapidly and his hind end kept fidgeting. He whined in a high-pitched, pathetic wail.

"I know, buddy. It's okay." Nik patted the top of the beast's head.

"I-It's not okay. What's he doing in there?"

The detective shrugged. "Checking out his new home, I guess."

"Wh-where is his owner?" I knew the answer, but I just couldn't wrap my bruised and battered brain around it.

"You're looking at him." Nik the nice guy was gone, Detective Stevens the cunning cop was on break, and Nikos the smug Greek was back in full force.

"Good night, Detective," I said stiffly as he stood there grinning like a fiend over my reaction to his beast. I quickly squeezed through my door and slammed it shut behind me, then leaned against it, thinking, *Great, just great*!

I hated chaos, I hated unpredictability, I hated change. What more could possibly happen to upset the peaceful, steady order of my life?

Chapter 3

Maybe it was all just a dream.

I woke up the next morning and stretched, feeling the back of my head. No bump. I listened for sounds from next door, but there was no sign of the beast—man or canine. I padded over to the window and glanced outside. No car except mine, which if last night had happened, my car would still be at the restaurant.

Things were looking up.

But Jaz's car was gone. I pursed my lips. Then again, she was an early riser and would be at the boutique already, I reasoned. If last night *had* happened, she'd still be up in her nookie nook—a Jazism for the loft. Same with a booty-que call being a Jazism for a booty call in her boutique. I cringed. I would have to disinfect the loft all over again if I planned to get anything done up there. If she still let me up there after my little incident. I had my work cut out for me today.

I shook off those thoughts and decided to remain positive. Today was a whole new day. A day to start fresh. A day filled with infinite possibilities, I thought, having no clue that in a little while today would become one of the worst days of my life.

I quickly showered, washing my hair three times, and then dressed in yet another practical suit. I already felt more like myself. I rechecked my house three times, making sure the throw pillows were at the precise angle and every knickknack was in its place. I fed Prissy and then headed out the door with a positive outlook.

Until I ran smack dab into Detective Stevens.

His bag of groceries and cup of coffee flew from his hands. He wrapped his arms around me and twisted so I landed on top of him as we fell to the hard ground with an oomph. "Whoa, there. You okay?" he asked. *Damn she smells so good. Feels good too. Soft curves in all the right places. I just wish—*

"Oh, my God. I don't want to know." I quickly rolled off him and sat up, pulling my suit coat down and searching my pockets for my hand sanitizer. I finally found it, and my heart rate slowed as I scrubbed my hands.

"What's wrong? You don't want to know if you're okay?" He rolled to his feet in his jeans, more casual sport coat, and T-shirt this time, then reached down to help me up.

"Yeah, that's it. I'd rather not know." I scrambled to my feet on my own, sure, now, that last night was *definitely* not a dream. And he smelled great too. Oh, man, was I in big trouble.

"Okay, then. I'll, ah, see you later. I have to feed Wolfgang." He picked up the bag of groceries and held up the dog food he must have gone to the store for, then scooped up his empty foam coffee cup. "I'll just grab a cup at the office. By the way, I had your car towed back early this morning. I figured you'd need it for work."

"You figured right. Thanks. See you later, Detective Stevens." Much later, I hoped.

"It's Nik," he hollered after me.

I scurried to my car before he let Wolfgang out. So much for it all being a dream. I could still read minds, the beast still lived beside me, and Nik the "nice one" had decided to stick around. Where was Nikos when I needed him? This wasn't a dream at all. It was more like a living nightmare.

Spring showers I was used to, but today looked like the Heavens were about to open up and shower their wrath upon us. Black clouds, a streak of lightning, a crack of thunder. Why did my gut tell me it was a sign that things were about to get worse?

My phone rang while I was still sitting in the driveway.

Glancing at the caller ID, I prayed for strength as I answered. "Before you even get started, I'm okay, Ma."

"I want you to come home, right now. Your yiayia Dido is having heart palpitations. You'll never be able to forgive yourself if you send her to an early grave. She says your papou Homer knows a guy, and your father agrees he comes from good stock. He mostly works with animals, but I know how you don't like doctors, and—"

"Ma, stop. Grandma and Grandpa will be just fine, but tell them thanks for me. And tell Pop not to worry. I'm not going to a doctor of any kind. I'm fine. It's just a bump on the head." I refused to dwell on it being anything more before I hyperventilated.

"At least rub some superglue on it and wrap it in Duct tape, or use some of that aloe from the plant I gave you."

Superglue and Duct tape were my father's answers to fixing everything, and my mother swore by aloe as her cure-all.

"Falling fifteen feet is not just a bump on the head," she rambled on, not surprising me in the least that she had already heard the details. This town was small, and Ma had eyes and ears everywhere. "Are you out of your mind?" she continued. "You can't take these things lightly. Remember what happened to your cousin Frona when she fell off the apple wagon? That was only four feet off the ground, and her head swelled to the size of a watermelon. She never was the same after that. There could be something seriously wrong with your brain."

I stifled a hysterical laugh and thought, *If you only knew.*

She went into a whole monologue about brain injuries, but I stopped listening as the detective walked out the door. He stared up at the sky as the first few sprinkles started to fall, and then he looked at me curiously. I pointed to the phone and rolled my eyes.

He laughed and gave me the OK sign and a sympathetic look, then climbed into his car. I watched him answer the CB radio thingy, say something, then shoot me an odd look. Seconds later, he disconnected and turned on his lights, then peeled out of the driveway without another look in my direction.

Well, that didn't seem good.

"Ma, I gotta go."

"You always *gotta* go these days."

"I promise I'll make it up to you just as soon as I finish my book of designs. I want to make some progress before I meet my PR person later today. We're supposed to go over a promotion plan for my new spring line, so they're pushing me to finish on time. Unfortunately, you can't rush creativity, and I haven't exactly had a whole lot of peace and quiet lately."

"You would if you lived back home. When are you gonna get a real job and design something respectable lik—"

"Look at that, my phone is dying. Sorry, Ma. Talk later." I hung up and pulled out of my driveway, heading toward Full Disclosure. Stealing a move from the detective, I was just about to turn my phone off completely when it rang once more. I glanced down at the ID. Speaking of Full Disclosure...

Turning on my Bluetooth, I answered the call. "Sorry I'm late, Jaz. I got hung up talking to my mother, but I'm on my way now. Anything wrong?"

"Everything's wrong," she wailed, completely out of character for her.

"Oh my gosh, what happened? It's Darrin, isn't it? I knew there was something off about him. Did he hurt you?"

"I'm fine...he's the one who's not. Oh, my God, it's so awful."

"Jaz, focus. What's wrong with him?"

"He's dead, Kalli. Deader than the doorknob to Disclosure, and they think I killed him."

"You can't seriously think Jaz is the one who killed Darrin," I said to Detective Stevens later that day at the police station as we sat across from him in his new office with his partner, Detective Boomer Matheson. "You know her," I added, appealing to the Nik I knew resided within him.

"Not really," he replied with an emotion as blank and bland as the white walls in the room. "Look, I'm not saying she did kill the victim, Miss Ballas." The detective was in full cop mode now, with Nik the "nice one" nowhere to be found as he put forth his best professional side in front of his partner. Go figure. "I'm just saying she was the last person that we know of to see him alive, and he was found dead in her boutique with a bullet to the gut from the same type gun registered in her name. My hands are tied. I have to follow all leads. She has no alibi and admits to being with the victim all night long."

Detective Matheson sat on the edge of his desk and grunted over that last comment, obviously not worried about looking professional himself. If this was good cop, bad cop, he was definitely the latter. Of course, it didn't help that he was one of the many broken hearts Jaz had left in her wake. A decent-looking man with russet-colored hair and hazel eyes, but his personality was seriously lacking.

Jaz scowled at Boomer and focused on Nik. For the first time since I'd known her, she didn't look glamorous. She was free of make-up and in a sweat suit. A designer sweat suit, but a sweat suit nonetheless. She pulled herself together and said, "I've had the gun for years. From back in my city days. You must know how it is, being from the city yourself. Small town or not, old habits die hard, Detective." She blew her nose, genuinely upset. "I keep it behind the register, but it hasn't been fired since I learned how to use it years ago at a pistol range."

"Maybe someone tried to rob her, found the gun, and shot him," I said hopefully.

"How could she not hear the gun go off?" Detective Matheson asked, sounding like he didn't believe a word that came out of her mouth.

"How could no one else hear the gun go off?" Jaz snapped back. "Besides, we'd had a lot to drink."

Again, Boomer grunted. "This is the business district. Most people go to their homes in the residential district to sleep," he pointed out. "No one would have heard the shot from a puny gun like that."

"Normally size matters," Jaz shot him a fake sympathy look, "but in this case, a gunshot sound is a gunshot sound. Loud and ear piercing."

"Kind of like someone else I know," he countered back.

"Unless someone was walking or driving through that area in the middle of the night. I don't think the real killer would have risked it," Detective Stevens cut in.

"The throw pillow Jaz sits on behind the register was missing," I said. "Maybe someone used it as a silencer."

He and Jaz both stared at me, looking surprised.

"What can I say? I'm observant." I felt my cheeks heat.

Detective Matheson's eyes narrowed, and I was sure I didn't want to know what *he* was thinking.

"Okay, fine. I've always thought it was highly unsanitary and secretly sprayed it with disinfectant when she wasn't looking. Same as I do with half the things in her shop." Jaz gasped, and I winced with a sorry look, then turned my gaze back on Boomer. "I notice things like that. Satisfied?"

He just grunted again, making some notes—and making me seriously irritated. The man was not very likable.

"You were saying?" Detective Stevens asked encouragingly, showing the first genuine signs that he really did want to help clear Jaz's name.

I clung to that and continued, ignoring Boomer the Butthead. "Anyway, when I got to the store today, I couldn't stand the mess. There was so much blood." I swallowed hard, my throat suddenly dry and my skin feeling like it was crawling. I took a breath and continued, "So I did what I always do. I started cleaning, as much as the CSI team would allow, that is. That's when I noticed the pillow was gone."

"Did you move it?" he asked Jaz.

"Moving my butt pillow was the last thing on my mind last night. Darrin and I headed straight up to my nookie nook—my loft—with a bottle of wine and didn't come down until this morning. Or at least I didn't. That's when I found him lying on the floor by the front door in a pool of blood."

"Yet nothing was taken and there was no sign of a break-in, correct?" Detective Stevens checked his notes.

"Correct. I don't know how anyone could have gotten in. I just know I didn't do it."

"No gun, either," said Detective Matheson, taking over. "Like the killer hid it just before we got here. Yet you admit to having the same type of gun that it appears the killer used, which is also missing. Convenient if you ask me."

"Why would I admit to that if I killed him with it?" Jaz stood up and started pacing.

"We would have found that out in time." Detective Matheson shrugged.

"Look, I'm cooperating," she said right in his face. He didn't even flinch. "I might not have an alibi, but I certainly don't have motive, either. And I have no idea where the stupid murder weapon is."

"Isn't your MO to meet them, love them, and leave them?" Boomer sneered.

Given Boomer's history with Jaz, it wasn't out of the ordinary for him to make a comment like this. However, the way he used the exact words I'd said to Nik made my stomach turn.

Jaz shot me a horrified look, and I nailed Nik with a *How could you* look. He must have repeated what I'd said to his partner. I'd only meant Darrin was her type because he wasn't the serious sort. Detective Stevens didn't quite meet my eyes.

"Hence the word *leave* them, not kill them," I sputtered, shooting Detective Matheson a murderous look.

"We're just trying to prepare you for what type of questions you'll be asked. Are you sure you don't want your attorney present?" Detective Stevens asked quietly.

Jaz thrust her chin up defiantly. "I have nothing to hide."

"Then why didn't you call 911?" Detective Moron asked, butting in again.

"I told you I overslept. I woke up to sirens wailing and came down to find Mrs. Flannigan pounding on the front door. She's one of my regular customers and knew I was having a sale today. She's the one who called 911. You know the rest."

"Are we done here? I think Ms. Alvarez has been through enough for one day. Don't you think so, Detective?" I shot Detective Stevens a look that said *You owe me*.

"Well, I don't know—" Matheson started to speak.

"I think you're right, Miss Ballas. We're done here," Detective Stevens said, giving his partner a firm no-nonsense look.

His partner stared him down, then finally backed off. "Fine. You know the drill. Don't leave town, Ms. Alvarez. And call us if you can think of anything else. We'll be in touch."

"Oh, don't worry. I've got your number," she snarled.

And I had an edge, I thought. I shuffled her out the door as quickly as I could. I truly believed everything happened for a reason. Maybe this mind-reading ability had happened to me at the perfect time. My best friend needed me, and I had access to information others didn't. Whether it would be admissible in court, or even believable to the average person, didn't matter. I would find a way around that. I wouldn't stop until I found a way to clear my best friend's name. I owed her that much. One thing was certain…

I wouldn't stop until I found the real killer.

Episode 2

Chapter 4

"I don't like her." My mother rubbed her hands on her olive oil–splattered and spice-stained apron, having sampled most of the menu today alone. What could I say? My family liked to eat.

"You don't even know her, Ma." I sighed, having a sinking feeling that tonight was going to be the longest dinner of my life.

My new PR person for Interludes, Natasha Newlander, had called earlier, letting me know she had arrived in Clearview. We were supposed to meet for dinner to go over the promotion plan for my new Kalli Originals spring line. Of all the restaurants she could pick, she had to choose my parents' place, Aphrodite. The goddess of love, beauty, and all things Greek filled every inch of space, with plenty of marble statues scattered about just short of overkill.

Ophelia Ballas squinted her dark-brown eyes and stared at the overly thin woman who was fashionably late and had made my cousin Eleni seat her at three different tables until she was satisfied. Strike one. She wore her short-cropped dark-red hair slicked back in a sleek style that somehow matched her perfectly tailored purple suit and four-inch heels. Apparently purple was the new "it" color. The woman couldn't be more than five feet tall and looked as though she hadn't had a decent meal in weeks. Strike two. Things were *not* looking good. If she reached strike three, there was no telling what my family would do.

"Oh, I know her, all right," my mother said, her Greek accent growing thicker with her irritation. "She's from that big fancy city that put stars in your eyes, but her kind are no good I tell you. They come in here thinking they are better than the rest of us with their expensive clothes and fat wallets."

"She chose your restaurant, so she must have good taste. She can't be all that bad, right?" Flattery was my only hope of salvaging the evening that had barely started. "All I'm asking is that you give her a chance."

My mother's scowl diminished slightly as she squared her shoulders with pride. Other than me, Aphrodite was the apple of my parents' eyes. Their firstborn. Something they'd actually birthed on their own. "Well, who wouldn't like Aphrodite with her beautiful Greek culture on display and food prepared with skill and pride." My mother's scowl was back. "If that pointy-nosed bird only orders a salad, I'm throwing her out. Who eats this late at night, anyway? Most people around here are finishing dessert and heading home."

"Things are different in the city, Ma. Most people from there are just getting started as you're heading to bed."

"No wonder she can't eat. That's horrible for your digestion, and just one more reason why you should never move away from home. That city is not good for you."

"I'm not moving there, my designs are. At most I'll make an occasional trip for business, so you can relax." I patted her shoulder. It was the closest to a hug I could get.

Her expression softened. "I'll relax when you stop hanging around with troublemakers. First, that hussy you work with scandalized everyone with being involved in murder."

"Allegedly involved."

"Same difference."

"Not really."

She went on as though I hadn't even spoken. "Then you start fraternizing with a woman who wants to starve you and take you away from me."

"She's not taking me away from you. She's helping me launch my new line."

"That's another thing. Your work is fifty shades of embarrassment to this family. Why can't you be a good girl like your cousins? Settle down, get married, and give me some grandbabies. At the very least get a boyfriend."

"Ma, you promised . . ." I had to force myself not to whine. My mother had a way of bringing out the child in me, and right now I felt like throwing a temper tantrum.

She threw up her hands and shook her big poof of black teased hair. "All right, all right. I'll stop for now. Go eat before you faint, Kalliope, but know I'll be watching that woman. One wrong move, and I'll—"

"Throw her out. I get it. Just behave yourself, for my sake, please."

She let out a heavy sigh, then patted my cheek before I could protest. "For you, my darling. Only for you. And then you can do something for me, no?" She grinned as she walked away with a spring in her step.

I rubbed my cheek with the sleeve of my suit coat and frowned. Why did I feel like she had just won some secret battle I knew nothing about?

Shrugging off my unease, I pasted on a smile and headed to Natasha Newlander's table with the stars in my eyes shining brightly. I was so excited to start this new venture,

I could barely contain myself. I still couldn't believe it was actually happening. "Ms. Newlander, it's a pleasure to finally meet you."

Natasha stood as I arrived and smiled back, looking professional and sophisticated. Someone I aspired to be. "The pleasure is all mine, Ms. Ballas. Sorry to have missed you last week. I had some urgent matters with another out-of-town client that had to be dealt with in person, but I'm here now." She held out her hand, and I didn't even freak out. I had prepared myself, knowing I would have to shake her hand. Discreetly holding my breath, I shook her hand firmly.

Her smile might be pleasant, but her grip was tight and she held on longer than necessary. A wave of distaste and resentment swept over me and then I heard, *Great. Erickson assigned Marcus to a top designer while I get Little Miss Sunshine. It's so unfair. Why do women have to work so hard to get ahead in this business?*

I tugged my hand away, lost my smile, and sat down as the stars faded from my eyes big-time. I was going to excuse myself to slip away and rub some hand sanitizer on, but my stubborn streak emerged. I pulled out the small bottle I always carried with me and blatantly squirted a generous amount into my palm and scrubbed hard.

Natasha narrowed her eyes a bit and asked as she sat, "Is something wrong?"

"I just feel a bit icky all of a sudden, but don't worry. I'm tougher than I look."

She arched a sleek auburn brow. "That's good. This business isn't easy." A flash of vulnerability crossed her face, and I decided to cut her some slack. I couldn't blame her for wanting to get ahead. I'd been around Jaz long enough to know getting ahead in any business was tough for women. Maybe Natasha wasn't as mean as she seemed. Maybe she was just ambitious. Now *that* was something I could relate to.

"So it would seem." I relaxed and gave her a genuine smile.

She studied me curiously, looking like she'd never come across a woman like me before. "Something tells me you'll do just fine." She actually gave me a genuine smile back.

Eleni stopped by and took our order. She was the perfect waitress: pretty, personable, and polite. Yet even her smile faded a bit by the time Natasha was through with her. Then my cousin Frona appeared out of nowhere, her dark hair in cockeyed pigtails and her apron on inside out. She refilled our coffee mugs with water, our water glasses with coffee, and then opened Natasha's napkin and stuffed it down her shirt before skipping back into the kitchen.

Natasha gasped. "What was that? This is unacceptable. I'm speaking to the manager."

"Wait," I quickly said. "Let me. I know the owners. Don't mind the poor woman. She fell off an apple wagon and hasn't been the same since. She's supposed to be on dish duty, but sometimes she gets confused. Excuse me." I slipped into the back, yelled at Ma, gently scolded Frona, and bribed Eleni to keep an eye on her before returning to my table. "Our dinner is on the house," I stated apologetically.

"Well done, Ms. Ballas, though I would have had her fired." She studied her manicured nails, then flicked a piece of lint off her arm. "Let's hope you are even more efficient with your book of designs. Speaking of the book, when can I expect it to be ready?"

No pressure, I thought, and so much for giving her the benefit of the doubt. Her ambition clearly outweighed her compassion.

"Well, Mr. Erickson told me I had a month."

"And I'm telling you we need it in two weeks." She stared me down, but I refused to look away. "Erickson might be the CEO, but the PR department is your bread and butter. We can make or break a new line. If you want a stellar launch, we need all the time we can get. I need that book ASAP."

"I don't want to hold you up any longer than necessary, but you can't rush creativity," I replied carefully.

Her face stiffened ever so slightly, but her smile remained in place. "Understood, Ms. Ballas, but creativity alone doesn't pay the bills. I need that book to get started on a proper PR plan. I am at your disposal. Maybe I can take a peek at the book and—"

I shook my head before she had half the words out. "I'm sorry, but I don't let anyone see my work until it's finished. That's one rule I won't break for anyone."

"Oh, you artists are a funny lot," she said with a chuckle. I didn't have to be a mind reader to imagine the mental eye roll she must be giving me.

"We do have our quirks." I chuckled back, albeit a bit more like hysteria than a chuckle. "I really don't want to hold you up, but I'm kind of going through something that might hinder my creativity even further. Why don't you go back to the city, and I can contact you when the book is ready."

"Oh, I'm not going anywhere without that book, Ms. Ballas. My orders are to stay here and help you in any way that I can. Now, what exactly are you going through? Maybe I can help resolve the issue."

"Unless you can help me catch a killer and clear my friend's name, there's not much you can do."

She blinked. "Pardon me?"

"Murder, Ms. Newlander. I need to solve a murder before anything creative can flow."

Her shock quickly passed to resolution. "I'm sorry for your trouble, Ms. Ballas, but make no mistake. Murder is what's going to happen to your new line and your book of designs is going to become a book of death if I don't get it soon."

And just like that I lost my appetite. I hated when my mother was right.

I'd stayed up all night trying to work on my book of designs with no success. Poor Jaz was pacing relentlessly, going stir crazy at home, her place of business still a crime scene. I had her making a list of possible enemies for herself while I tried to be creative. *Tried* being the operative word.

After giving up at the crack of dawn and sleeping a measly two hours, my mother woke me up by phone for mass at our Greek Orthodox Church. I spent the whole hour wondering how many days sleep deprivation had just stolen from my life. If that wasn't bad enough, we'd run into Nikos in full Greek mode. His mother was in town visiting, so of course my mother invited them both over for our weekly Sunday brunch. This time she couldn't blame me for not eating. It was all her fault that I'd lost my appetite.

"I like your nice Greek boy," Dido said. She was short and plump with her gray hair pulled back in a bun and her ever-present apron tied around her waist. "He's a keeper." She rubbed my back. *I just hope it's not too late and your eggs haven't dried up.*

I bent down to fix my heel, which didn't need fixing at all, but since I was there I readjusted it three times, trying to ignore her mental sigh. The action removed her hand from my back, which was my main goal. There were some thoughts I really didn't care to hear. "He's half Greek, Yiayia, and he's not my anything," I responded, hoping to squash my grandmother's plans before she put them in motion.

Yiayias were far worse than mamas.

"He's Greek enough, considering…you know." She shrugged sympathetically, but then a mischievous twinkle entered her faded brown eyes. "He might not be yours yet, but Ophelia says it's only a matter of time."

She locked eyes on my mother, who had her head bent close to Nikos's mother, Chloe. The women were about the same age, but that's where the similarity stopped. Chloe had short black hair styled chicly and wore fancy clothes, whereas Ma wore her hair in a beehive and preferred a flashy polyester look. That didn't matter one bit when it came to scheming mamas.

I rolled my eyes. "Don't believe anything Ma says. You know how desperate she is for a grandbaby."

"She's not the only one. Look at Homer. He's beaming at Nikos. I can see the longing in his eyes all the way over here. My poor boy. Why you deny him the son he never had? And look at Amos. Your papou only wants to see his granddaughter happy. Is that so wrong?"

The drama gene ran rampant in my family. Every day was like a three-act play with them. It didn't matter how many times I yelled "cut," they never stopped. I loved them, but they were exhausting.

"Opa! Opa! Opa!" Frona yelled as she skipped about, supergluing the napkins together and wrapping Duct tape around the gazebo poles.

"Frona, no." Yiayia scurried off after her. "Eleni, take your sister inside and keep her there."

Frona giggled hysterically, poured olive oil all over herself, and zigzagged around the yard. All chaos erupted as everyone tried to catch the slippery waif to no avail.

Detective Stevens walked toward me, wearing khaki pants and a baby-blue polo shirt that brought out the amazing color of his eyes. His thick, coffee-colored wavy hair accented his olive skin and five-o'clock shadow perfectly, causing my insides to flutter in a most uncomfortable way. I was pretty sure that could *not* be good for me. He came to a stop beside me with a concerned look on his face and hooked his thumbs into his pants' pockets. "Hey," he said. "How are you?"

Great, he'd left his detective personality at work and his Nikos one under the gazebo, choosing to don Nik the nice guy instead. *So* not what I needed right now if I was going to have a chance at all of staying strong.

I smoothed my chignon and smiled pleasantly. "I'm fine, Detective. I'm used to this behavior. I told you my family was unique. The question is, How are *you*?"

He studied me for a moment, and then a slightly sad smile crossed his face, as though he wished we could start over. "And I told *you* my family is just as crazy. I meant: How are you with everything that's happened to Jaz?"

"Oh." My shoulders slumped a bit. "We're okay for now, but she'll go stir crazy if her shop is closed for long. Not to mention she's a little shocked and upset. She might not have known Darrin that well, but still . . . he died in her store while she was right upstairs. I have her making a list of any possible enemies that she might have. We have to start somewhere."

Nik slid his thumbs out of his pockets, and his eyes narrowed as Detective Stevens came back on duty. "Why?"

"What do you mean why?" I frowned. "Why on earth not?"

"Because you're not a detective."

I stiffened my spine and crossed my arms in front of me. "Apparently, neither are you. Why aren't you out investigating?"

"Because it's Sunday. And everyone deserves a day off. And my mother's in town. And missing church was not an option. You of all people should know that, and why the hell am I explaining myself to you?" He scowled, pure frustration written all over his handsome face.

"Jaz doesn't get a day off, does she? She's looking at twenty years to life if we don't catch this guy. That's why."

"Let me make myself perfectly clear. There is no *we*, Kalli. You are way too close to her to be of any help. Not to mention that if she truly is innocent, then there's a killer on the loose. You could be in danger. So could she, for that matter."

"What about you? She's your landlady, for crying out loud. I might not be Sherlock Holmes, but I'm pretty sure I can deduce that's a conflict of interest or something?" I gave him a smug look.

"And Detective Matheson is her ex-lover. I'm pretty sure that means I'm the better man for the job in a police department this small." He smirked, but then blew out a large breath and rubbed the back of his neck before adding calmly, "Look, we both want the same thing here: to get to the truth. All I'm asking is that you cooperate."

"Well, what do you suggest I do?" I put my hands on my hips and glared at him.

He mimicked my movements and I jumped back, nearly having a heart attack at his nearness. "Stay away from this case, and let me do my job," he said with a growl.

I huffed.

He grunted.

And Frona screamed for all she was worth as someone finally caught her.

Chapter 5

Later that night, we were having unusually warm spring weather so Jaz and I sat on our back deck. When the house was divided, she'd had the fenced-in backyard divided as well, along with two decks put on. Detective Stevens was nowhere in sight and neither was his beast of a dog, Wolfgang, thank goodness. His yard was a mess already, and he'd barely moved in.

My Calico cat, Priscilla, leapt on top of the railing and stretched out, staring over the perfectly groomed yard and landscaping. The snow had melted early this year. Flowers hadn't bloomed yet, but the promise of their glorious splendor was in the air. I adored spring when everything was fresh and new and... clean.

Jaz still wore her track suit, and quite frankly still looked like a hot mess, but I'd convinced her to have her favorite toddy to help her relax. I'd fixed her a Bahama Mama while I sipped on a crisp glass of chardonnay. Usually Jaz was the strong one, pulling me out of my funk. It felt so strange to reverse our roles, but I knew she needed me. No matter how uncomfortable, I would do whatever it took to clear her name.

"So... how was your day?" I asked tentatively.

"Awful," she responded, leaning back in her lounge chair and crossing her legs before her. "I can't stand not being busy. I don't know how people who don't work manage their days without going crazy."

"You need to keep busy. Find a hobby. Focus on something." I paused for a second to let my words sink in, and then I asked, "Any luck on making a list of suspects? Who would like to see you get into trouble and suffer?"

She snorted. "Pretty much everyone in town."

"Well, that narrows it down," I said dryly, then adopted a no-nonsense tone like the one she had used plenty of times on me. "Jaz, if you honestly want to get your life back, you have to get serious about this."

"I know." She sighed. "I just needed a little pity party." She pulled a folded up sheet of paper from her pocket and opened it fully. "For starters, Maria Danza hates me."

"You mean the pastry chef across the street from your shop?"

"One and the same."

"What did you do?"

"Remember the carpenter, Johnny Hogan, I hooked up with six months ago?"

"Yeah, the one who split this house in two? Why?"

"Well, he kinda sorta was her boyfriend."

"What?" I slapped my forehead with my palm. "Oh, no, Jaz...tell me you didn't."

She winced. "I did. Several times in fact. What can I say? I'm a sucker for muscles, and the things he could do with those big hands were—"

"Jazlyn, honestly!" I puckered my face. "Why didn't you tell me?"

"Because I knew you would disapprove, just like you are now."

I relaxed my features and adopted a nonjudgmental tone. "It doesn't matter what I think, you need to tell me everything if we are going to stand a chance of solving this case."

"Okay, but in my defense, they were having trouble before I came along. Maria grew up in this town, just like you. While Johnny was an outsider, same as me."

Jaz had purposely chosen a small town to start fresh and put her name on the map, knowing her mother would never step foot there. Johnny, on the other hand, *was* small town.

"Maria and Johnny were complete opposites, but she was the first person he met, and they formed a special bond, kind of like you and me," Jaz continued. "They would have been better off remaining best friends, but he had to go and ruin it by sleeping with her and giving her hope for something more. Unlike you and most definitely like me, he has a hungry appetite, so to speak. It was only a matter of time before Maria's pastry cakes wouldn't be spicy enough for him. I can't help it he prefers hot tamales."

"Oh my." I fanned my cheeks.

"Oh yeah. And it gets better. I knew it was wrong, and you know that I can't stay with anyone for too long. I wanted to do the right thing and get them back together. But when I tried to break it off, Johnny wouldn't accept no."

"Oh wow." I pressed my lips together.

"Mmmhmmm." She cleared her throat. "I can feel you judging me."

"I didn't say a word." She was right. We were best friends. She didn't need a gift to read my mind. I smiled brightly, then quickly added, "Moving on. Let's talk this out. Maria could have had a grudge against you and killed Darrin out of desperation. If she framed you for murder, then you would be out of the way in prison, and Johnny would get over you and come back to her."

"That sounds like a legitimate possibility." Jaz stared up into the sky, pondering my words.

"On the other hand, if Johnny couldn't accept no, then maybe *he* killed Darrin out of heartbreak. Maybe he thought if he couldn't have you, then no one could."

"I never considered that."

"Trust me. I've seen your exes in action. You leave a lasting impression on them, making that a definite possibility."

"I can't help it I'm so memorable." She fluttered her lashes.

I shook my head with a grin, knowing that keeping things light was her defense mechanism. "What else do you have?"

"Well, there's also Anastasia Stewart."

"You mean the owner of Vixen?"

"Exactly. My one and only competition for your lingerie line. Before I added you, she was the only game in town. When I sold everything else except lingerie, she acted like my best friend. But the minute I added Kalli's Originals, she turned into a she-devil."

"Oh, my gosh. She could have killed Darrin out of greed. She had to know if you take the fall, then Full Disclosure will fold, and she will be the only game in town once more. She probably thinks I'd work for her, even though I've turned her down every time she's made the offer. Is she really that greedy?"

"And then some. She was angry that you went with me and not her."

"Like there was ever any choice." I scoffed. "So is that it? Johnny, Maria, and Anastasia?"

Jaz frowned and bit her bottom lip. "Well, there is one more? It's probably crazy, but it is a possibility."

"Who?"

"Boomer."

My jaw fell open until I finally sputtered, "Nik's partner? But he's a cop."

"Exactly. He would know how to get away with murder and make me look guilty. He could have killed Darrin for revenge. I think he's trying to punish me for humiliating him."

"But you two broke up a year ago. Don't you think he's moved on by now?"

"You've seen the way he acts around me. He's so bitter and angry still, and he hasn't dated since. Every time I date someone new, it gets worse."

I thought about that for a minute. "He's handsome enough in his own way, but he wasn't your typical type of guy. Yet you two seemed so serious for a while. And didn't you date for nine months?"

"That was the problem." Jaz looked sad for a fleeting moment, but then her stubborn side won the battle. She downed the rest of her drink before saying, "Boomer had to go and get serious on me. He *wasn't* my usual type. That's what I liked about him. He knew where we stood right up front, but he thought I would change my mind over time. Big lesson learned there: stick with my type."

"Would getting serious really be all that bad? He seemed great back then."

"He was great. The problem was me. Men are fun to play with but a whole lot of work to keep. My father was so needy, but my mother was a free spirit like me. Always off to some model gig while he stayed home with me and worked at the bank. He acted content and happy and never held her back, but I could see what it did to him. Boomer looked at me with the same puppy-dog eyes, and I just couldn't put him through that. I might not be off on some photo shoot, but we both know it would only be a matter of time before my eyes would wander. So I ended it before either of us could get hurt. I just don't want a serious relationship." She nailed me with a pointed stare. "Do you?"

"Touché." I held up my glass of wine and then took a dainty sip. "Wandering wouldn't be the problem for me. Intimacy would." I shuddered. "And his beast would always come between us."

"And that's a bad thing how?" Her lips twisted into a mischievous grin.

"I meant his dog, and you know it." I stood up and pulled my sweater tighter around me. "It's getting chilly," I said, even though I knew my face was fire red. "We should probably go in."

"You're right, but in a minute." She stood beside me and we leaned over the deck rail, looking out into the yard. I was planning my vegetable and herb gardens, and maybe some olives and grapes—all organic, of course—when she spoke again. "I'm sick of my own house already. Now that we have some suspects, what do we do next?"

I used a page from Detective Steven's book. "*We* don't do anything. You stay far away from this case and keep out of any more trouble."

Jaz scowled. "I can't sit here and do nothing, Kalli."

"We have to eat, right? I will get us some pastries in the morning and have a chat with one Maria Danza for you. We'll start there."

"Why do you get to have all the fun? It's not fair."

"Trust me. Watching you two go at it would not be fun, or helpful to solve this case. I'm doing this for your own good."

"Fine, but I'll tell you one thing. I need some kind of excitement soon, or I'm never going to survive." She began to pace, so I turned around to face her and leaned back against the railing. She might act all nonchalant like Darrin's death was tragic but didn't really affect her. Except I knew her better. She might not want a serious relationship, but she had a heart. It bothered her that she was the last woman he had been with, and essentially in the same room with him when he had died.

"It's okay to be sad, Jaz. It's normal."

A flash of emotion crossed over her face, but then she let out a small laugh. "I'm fine. Besides, I've never been normal. You of all people should know that."

I chose my words carefully. "All your excitement has done lately is get you into trouble. I know you don't like to hear it, but I think a little boring would do you some good."

At first she looked taken aback, but then some birds flew out of the bushes in our yard and startled me. She stared off at them for a moment, her eyes widening a fraction, until she looked back at me all calm and innocent. "I think you're right. It's time I left the excitement to you. It's like you said. I'm doing this for your own good." She stepped through the screen door, but closed it before I could follow.

"What exactly does that mean?" I asked, standing up straight and frowning at her.

"You'll see," she said with a cat-ate-the-canary grin, sounding like her old self for the first time since the murder, and then turned the lock with a foreboding click.

Ten minutes later, after relentless knocking to no avail, I was about to gather Prissy and head around front. That's when I heard the snuffing and snorting behind me.

Miss Priss's white fluffy hair stood on end, and she bolted to her feet. With eyes wide, she stared at something across the yard, and I was afraid to look. Swallowing hard, I ignored my crawling skin and turned in that direction. I was still terrified but relieved to see that Wolfgang was on the other side of the fence in Detective Steven's side of the yard. Nik chose that moment to wander out on his deck in jeans and a sweatshirt with a beer in his hand. The dog jogged over to him, whined, and then pawed at the door.

"For the last time, boy. No more treats. Now, go do your business." He glanced to the side and spotted me, smiled a pleasant smile, and held up his beer in greeting. I smiled weakly back and gave him a small wave. My gaze darted to the sliding glass door, and I choked on my own breath. Jaz had made popcorn, refilled her drink, and was sitting contentedly in a chair, thoroughly enjoying the show.

I gave her an evil look and was about to walk around to the front of the house to get inside that way when Nik spoke.

"Nice evening, isn't it?" he said.

It was, I thought, but responded, "It sure is, but I think I've had enough."

And that was all it took for Wolfgang to notice my presence. He bolted to the fence, looking over the top while still on all four paws, wagging his tail and whining pathetically. His tongue hung out and dripped saliva while I tried desperately not to gag. I didn't care how clean they said a dog's mouth was, that could *not* be sanitary.

"He likes you," Nikos said with a knowing smirk.

I couldn't say the same, so I simply said, "Mmmm, does he? That's nice. Well, it's getting late. I'd better head inside."

Prissy hissed, and Wolfgang froze. His tail stopped wagging, his tongue stopped flopping, and his adoring eyes narrowed with a look that said, *Mine*! He let out one loud bark, stood on his hind legs, and leaned on the fence. It didn't take much for that sucker to fall to the ground, and for all hell to break loose.

I screamed as the beast charged into my yard.

Nik jumped over the deck railing and bolted after him.

Prissy let out a yowl and headed for the nearest tree.

"Wolf, heel!" Nik yelled, but the St. Bernard ignored him, blocking Prissy's escape route.

She shot across the yard in another direction, and he gave chase once more. Nik ran after him, slipping and sliding on the slick grass wet from the recent rain as the dog kept evading him by mere inches. Meanwhile, I ran after Nik and followed Prissy. I almost caught her when she let out one more hiss and bolted up the tree to safety. Relief swept through me until I heard the whine again.

Now that Prissy was out of reach, Wolfgang had turned his attention on me. His enormous tongue made an appearance once more, and his entire hind end moved back and forth with the wag of his tail. His large paw scraped the ground a couple of times, making him look more like a bull than a canine, and then he charged.

Nik commanded, "Stay!" but once again the beast ignored him.

I shrieked, "Don't let him get me!" as I backed up against the tree.

Nik slid in between us, and Wolfgang stopped short. "Hop on," he said. I didn't hesitate. I jumped on Nik's back and he held on tight, keeping me behind him and Wolfgang in front. "Heel, Wolf. I mean it," he said louder this time, and finally the dog obeyed, plopping his fanny on the ground and thumping the dirt with his tail. *You are not helping her like us any better, buddy.*

"Ya think?" I sputtered.

"Excuse me?" he asked, and I could hear the confusion in his voice.

I cleared my throat. "Do you think he will stay?"

"Sure," he said confidently. *But for how long I have no clue.*

"Great," I said with an entirely different meaning. "You can let me down now."

"Oh, whoops." He laughed and set me down, but I could feel his hesitation and regret in his every move as he let go and turned to face me.

Wolfgang jumped to his feet and started his whining again, his massive head trained on me.

I threw myself into Nik's arms and held on tight.

"Home, Wolf! You want a treat?"

The dog's ears perked up at the word "treat," and he ran back to Nik's sliding door, sitting down and waiting patiently like the most obedient good boy ever. Like he'd known all along it was only a matter of time before the detective would cave. I couldn't help being a little impressed with the dog's cunning way of getting exactly what he wanted—he had the detective wrapped around his big ole paw.

Nik's arms were circled around me gently, and he was rubbing my back. When had that happened? I wondered, but then his words distracted me. "He won't hurt you, you know." *Dammit, what is it about you? Why do you make me want to protect you so? I don't need this complication in my life right now,* I heard him think.

Just then I realized I was *still* in his arms, and for the first time in my life, it hadn't been horrible. I stepped away and took a deep breath as I stared at him in wonder and shock.

"What's wrong?" he asked.

"Nothing." *Everything*. Suddenly, I wasn't afraid that the dog would hurt me, but I had a suspicious feeling that the detective just might.

Chapter 6

Monday morning dawned stormy and cool. Not a good sign for the start of my investigation. Detective Stevens had made it clear he didn't want Jaz or even me butting into this case. He said it was because he didn't want us to put ourselves in danger, but I suspected the real reason was he didn't want us to compromise his investigation. I couldn't blame him, really. I mean, I didn't have a clue what I was doing. I just knew I had to do something.

Sinfully Delicious was busy as always when I walked inside. Half the town stopped by every day for their morning coffee and pastries, both of which lived up to the name. Maria Danza really did have a gift. I ordered a cup of coffee with cream and sugar, as well as several delectable delights to bring home to Jaz. Then I wiped down a table with an antibacterial wipe from my purse, earning me a few odd stares. I ignored the looks, which I'd grown accustomed to, sat down, and sipped my coffee, waiting for a lull to question Maria.

Once the crowd died down, she headed right for my table.

"I take it since you're still here, you want to speak with me?" Maria sat down, her black hair pulled back in a ponytail—encased in a hairnet, bless her soul—and plump rosy cheeks glowing brighter than ever. She looked cherubic, yet her eyes were full of steel. "I'm not stupid. The whole town has heard what's happened by now. I know you and Jaz are close, so you must know we're not exactly on friendly terms. What I don't get is what I have to do with the situation she's landed herself in?"

Not exactly on friendly terms? I thought. That was putting it as light as a cream puff. According to Jaz, the whole town had heard Maria vow to make Jaz pay for ruining her life. Well, the whole town except for me. If it wasn't for Jaz, I'd be completely out of the loop since I wasn't exactly plugged into town gossip.

"She didn't land herself in anything," I responded, finding it really hard not to get defensive, yet I knew that would get me nowhere. I folded my napkin into a perfect square and thought about what to say. "Look, you're right. I know you two didn't exactly get along, but that's not why I'm here. Your shop is right across the street from hers. I was just wondering if you saw anything at all out of the ordinary." That wasn't completely a lie, and I sensed that if I didn't come across as more friendly, then she'd probably never open up.

"Oh," she said, sitting back and relaxing for the first time since I'd entered her shop. "Well, at that time of night, I was sound asleep at home like most respectable people would be."

"Alone?" I regretted the words the second they slipped out. I'd simply wanted to verify her alibi, not set off the pressure cooker within her.

Her face flushed bright red, and if I didn't know better, I'd swear there was steam leaking out her ears. "I said respectable, didn't I?" she snapped.

"Absolutely. I meant no disrespect. I just know you come from a big Italian family, kind of like my Greek clan. Just between you and me, we're never alone, are we?"

Her face cooled a bit, and she nodded on a sigh. "Ain't that the truth?" After shaking her head, she frowned slightly. "Back to the floozy. She doesn't have a big family at all, yet she never lacks for company. I see men there all the time. That night was no exception. I was just getting ready to close up shop when I saw her and some big blonde guy stumble into her place. What is it with her and blondes?" she grumbled, half to herself, then continued. "Jaz has a house, but no no no. It's bad enough she stole my man, and most of the men in town, but to bring them all back to flaunt right in front of my face is just wrong, I tell you. Flat-out wrong. No wonder she has to turn to outsiders."

"I don't think she's trying to flaunt her men in front of you. She just likes the excitement of her nookie nook."

"Her what?" Maria raised her eyebrow like she thought I was two donuts short of a baker's dozen.

"Never mind," I said, wanting to distract her from Jaz's secret hideaway. "The point is Jaz bringing a man back to her store isn't unusual. Did you happen to notice anything else that was?"

Maria shrugged. "I thought I saw a shadow peering into the storefront window, but I didn't have my glasses on. When I finally found my glasses and looked again, there was nothing there. All I saw was the floozy come back downstairs and lock up. And then I went home."

"Thank you for your time, Maria. The coffee was great." I held out my hand, hating this part of my so-called gift. At least she had just washed hers.

"You're welcome. Anything to help put the scum of this town behind bars." She grasped my palm, and I tried not to squirm. *And by scum I mean the back-stabbing, lying, cheating whore. She deserves to be behind bars. She should have been the one to die.*

I pulled my hand away, feeling uneasy by the crazed look of hatred in Maria's eyes. Attempting to cover my abrupt gesture, I pointed to the back of her shop. "Is something burning? I think I smell smoke."

Her eyes sprang wide. "My muffins!" She jumped to her feet and bolted to the back without another word—or thought, thank goodness!

Meanwhile, I fetched the hand sanitizer out of my purse, poured a huge amount into my palm, and scrubbed hard. Then I quickly made my escape. Once I was outside in the eerily darkening sky, I pulled my coat tighter and made my way across the street to the front of Full Disclosure.

I played Maria's words over and over in my mind as I stared through the window much like the killer must have, and then it hit me. If she truly had seen a shadow peering into the store, then looked away, and then looked back to see Jaz lock the front door, then it was possible the shadow had already slipped inside. That was why there was no sign of a break-in. Jaz hadn't locked up immediately. She'd told me she'd gone to her office first to disable the cameras that ran throughout the store. Jaz might like to play out her fantasies in her nookie nook, but she wasn't a sicko, and she definitely wasn't into taping her rendezvous.

The person who had slipped inside could have hidden while Jaz finished with the cameras and then locked up. If they'd wanted to rob the place, they could have easily taken whatever they wanted while Jaz and Darrin were preoccupied upstairs and then made their escape with no one the wiser. But the person hadn't taken anything, except the throw pillow which could have been used to silence the gun. Looked like Jaz had a secret enemy, and I had my first clue.

And after the look I saw in Maria's eyes, that person could be her.

Midmorning I was returning home to give Jaz her pastries and tell her what I'd discovered when I saw a truck in my spot in the driveway, right next to Jaz's car. I parked next door in the detective's driveway because I knew he was at work. I didn't know for sure whom the truck belonged to, but I had a pretty good idea.

Johnny Hogan.

Unbelievable. Of all the people Jaz could call to fix the fence, she had to call Maria's ex-boyfriend and her ex-lover. And of course he'd come running, even though it was clearly about to storm. Who in their right mind would start a fence now? He was obviously here for more than just work. Good thing Jaz didn't have any neighbors, because if Maria found out, she'd kill Jaz for sure.

I knew what Jaz was up to. She might not want a long-term commitment because she'd seen the toll it had taken on her father, but her mother's actions had done a number on Jaz as well. She craved attention and affection because her mother was always gone and her father was busy working. Jaz hated being alone, but calling Johnny was not the answer, especially after we'd labeled him a possible suspect. Just wait until I got her alone.

I walked out back with our treats from Maria's, and sure enough there was Jaz, sipping her coffee and flirting shamelessly with an adoring, drooling Johnny. Today Jaz wore skin-tight yoga pants with a long-sleeve form-fitting t-shirt, her hair scooped high in a ponytail. I could smell her heady perfume from ten feet away.

Johnny had on faded worn-out jeans, work boots, and a tight T-shirt, despite the cool temperatures. His skin was a dark tanning-bed tan, and his hair a sandy surfer-style blond that made my skin burn and scalp itch over the thought of what those rays and chemicals must doing to his insides. Jaz tended to go for big blonde beefcakes. You'd think she would have learned her lesson by now. A rumble of thunder sounded in the distance.

"Morning, John. Care for a pastry?" I asked sweetly as I held up the bag clearly labeled Sinfully Delicious, when all I really wanted to do was give him a lecture.

His eyes locked onto the bag, and his smile faded as he cleared his throat. "Ah, no thanks. I don't have much of a sweet tooth these days."

"Interesting," I said.

"Not really." Jaz glared at me. "Not everyone is into sweets."

"Hmmm." I took one out and nibbled daintily, worried about my arteries clogging but wanting to make a point. "I thought maybe he was on a break, with you out here talking his ear off. Are we paying him by the hour?" I fluttered my eyes innocently at Jaz, earning me a scowl from her as she huffed off back into the house, then I glanced back at the carpenter, who didn't look happy with me. Time to change tactics. "So, how's the fence coming? I have to say, I was surprised to see you here with the impending storm, and all."

"Ms. Alvarez said it was an emergency. Something about a beast." He eyed me warily and got back to work. "I think you need a bigger fence with your new neighbor sharing the yard."

I looked next door and saw Wolfgang pawing at the sliding glass door, his long tongue hanging out as he stared at me with pleading eyes.

I dropped my half-eaten pastry back in the bag and said, "Give me the biggest one you've got."

"Yes, ma'am."

"Please, call me Kalli," I said casually, trying to put him at ease. I shot a glance at the house and saw Jaz in the kitchen window doing the dishes and Prissy lounging by the window, safely inside where I longed to be, but I had a job to do. I glanced at the ominous clouds and then focused on the task at hand. "It was nice of you to come out on such short notice. You must be busy now that it's spring."

He shrugged a beefy shoulder. "Things are picking up, but our busiest time is summer. Besides, I figure Jaz—I mean Ms. Alvarez—has been through enough."

"So you've heard."

"Kind of hard not to in a town this small. I knew that guy she was seeing was bad news," he said more to himself than me. "Crazy woman can't see what she has right in front of her."

"And what's that?"

He blinked as though he just realized he'd spoken out loud. "Uh, you know, a successful store. Good friends. She has everything going for her right here. Why mess it up by getting involved with online dating. It's a crazy scary world out there. She didn't know a thing about that guy."

"I don't know. What do we really know about anyone? I'm sure we all have our secrets, right?" I borrowed a move from Jaz and leaned forward, giving him a coy smile and placing my hand on his forearm.

His eyebrows shot up, and he stared down at my hand, then back at me. He let his eyelids close halfway and a cockeyed grin hooked the corner of his mouth. *I came here to get even with Jaz for dumping me. Show her what she was missing out on. Maybe the best way to do that is by sleeping with her best friend. I've always thought all the Ballases were a little weird, but this one sure is pretty.* He flexed his pec muscles.

I gasped and dropped my hand. "You pig."

"Excuse me?" he said, narrowing his eyes.

"I said you're big." I discreetly rubbed my palm on my skirt, feeling my skin crawl. "Your job must give you a great workout."

His frown faded and a smug look swept across his overly tanned face. "It has its perks, and I have great genetics." He took a step toward me. "Big family, big fence, big muscles . . . I take it you like big."

"Big mistakes." I wagged my finger at him as I took a step back. A streak of lightning lit up the sky. "I've made my share of them. I'm trying to quit."

"If you mean quit butting your nose in my investigation, then that's the first smart idea you've had all morning," said a booming familiar voice from behind us.

I whirled around and sure enough, there stood Detective Stevens in all his naturally tanned glory, looking amazingly handsome in his sport coat and jeans. Not too big, not too small, this one was just right.

"Detective, what are you doing home?" I asked.

"Catching you red handed, apparently." He grunted.

"What is he talking about?" Johnny looked suspiciously back and forth between us.

"I stopped home for lunch, if you must know," the detective responded to me, "Only to find you questioning yet another person of interest. First Maria and now him? You don't listen one bit, do you?"

"Wait, how do you know about Maria?" I asked before thinking. "I mean, I was just picking up breakfast," I quickly added.

"I know everything," was all he said, but his eyes screamed he knew much more than he was letting on.

Johnny dropped the piece of fence he was holding and stared at me accusingly. I didn't need to read his mind to know he was pissed. His expression was plain as day. He knew I was using him, same as Jaz had done, and now I'd made an enemy of my own.

"You just made your biggest mistake yet, baby." He grabbed his toolbox and headed for his truck, followed by a clap of thunder. I counted the seconds and briefly wondered what the odds of getting struck by lightning might be.

"Wait, what about the fence?" I yelled after him, trying to focus.

"Do it yourself. It's a nice big project. I'm sure you'll be *real* into it."

"What is the matter with you?" I turned on the detective. "This is all your fault, and you'd better not let your dog out until you finish this fence."

"My fault? That's a good one. If you hadn't been all over him, we wouldn't be having this conversation right now."

"Are you kidding me? All I did was touch his arm."

"I thought you didn't like to be touched?" Nikos the Greek made an appearance, wearing a full smirk.

"I don't," I ground out.

"Could have fooled me," he snapped, his smirk replaced with anger and what sounded suspiciously like jealousy. "Maybe it's just me who makes you skittish, because I sure as hell did last night with the way you took off."

"Actually, that's not why I took off. You're the only one who doesn't make me squirm," I muttered, "I mean you do, but not as much, and I was just . . . wait, *why* am I explaining myself to you? You're the one who said I wasn't your type." Somehow we had ended up a mere inches apart as the first few raindrops began to fall.

"Well, you said I wasn't yours either," he said, his frustration clearly evident.

"Then why are we having this conversation?" My heart started beating heavier with his nearness.

"Damned if I know," he growled, plunging a hand through his hair. "All I know is that you make me crazy."

"Well, what am I supposed to do about that?" A fat raindrop rolled down my cheek.

"I don't have a clue," he said softer as he tracked its path with his gaze. He lifted his hand as though to wipe it away, and I held my breath.

"Guys, come quickly!" Jaz yelled out the kitchen window. "Meet me out front."

Nik and I gave each other one last intense look and then took off toward the front of the house. When we got there, my jaw fell open. Jaz's car had been ransacked. The trunk was pried open, the driver's side window broken, and door left wide open. The visor hung off one hinge, and the glove compartment looked broken. And then there were the flat tires, which had been slashed in a violent, angry manner that spoke volumes. This didn't look like an ordinary break-in. It looked like an act of revenge.

The rain started coming down in a sprinkle, so Nik sprang into action. I followed his lead as we rushed to the car.

"Don't touch anything with your hands," he said.

"No worries there," I said, eyeing the car. It was in dire need of a wash, and who knew if the culprit had worn gloves or what Jaz had done in there. I tried not to think of the germs I could encounter as I slammed the trunk closed with my elbow and he bumped the front door shut with his hip. Just then the heavens opened up and it poured. He nudged me toward the front porch, where we ran to join Jaz.

"What happened," Detective Stevens asked, all business once more.

"I don't know. I didn't see or hear anything," Jaz said, handing us each a towel.

"Do you think it was Mr. Hogan?" I asked.

"I don't think Johnny would do anything like that to me," Jaz responded.

"Trust me, you didn't hear his thoughts." I scoffed.

The detective frowned. "No kidding, Kalli. Who on earth could?"

Jaz and I locked eyes and I laughed, sounding like a nervous hyena. "Right, I just meant, you should have seen his face. He has not been a happy camper ever since Jaz broke up with him."

"Is that right?" the detective asked Jaz.

"Uh, yeah, I guess," she responded, looking at me questioningly.

The detective kept watching us keenly. I was sure he knew something was up, but there was no way he could know exactly what. I intended to keep it that way.

"Why would you call Mr. Hogan to fix the fence then?" he asked her.

"Because he's the best," she said simply. "Whether he likes me or not, I am first and foremost a business woman. I always hire the best." That much was true, and it seemed to pacify the detective.

"Okay. I'll talk to Hogan, but let me make myself clear. You two stay far away from this case, or the consequences won't be pretty. Hogan left pretty angry after Ms. Ballas acted like a tease, so he could have trashed your car on the way out."

"Wait a minute…Ms. Ballas did what?" Jaz squeaked, nailing me with a look I didn't want to face alone.

"Later, ladies." Nikos the Greek winked at me before the detective finished with, "My work here is done, and I've got a job to do." Then he walked out the door just as the rain let up.

I sat there stunned, thinking I had a job to do as well and it started with a little thing called payback. But first, I had another mess to take care of. I slowly turned around to the murderous look on Jaz's face.

"Now, Jaz—my favorite person in the world and best friend on the planet who would be really sad and lonely if anything bad should happen to me—let me explain…"

Episode 3

Chapter 7

Tuesday afternoon Jaz and I went to Diner Delights for lunch. Since my family ran half the businesses in town, it made the choice of a place to eat difficult for Jaz. My cousins, Kosmos and Silas, were the only members of my family that Jaz got along with. Probably because they were young, single, attractive men . . . and off limits, which made them that much more appealing. Just because we had an agreement that she couldn't date my family members did not mean that would stop her from flirting outrageously with them every chance she got.

Kosmos was on the short side, but built like a tank. He kept his dark hair cropped short, and it somehow matched his stature: tough as nails. But his eyes gave him away. They were the soft, dreamy, sleepy bedroom eyes that all women fell for. Then there was Silas. He was the biggest flirt of our family. Thinner but taller, with thick curly black hair and dimples that worked their charm every time.

Kosmos stood behind the deli counter, making sandwiches. He gave us a friendly wave when we came in and sat down. Meanwhile, Silas ran the register. He shot me a quick grin, but focused his sexy smile on Jaz and tossed her a wink. Jaz laughed and blew them both kisses. I just rolled my eyes. At least they'd cheered her up a bit, which even I had to admit she desperately needed.

The rest of my family thought she was a bad influence on me. Now that she was the prime suspect in Darrin Wilcox's murder, they were on my case more than ever for me to move out. My cousin Eleni had a gypsy boyfriend who had a sister who dabbled in voodoo. I'd caught them whispering about Jaz and was pretty sure they'd put a curse on her. Normally I didn't believe in such nonsense, but ever since I woke up with my "gift," I'd come to realize that anything was possible.

"Why do you keep staring at me that way?" Jaz asked me after finishing her bite of Caesar salad. We hadn't even needed to order. My cousins had prepared our salads and brought them to our table, even though the restaurant was normally self-serve. Today was the first day she'd dressed in a flowy dress and not yoga pants or a warm-up suit. She wasn't back to work, but she was beginning to get back to her old self.

"Now you know how I felt the day I realized I could read minds," I responded, wearing yet another suit. I kept hoping if I dressed the part, the rest would follow, but so far I'd had no such luck in creating more designs for my book. "You kept looking at me like I was possessed the other day," I went on. "I'm just making sure you're okay." I took a bite of my own salad.

"Would you forget about that stupid curse? I'm fine." She set down her fork, and I regretted killing her appetite.

"That's what I said," I pointed out, unable to ease my mind. I was worried something bad was about to happen, but I had no clue what or when.

The bell over the door chimed and in walked Detective Stevens. "*There* you are," he grumbled as he sat down. "Why aren't you home?"

"I'm a person of interest, not a prisoner. Last time I checked, I couldn't leave town. No one ever said anything about leaving my house." Jaz scowled.

"That might be true, but there's still a killer on the loose and someone did just break into your car," he pointed out to her.

"Good." She studied him.

"Come again?" He rubbed his whiskered jaw.

"It's good that you don't think I'm a cold-blooded murderer like your joy of a partner."

He sighed. "No, Jaz, I don't. But I do think you've made some poor choices as of late. I'm just trying to keep you safe and do my job."

"It's just lunch, Detective," I said gently, drawing his attention. "We did like you asked and stayed away from the case the rest of the day yesterday and all this morning. When we didn't hear anything from you, Jaz got restless. I thought a change of scenery might do her good. That's all."

"Now that we've established I'm being a good girl, what's the scoop? Did you find out anything from Johnny?" Jaz asked.

"He says he didn't trash your car. He was pissed that Kalli was just using him—"

"Only to find out information," I quickly added, my gaze darting apologetically to Jaz.

"Amateur." Jaz rolled her eyes, not nearly as mad as she had been when she first thought I was hitting on him for real.

"Yet another reason you need to leave the investigating to the pros." The detective leveled me with a pointed look.

"Continue please," Jaz said.

"Hogan said the car was fine when he left your place, but that you had plenty of other enemies who would do something as petty as that. When he said he could think of better ways to get back at you, I did some digging. Detective Matheson and I discovered that John Hogan ran into Darrin Wilcox when he first arrived in town. Hogan was doing some renovations at the Clearview Motel for Larry Miller. When Hogan found out who Wilcox was, they got into an argument right before Wilcox left to meet you at Rosalita's Place for dinner. Everyone heard Hogan say Wilcox would be sorry he'd ever set foot in Clearview before the night was over."

"I couldn't have had a relationship with such a monster," Jaz said on barely more than a whisper. "You don't really think Johnny could have killed Darrin, do you?"

"I don't know him well enough to speculate. What I do know is that after Wilcox left, Hogan headed to Flannigan's Pub. Michael Flannigan said Hogan came in and stayed all evening, well on his way to getting smashed. So he took his keys. Hogan wouldn't let him call a cab, so he stormed out to walk it off. He said he was headed home. He can't prove he actually did go home, but there's also no way to prove whether or not he made a pit stop at Full Disclosure along the way. He didn't return until the next day to pick up his truck."

Mr. Flannigan was married to Lois Flannigan—one of Jaz's regulars who had shown up for the sale on Saturday morning, only to discover Darrin's body as she peered through the storefront window. She was the one who had called 911, and apparently she hadn't been the same since, heart palpitations and all. Jaz had promised her a permanent discount once she reopened, but Lois wasn't sure she would ever be able to set foot inside that store again.

I had to admit I was worried Jaz would lose business in town after this whole mess was over, but Jaz was a savvy woman with a strong business model. She still had an online component to her store that would work as a fallback for her while she figured out the rest. At this point I just wanted to keep my best friend out of jail. The only problem was the evidence was stacking up against her, and things weren't looking so good.

"What do we do now?" I asked.

"You two behave while I try to find Darrin Wilcox's next of kin. It's very strange." Detective Stevens puckered his brow as he scanned his notebook.

"What is?" Jaz asked.

"Well, there's not much information on the guy. It's like he has no family and not much of a past," Nik said to her, then turned to me. "When I checked out his social media profile for Jaz, he had said he was an international businessman, but then I found a reference he made to selling cars. I had assumed at the time that he'd just slipped up to what his real occupation was. At the time Jaz hadn't cared that he'd fudged a few details about his occupation to make himself look better, because she wasn't interested in anything long term. Now I wish I had done an actual background check on the guy. Maybe then we would have avoided this whole mess. Now that I've had to do some deeper digging, there's no other paper trail on the guy. It's like he never existed."

"What does that mean?" I asked.

"Nothing good," the detective responded, giving Jaz a meaningful look.

"Yeah yeah, I get it. Poor choices." She sighed. "Story of my life."

"I suggest you write a new story, or you won't have much of a life left," he said gravely.

Speaking of having no life, the door chimed once more and in walked my PR rep, Natasha Newlander. "Well, thanks for the update, Detective, but Jaz and I have to go. Lots of work to do, right Jaz?" I smiled brightly as I stood and grabbed my purse.

"Uh, sure, yup, you got it." She stood beside me, glanced at the detective, and shrugged. "Later gater," she said to him as she followed me out. "Hey, boys," she hollered to the back, drawing everyone's attention, which was the last thing I wanted to do. "Put our lunch on my account. Thanks darlings." She wiggled her fingers.

I glared at her. "Did you have to be so loud?"

"What's up with you?"

"Her," I said in a low voice, jerking my head to the side.

"You mean the stylish woman staring at you from across the room?"

I closed my eyes. Just peachy. Then opened them wide and worked up a smile as I turned around. "Great to see you, Ms. Newlander, but as you can see we were just on our way out. Lots of work to do, and all. You know how it is."

She didn't say a word. Just tapped her watch as if to say, *Clock's ticking, Ms. Ballas, and we both know how it will be if you don't turn in your book of designs soon.*

"What on earth was all that about?" Jaz asked.

"Story of *my* life."

On our way home, Jaz begged me to stop by Full Disclosure. There was crime scene tape across the door, letting everyone know it was closed, but that didn't matter to Jaz. Her store was her baby. She'd worked long and hard to make this place a reality.

"I hate seeing it this way," she said as she stared in the front window. "I might as well be wearing a scarlet letter. People have always judged me, but I owned that judgment. I am who I am, like it or not. But this . . . this isn't fair at all. I'm being punished for one stupid mistake, one more bad choice. I certainly didn't want Darrin Wilcox dead, but I wish I'd never laid eyes on him."

"I know. This stinks for sure. Innocent until proven guilty, remember? And we both know you're not guilty, so you have nothing to worry about."

"Tell that to the judge." She snorted, then stared down at the ground, her shoulders slumping a bit.

"It'll be okay." I dipped my head down so she could see my face. "Just know I'm hugging you on the inside."

That got a lopsided grin out of her. "I know."

"Unfreakingbelievable!" Maria Danza came charging out of her pastry shop across the street, followed by some mousy-looking woman who seemed dazed and confused.

Jaz snapped her spine straight. "Always good to see you too, Maria."

"Save it for the jury. I don't think you'll be seeing anyone for quite some time after they get through with you." She dusted flour off her apron-covered curves, a fine white powder drifting in the air around us.

"Maria, I don't think—" I started to say, then coughed, wondering if flour dust would act like secondhand smoke in my lungs and what kind of damage it could do.

"And you!" She thrust her plump finger in my face, and I was more than happy to take a step back where I could take in clean air. "Don't even get me started. For some reason, she has completely fooled you. You're so blind you can't see her for who she really is."

"And what's that, Maria? Please enlighten us." Jaz crossed her arms over her chest.

"A man whore."

"Well, that's original." Jaz smirked. "And actually incorrect. A man whore is a guy who acts like a whore, not a woman… kind of like your ex."

"Well, you would be the expert. I wish you'd *be* more original," Maria spat. "You're such a cliché. A hot South American woman who's so insecure she can't be happy with a man of her own so she has to steal everyone else's."

"Look, I've told you a thousand times that Johnny said you two were through. I was under the impression he had already ended things. I had no idea you were still dating."

"Yeah? Then tell me something. Is it your fault that Darrin was still married?"

"What?" Jaz and I both shrieked at the same time.

Maria looked smug, and the poor woman beside her looked ready to burst into tears.

"I can't help it that men like me, but a husband stealer I am not. What the hell are you talking about?" Jaz asked.

"Like you didn't know Darrin Wilcox was married."

"*Is* married," were the first words to come out of the mousy woman's thin lips. "*Is*," she repeated quietly.

"Then why on earth was he on a dating website?" I asked, unable to process what I was hearing.

"I don't know. Daddy made him manager of his biggest car lot. We had everything we could want. He said he was going on a business trip, but I found out from Daddy that was a lie. Then I found his email to you, and his profile on the dating website. That's how I knew to look for him here," the woman said, finally staring Jaz in the eye. For the first time, she didn't seem so mousy. She looked confused and hurt and angry enough to commit murder.

"I'm sorry. What's your name?" Jaz asked, appearing poleaxed.

"Wilma Parks. Scott Parks is my husband. Darrin Wilcox is the alias he used to lure in floozies like you."

"In Jaz's defense, she had no idea you existed or she never would have agreed to go out with him," I said, having a hard time believing someone like him could have been married to a woman like her. They seemed worlds apart, unless he'd been in it for the money her father obviously had.

"Oh, sure. I'll believe that when my pastries sprout wings and fly off to Neverland." Maria snorted.

"I can't believe he was married," Jaz said, still in a daze. "This has to be my poorest choice yet. Scott Parks? No wonder they couldn't find his next of kin."

Wilma gasped. "Next of kin? W-What are you saying?"

"That this hussy didn't just steal your husband. She killed him," Maria said, her voice hissing with venom. "Darrin Wilcox. Scott Parks. It doesn't really matter what he called himself. The man's dead."

Wilma's face turned ghostly white, her eyes rolled back in her head, and she hit the ground hard. And that's the night that the lights went out in Clearview. All I could do was hope that no one was out to hang an innocent woman.

CHAPTER 8

"I can't believe Maria didn't tell Mrs. Parks about her husband's death," I said to Jaz. "She had plenty of time, since they'd obviously been talking long enough for Maria to find out about his alias and his cheating."

"Maria claims she was about to direct Mrs. Parks to the police station and let them deliver the bad news, but then she got distracted when she noticed us outside. I bet she was stalling, hoping I'd show up so Mrs. Parks could confront me. That sounds more like the Maria I know."

"Either way, she handled the whole situation badly if you ask me," I said, staring at the ambulance, hoping the woman would be okay. Just then the doors in the back opened and a man helped her out. He looked around, spotted us, said something to her, and then walked in our direction. Just my luck it had to be him.

"How is she?" I asked Max Rolland the EMT-slash-firefighter whom I'd grown up with. He had a sandy-brown flattop hairstyle, gray eyes, a great body, and a big crush on me. He'd had a thing for me ever since we were teenagers. He knew about my quirks, but he said they didn't matter to him. He found them charming. Of all the men in the world, I knew he would be the one who would never hurt me, but he just didn't make my heart sing like... I derailed that crazy train of thought and added, "Will she be okay now that she knows her husband is dead?"

Max came to a stop in front of me and placed his hands on his uniformed hips, looking like the centerfold in a Hunky Heroes calendar. "Hi, Jazlyn." He smiled kindly at Jaz, who two-finger saluted him with a weary tilt to her lips, then he locked his gaze on me. "Kalli. It's good to see you. It's been a while."

"Sorry. It really is great to see you again. I'm just a little frazzled with everything that's gone on." I twisted my hands together. "How's the family?"

"Hangin' in there. How's yours?"

"Resilient." I blew out a breath, and he chuckled.

"Mrs. Parks will be fine physically. Emotionally I'm not so sure. She finds out her husband cheated, only to learn he's been murdered. That's a lot to handle all at once." Jaz groaned, and Max's gaze shot to her. "Sorry, Jaz. No offense meant."

"None taken, Maximillian. You couldn't possibly offend me any more than everyone else in this town has." She stared off past him and then sighed deeply. "And here comes the most offensive person yet."

Detective Boomer Matheson pulled into the parking lot of Full Disclosure and cut the engine to his cop car. He slid his long, lean body out of the door and ran a hand through his unruly russet-colored hair, scanning the area. He really wasn't Jaz's typical type—big, blond, and buff—yet she'd gone out with him longer than she had any other man. No matter what she said, I had always thought the only reason they broke up was because he wanted more and she got scared. I couldn't imagine him as the killer, but

I supposed anything was possible. And she was right. If anyone would know how to commit murder and get away with it, he would.

His hazel eyes settled on Jaz, and for a fleeting second I could swear I saw them soften, but then he donned a neutral expression, squaring his shoulders as he made his way over to us. "Hey, Rolland. Any updates on the widow?"

"She's well enough for you to question, but go easy on her. She's a bit fragile."

I remembered the look she'd given Jaz, I thought, and *fragile* had been the last adjective I would have used to describe her at that moment.

"Great," Detective Matheson responded. "Why don't you get her settled in my cop car and let her know I'll be there in a minute."

"Will do." Max gave me one last, longing look, nodded once, and then walked away.

"Poor Boomer. Nothing better to do than torture innocent victims. Must be a slow day," Jaz said, her voice dripping with sarcasm.

"Torture innocent victims?" He barked out a laugh. "That's rich coming from you. Last I checked you were the one leaving innocent victims in your wake."

"Oh, please." She flicked her hand in the air. "Sounds to me like someone can't handle rejection."

He parted his sport coat, dropping his hands to his hips and leaning in close. "More like someone can't handle genuine affection."

They stared into each other's eyes as though I wasn't even there, and my gut told me I was right. Jaz did care about him, a lot more than she was letting on.

That was the problem.

She was the first one to look away. "I can handle affection just fine, but the last thing I want is an adoring puppy dog. I prefer cats."

"And that's exactly what you're going to end up being if you don't change your ways. A little old spinster cat lady."

"I could think of worse things."

"So could I... like life in prison."

"I'm sure it won't come to that because Jaz is innocent," I interjected.

Boomer looked at me like I didn't have a clue. "Jazlyn Alvarez might be a lot of things, but innocent isn't one of them." He sounded sincere, but innocent of what I wasn't quite sure. His gaze shot back to hers and held her captive. "Everyone has to pay for their sins at some point, Jaz. Looks like yours are finally catching up to you. Enjoy your freedom while you can, princess."

"I always do and don't plan to stop now." She licked her lips and blew him a kiss.

He clenched his jaw, and a muscle pulsed in his cheek. For the first time ever, I actually felt something like sympathy for him. I reached out and touched his arm without thinking and was bombarded with his thoughts screaming in my ear. *Damn you, woman. Why do I let you do this to me? Why do I even care?*" He shrugged off my hand, still glaring at Jaz, and then stormed away.

"Oh, that man makes me so angry I could scream." Jaz clenched her hands into fists.

"And why do you think that is?" I asked her, crossing my arms and tapping my foot. My own frustration with her was quickly rising to the surface.

Her gaze snapped to me. "What are you getting at?"

"Just that love and hate are two emotions that are much closer than you might think. You, my dear, are your own worst enemy."

"Oh, no. Don't even go there, sister. You have no room to talk, and that man makes me crazy."

"Which is exactly why you care more about him than you are willing to let on, and you're right. I do know what you're going through. I'm going crazy too, I'm just not a suspect in a murder investigation."

"Now *you're* the one making me crazy."

"Well, if you had heard his thoughts, you'd know where I was coming from. That's all I'm saying."

She frowned. "He hates me."

"Like I said . . . love and hate—one and the same. You'd be surprised how much he still cares as well."

"He sure has a funny way of showing it, and it doesn't matter anyway. My life is a mess."

"I hear that loud and clear, and trust me when I say I feel your pain." I wasn't much of a partier, but right now I thought she could use something to lift her spirits. "Wanna go get a drink?"

"I thought you'd never ask."

Later that night, Jaz and I finally returned home. I'd only partaken in one drink hours earlier, being the designated driver, but Jaz had quite a few. Tipsy didn't begin to describe the overstressed fiery woman who had needed desperately to forget her troubles, if only for a moment, and let loose. And let loose she had, all over anyone within earshot.

I noticed Detective Stevens' car next door, so he must be home. Ignoring the odd pull in that direction, I helped Jaz into our half of the house. I went to unlock the door, but it already was. For a moment, I thought maybe I'd left it unlocked, but that couldn't be. I always checked the locks three times before going anywhere. I was afraid to open the door and find out what that meant. Sucking in a fortifying breath, I pushed the door open wide and stepped through, hauling a giggling Jaz along with me.

Her giggling stopped.

We both stared.

And then Jaz screamed for all she was worth.

"What's wrong?" Nik bellowed as he charged through the door in record time, almost as though he'd sat ready and waiting for something to go wrong. Yet he wore sweatpants, a tank top and bare feet like he'd been relaxing before bed.

"Someone knocked my plant over. Look at my white rug. It's a mess," Jaz wailed.

"Are you kidding me?" Nik gaped at her. "That's why you screamed?"

Jaz just shrugged. "I needed a good scream, but I feel better now."

"Glad to hear one of us does," he muttered, running a hand wearily over his whiskered face.

"I think we've been robbed," I said, pointing to the mess before me to take my mind off his way-too-casual appearance. He was far more muscular than I had realized, and it disturbed me greatly. And Jaz's scream hadn't helped.

I focused on the situation at hand. Tables had been overturned, cupboards ransacked, drawers emptied.

"I still can't believe she screamed like that. I thought someone else had been murdered." He ran his hand through his dark waves before asking, "Do you see anything that's missing?" Detective Stevens was in full cop mode once more, but it was still hard to focus with him dressed that way.

"Just you, sillypoo," Jaz said, giggling as she poked him in the chest, her ruined white rug forgotten. "We missed you, Nikos. Or at least Kalli did. I'm not too fond of detectives at the moment." She hiccupped.

"She's drunk?" he asked me, raising his dark eyebrows sky high and ignoring her comment, thank goodness.

"That she is," I answered, closing the door behind us and kicking off my shoes.

"Why?" he asked, his gaze flicked down to my feet and then quickly back to my face.

"Detective Boomer Matheson," was all I had to say.

"Ahhh." Nik rubbed the back of his neck. "I should call this in."

"No!" Jaz stated firmly. "This is my house, and I choose not to report it. I have had my fill of cops, no offense, Detective Dreamy."

"None taken, but I think you're making a mistake."

"It's my mistake to make. Mmmm, and I'd like to make a milkshake with Kahlua." She headed off to the kitchen.

"Why not?" he said.

"Pardon me?" I sputtered.

"I'm off duty and frankly, I'm in the mood to join her."

"In getting drunk?" I asked, aghast.

"No," he called over his shoulder as he headed to the kitchen after her. "But I definitely think this never-ending day calls for something stronger than coffee."

"The cupboard over the stove. Jaz has all sorts of stuff. Help yourself. I'm going to put her to bed and change into something more comfortable."

"Okay. I'll be in the kitchen when you're ready to talk about whatever this is."

Oh my. By *this* he probably meant the break-in, but part of me wondered if he meant us. I blew off those insane thoughts, chalking them up to stress. I followed him to the kitchen and grabbed Jaz before she could start her milkshake and turned her in the other direction.

"Where are we going, and is Detective Dreamy coming with?" Jaz asked, tee-hee-heeing all the way.

"To bed. It's night-night time. Detective Dreamy isn't tired, but the sandman is calling your name."

"Really?" she asked, staring up at me like it was Christmas morning. "Is he cute?"

"Hot," I said. "Like desert hot, and he's waiting for you, so you'd better go right to sleep."

"Okay," she squealed, and by the time her head hit the pillow, she was already snoring.

Getting her tipsy had so not been a good idea.

I washed up thoroughly and then looked for something to wear. Today was laundry day, but the day had been completely thrown off kilter. I had nothing clean to wear except for the yoga outfit Jaz had bought me when she insisted I change my life and loosen up. Yeah right. Look where that had gotten her. I'd never worn the outfit, but it was clean, and I did need something comfortable to wear. I slipped them on before I could change my mind and headed out to the kitchen to join Nik.

He sat at our kitchen table, lifting a longneck bottle half-way to his lips, but then he paused when he spotted me, his eyes widening with surprise. "Hey," was all he said on a husky whisper.

"Hey," I responded and then cleared my suddenly tight throat—surely a side effect from my earlier dose of flour dust. "Beer. Good choice. I prefer wine." I headed straight for the refrigerator and poured myself a big glass of chardonnay before realizing I'd put my yoga pants–covered fanny right in his line of sight. Let's just say the pants lifted and separated a certain part of my anatomy much more than I was comfortable with. I took a healthy sip before turning around and joining him at the table.

"For the record, I still think you should call this in," he said.

"She'd kill me. And to be honest, it doesn't look like they took anything. It seems as if they were looking for something, but I don't have a clue what."

"Then why did you call me?"

"I didn't. You heard Jaz scream and came running, remember?"

"Oh, right. Price you pay for sharing a house, I guess. Everything sounds louder than it really is."

"Tell me about it. I thought Wolfgang was killing you the other day."

"He does get a bit excited now and then."

"Excited and fence-breaking crazy."

"No worries. I've got him under control."

"Something tells me he thinks it's the other way around."

"He's probably right, but don't tell him I said so." Nik winked. "So, any ideas who could be responsible for breaking in?" he asked.

"Gee, only half the town. Jaz isn't exactly the most popular person in Clearview, especially now that her name has been linked to a murder. It could be anyone from a jilted ex to an angry other woman or competition in the business world." I took another sip, hoping the wine would calm my body's strange reaction to that wink. "I have no clue, but rest assured, I plan to find out."

"And that right there is what worries me. You really need to install a deadbolt. A child could have picked that lock."

"I know. I'll make sure fixing the lock is a priority. I'm not stupid, you know. I'm not going to do anything to put myself in danger."

"Honey, you already are in danger."

"How so?" I asked, ignoring the ping in my stomach over his term of endearment as I raised my glass once more.

"Guilt by association." Nik walked to the refrigerator as if this was his kitchen, and helped himself to another beer. "You are friends with Jaz, work with her, and are now trying to clear her name. That doesn't exactly make *you* the most popular person in town these days."

"Well, it won't make me stop, either. I'm not afraid to stand up for what's right. I know Jaz. She is innocent. I would bet my life on that."

"Careful, Ballas, or you just might."

Chapter 9

Wednesday morning I decided that a little shopping trip was in order. I'd thought about what Detective Stevens and I had talked about. Possible suspects who could have broken into our house. The biggest name that came to mind was Anastasia Stewart. She owned Vixen and was Jaz's prime competition in this town. She used to be number one.

Or had been until I added my line to Full Disclosure.

Ana had tried hard to get me to join her store instead of Jaz's. Like that would ever happen. Jaz was so much more than my business partner. She was my best friend. So far, Ana hadn't found anyone with designs in the lingerie line, so Jaz was still on top. But I was terrified this whole scandal would ruin her.

I walked into Vixen and had to admit the store was pretty busy. The décor was high end, like Jaz's store, but a little less classy. I noticed my cousin, Eleni, and couldn't believe she was shopping here already. Some of my family might not approve of Jaz, but Eleni had always been pretty cool, other than the voodoo curse she'd had her boyfriend's sister put on Jaz for insurance. They wanted to be able to control her if she really was the murderer. I still had my business to think of. Turning on Jaz was the same as turning on me.

"Hey, what are you doing?" I hissed as I came to a stop beside her.

She flushed guiltily, her tanned skin turning a reddish-bronze hue. She smoothed her waist-length, dark curly hair. "You know I love Jaz's clothes, but I still have to shop. Vixen's is the next best thing." She glanced around, making sure no one could overhear us. "By the way, I'm in need of another *special* commission from you. I finally have a man in my life who knows exactly what to do with all my curves."

"You don't say," I said dryly. My family might act all scandalous over me designing lingerie instead of something respectable like wedding attire, yet half of my private commissions came from my relatives. With the understanding that everything would remain confidential, mind you.

"You're so good at showcasing a woman's best assets. When do you think you could have it ready by?"

"Now is not a good time. To be honest, I haven't been feeling very creative as of late."

"I get it. It has to be so hard with Jaz being accused of murder and all. I would hug you, cuz, but I wouldn't want to stress you out even more."

"Leni, she's not accused of murder." I huffed in frustration. "She's a person of interest. There's a big difference."

Eleni held up her hands. "Won't make much difference. Either way it's a death sentence to her career if things don't get back to normal soon."

Ana spotted me and headed our way.

"Gotta go. Sorry, but you know how it is. This sale is awesome. I can't be spotted associating with the enemy." Eleni scurried off, and my jaw unhinged.

My own cousin had turned on me, all in the name of fashion.

Ana looked a lot like Jaz. She might not be South American, but she was tall and chic and stylish. She had a good business sense, and she knew fashion. She stopped beside me, smiling pleasantly, but I could see the edge of steel beneath the surface. "Ms. Ballas, it's lovely to see you. I hope life has been treating you well."

"I've been better," I said honestly, feeling her out.

She pursed her lips sympathetically. "Yes, I heard. Such a shame. I always thought that one day Ms. Alvarez's lifestyle would land her in trouble. I'd hate to see you go down with her sinking ship."

"Hmmm, would you now?" I responded with a smile just as phony. "What exactly are you suggesting, Ms. Stevens?"

"That maybe it's time you jumped."

I narrowed my eyes a fraction. "You mean jump ship as in leave Jaz?" I had to wonder just how far she would actually go to get what she wanted.

"My offer still stands. Come work with me, and you won't be sorry. Did I tell you I met your PR representative, Natasha Newlander?"

"No, you failed to mention that." I clenched my jaw, reminding myself why I was here: to find out information. Would it be possible for Ana to frame Jaz for murder and ruin me in the eyes of Natasha all because I wouldn't work with her?

"Lovely woman with a bright head on her shoulders. She'll go far in the world of fashion, you wait and see. And so will you if you play your cards right. She has great things to say about you."

"I'll keep that in mind."

"You do that, but don't keep me waiting too long. The offer won't be around forever." She saw Mrs. Flannigan and made a beeline in her direction.

I couldn't believe it. Mrs. Flannigan looked right at me, turned a bright pink, and started fanning herself as though her heart was about to palpitate right out of her chest. I might not like Ana, but I had to agree with her. Jaz's ship was sinking fast, and at the rate she was losing customers, she might not have a business to come back to when the storm finally passed.

Feeling depressed and helpless, I headed toward the door. I had almost left the building when I spotted an outfit in the display window. Not just any outfit, but one of Jaz's brand new outfits she'd gotten from the city and had planned to display in this year's spring collection, but then the murder had happened. There was only one way that Anastasia could have gotten her hands on that outfit.

She had someone on the inside.

I left the store and parked my car down the road, then waited a bit until the morning shoppers had thinned out and headed off to lunch. My gut told me there was a mole working for Jaz. How else would Ana have known about that outfit? Once I was sure the coast was clear, I crept out of my car and slipped around to the back of Full Disclosure. The door there used a keypad with a code for a lock. Laying a tissue over the keypad, I punched in the code. I slipped inside, but didn't dare turn the lights on.

The first place I headed was to the back storage room. That was the last place I had seen Jaz store the outfit, along with the others she had put together for the collection.

Jaz had a great eye for what worked and what didn't when it came to fashion. I searched the entire room and finally found the clothes in a pile in the back. I looked through her file of invoices and sure enough the invoices were gone. Ana wouldn't be stupid enough to steal the actual clothes, and she didn't need to. As long as she beat Jaz to the punch and displayed the clothes first, then Jaz came off looking like the copycat. That's why both women kept each season's treasures locked up tight and tried to outdo each other with the best finds. So far Jaz had come out on top, until now. But which one of Jaz's employees would sell out to her?

Who had jumped ship?

Clunk!

A noise sounded from the front of the store. I froze. Who could it be? And where on earth was I going to hide? I glanced around the room. There were lots of boxes and clothing racks and outfits scattered about, but no real place to conceal myself. The noise was getting closer. My heart started pounding, and I wasn't quite sure what to do. At the last second I jumped behind the door. When it opened, I kicked it hard and it slammed into the person on the other side.

"Ooph!" came first, followed by a grunt as the person fell to the floor.

I didn't hesitate, running as quickly as I could, but not quickly enough, apparently. A hand reached out and grabbed my ankle and down I went...right on top of my attacker.

Darkness surrounded me.

No windows. No light. The door slammed and closed tight.

All I could hear was the sound of my attacker breathing. Or was that the sound of my own lungs gasping for air? I started to struggle, trying to figure out how to escape his grasp. It was most definitely a man lying beneath me. I might not have much experience, but there were some things a man simply couldn't hide.

"Dammit, Kalli, quit wiggling like that." *Before I embarrass us both.*

I stilled instantly, thinking, *Too late*. "Detective Stevens?" I squeaked and quickly rolled off of him, scooting away until we were no longer touching. "What are you doing here?"

"Me? I'm the cop, remember? The better questions is: What the hell are *you* doing here?"

I heard him fumbling about, so I got to my feet and found the light switch. We took a moment to adjust our eyes. I reached in my pocket, and a moment of panic hit me. I was out of hand sanitizer, and I'd left my purse in the other room. How had I let that happen? My heart started pounding and I could feel a bead of sweat trickle down my back, which made the situation even worse.

As though he could read *my* mind, Detective Stevens pulled out a handkerchief from his inside pocket and handed it to me. "Here," he said.

"Oh, thank you, but no. I couldn't possibly."

"It's no trouble." He took a step forward.

I held my hands up. "No, I mean, I seriously couldn't possibly. Do you know how dirty handkerchiefs are? Tissues are so much more sanitary. And when's the last time you had your jacket dry cleaned? Your inside pocket is undoubtedly loaded with germs. Who uses handkerchiefs these days anyway?"

"Never mind," he said, sounding exhausted. "I was just trying to help. And for the record, I'm very clean. As for the handkerchief, my ma gave me this." He pointed to the monogram of his initials on the front and shrugged. "She thinks if I keep it close to my heart, it will keep me safe. A lot of good that did me today when you tried to knock me unconscious." He grunted, slipping the handkerchief back in his pocket. He touched the back of his head, wincing.

"Well, if you hadn't scared me to death, that wouldn't have happened." I kept rubbing my palms down the front of my skirt, knowing I wouldn't feel completely clean until I showered at least three times.

"I wouldn't have scared you if you hadn't snuck in here. Do you know how much trouble you could get into just by being in here? You're lucky I was the one who saw you slip inside and not Detective Matheson."

"I work here, remember?"

"Nice try. You'd better not be trying to solve this case on your own." He loosened the knot of his tie and then pulled out a notepad and pen, jotting down Lord only knew what. "Don't make me lock you up for your own good, Ballas."

"Don't be silly, Detective. I came here to retrieve my book of designs."

"Then where is it?" he asked suspiciously.

"Oh, I don't let anyone see my book until I'm good and ready." I snapped my fingers. "Silly me. I've been so stressed, I completely forgot I had already brought it home, which is exactly where I'm about to head." I stepped forward, spotting a rag that only looked slightly cleaner than the doorknob, but I was desperate. I reached for it, but the detective's words stopped me in my tracks.

"Right. While I sympathize with your obvious discomfort, unfortunately, I don't think you're going anywhere."

"What are you talking about?" I swallowed hard, fearing what his answer would be.

"I'm guessing the door's locked. I'm no genius, but based on all the inventory in here, I'm sure Ms. Alvarez wouldn't have wanted anyone messing with her stuff. Kind of like your precious book."

"Oh, God, you're right," I moaned, instantly feeling the walls closing in on me. I grabbed the rag, cringing slightly, and tried the door. Sure enough, it was locked, and I knew for a fact that Jaz had the only key.

"Relax before you give yourself a heart attack." Nik stood.

"Don't touch me." I stumbled back a couple of steps.

"I'm not going to touch you." He slowly held his hands up in front of him, eyeing me like I was some bizarre creature from another planet. Sometimes that's exactly how I felt, but I was who I was. "I'm going to try the door," he said carefully.

"It's not going to budge. It's made out of steel. Jaz wanted to make sure no one could break in and see her latest treasures. Can't you just shoot it or something," I said, sounding hysterical even to my own ears. "There are no windows in here. I can't breathe." I fanned my face, feeling my throat start to close. "What if we suffocate?"

"I can't shoot it. The bullets could ricochet off the steel. We're not going to suffocate, Kalli." He pointed up. "There are vents near the ceiling, see?" He slipped off his jacket and rolled up his shirt sleeves. "If only they were big enough to crawl through," he mumbled to himself.

"Forget that. Just call for help, already. I need to get home now."

"I would if I could, but when a certain someone knocked me on my can, my phone went flying."

"Out the door?"

"Unfortunately."

"Stop saying that," I snapped.

"It's true," he snapped back, his patience with me finally waning. "This whole situation is unfortunate because you couldn't keep your nose out of places it didn't belong. If you had just done as I'd asked, you'd be home right now, taking a long hot bath."

"You obviously don't know me at all. Sit in my own dirt? Never." I shuddered.

"Fine, then. You'd be showering. Whatever." He swiped his hand through the air. "The point is you wouldn't be stuck in here with me."

"Don't say the word stuck." I wailed, seriously feeling claustrophobic. "There has to be something we can do."

"There is." He unclenched his fists and rolled his head on his shoulders, visibly gaining control over his emotions. "We can talk. You can start by answering my question for real this time." Nik sat down on a box and settled in.

Taking a deep breath, I found the cleanest spot I could, laid my coat over it, and gingerly sat, careful not to touch anything more than I had to. Maybe if we talked things through, we could figure out a way to escape. There was no way I could handle an entire night in this place.

"Fine," I finally said. "I went to Vixen to speak with Anastasia Stewart."

"I know," he said, not sounding the least bit surprised. "I tailed you."

I gasped. "That is a complete invasion of my privacy."

"Turnabout is fair play." He shrugged. "Keep invading my case, and everything's fair game, including your privacy. Now, you were saying?"

You're a big buffoon, is what I wanted to say, but growing up in my family had taught me to bite my tongue more than once. "I'm just trying to help, Detective. You were already looking into Johnny Hogan, and you knew I talked to Maria Danza." I wasn't about to tell him our suspicions regarding his partner, Boomer Matheson, but I could share the only other suspect we could think of. "Jaz and I both agreed that other than a jilted ex-lover or angry other woman, the person in town who would most want to see her locked up and out of the way would be her main competition in the business world, Anastasia Stewart."

"Agreed."

I blinked. "Wait, you agree with me?"

"Like I said, if you would have a little patience and let me do my job, you would realize I'm not completely incompetent."

"I never said that."

He arched a thick black eyebrow. "You didn't have to. Your actions speak volumes."

I bit my bottom lip and tried not to look guilty. "Okay, you go first, and I promise I'll share what I know."

He studied me for what felt like forever, then seemed to make up his mind about something.

"Deal," he finally said. "Maria Danza didn't just see Jaz and Wilcox from her shop across the street. Her pastry flour fingerprints were on the front window of Full Disclosure, and we have surveillance footage of her crossing the street just before Jaz shut off her cameras. Maria claims she went over to see if she could get a look at Jaz's latest conquest, but she couldn't see anything because they had already gone upstairs."

"I knew there was more to her story," I said. "And with the cameras off, there's no proof that she wasn't the one who went back in."

"Exactly," he continued. "I also looked into Ms. Stewart's finances and phone records. She made several transactions lately to the same anonymous account, and there were a number of phone calls to the same unlisted number. Whomever she was dealing with did not want to be found out. The question is why."

"The fashion world is very competitive. "

"I'm beginning to see that."

"Jaz and Ana have been competing for customers for years. At one time, Ana's store was the number one place to shop for high-end clothes in Clearview. As you know, Connecticut isn't that far from New York City. We have a number of wealthy residents who love nothing more than to spend their money on fashion, but making the trek into the city on a regular basis isn't always convenient. Having access to the latest trends in fashion right here in town is priceless to them, but they want to know they are getting the best.

Once Jaz added my Kalli Originals, she started edging out Ana. Ana didn't take that lightly, and she's been trying to find a way to get back on top ever since."

"The question is: Is she desperate enough to set Jaz up for murder?"

"Women and fashion can be a dangerous mix, and competition can make people do crazy things. All I know for sure is that the outfit in Vixen's storefront window is the same one that Jaz planned to use to launch her new spring finds. But since Full Disclosure is conveniently closed down for the moment, Anastasia beat Jaz to it. Jaz guards her finds with her life. There is only one way Ana could have known about that outfit."

"Meaning Jaz has a mole in her company."

"A mole with a much bigger paycheck as of late, it would seem. So what do we do?"

"We start there... if we ever get out of here, that is."

"That's not even funny."

"I'm not trying to be funny," he said in a serious tone. "The trouble with moles is they are dark and creepy and don't like to be found. There's a reason this mole took great lengths to remain anonymous. Something tells me he or she isn't above going to great lengths not to be found out."

"Great lengths like murder?"

The detective didn't have a chance to answer before the power was cut and the lights went out. I opened my mouth to scream, but the detective's hand covered my lips and pulled me behind a clothing rack just as the doorknob jiggled. I held my breath and tried not to think about all the places the detective's hands might have been and focused on the door as it slowly creaked open. The light streamed inside and temporarily blinded us, but one thing was for sure...

We were no longer alone and might very well be in the presence of a cold-blooded killer.

Episode 4

Chapter 10

Detective Stevens still held me tight against him, but his hand was no longer over my mouth—thank God, because who knew where it had been—as we hid behind the clothing rack in the storage room of Full Disclosure, awaiting our fate. The room was pitch black. With the loss of sight, my other senses came alive. I could smell his musky scent and feel his heart beating in time with mine. It still amazed me I wasn't completely freaked out by touching him. That wasn't to say I felt comfortable, but at least he didn't make my skin crawl. And that had never happened before. A step in the right direction, but I wasn't getting my hopes up. In my experience the only man who had the patience to deal with my quirks was Max, but I could never get out of the friend zone with him.

Thank God Nik was too focused to have any thoughts about me right now because I was terrified to know what he really thought about me. The doorknob rattled once more, bringing me back to the gravity of the situation we were in. I swallowed hard, my throat suddenly dry. What if the person on the other side of the door really was the killer?

As though reading my thoughts, he whispered, "It's going to be okay, Kalli. I might not have my phone, but I'm always packing." He unsheathed his weapon. *Get it together, Stevens. Both your lives depend on you keeping your cool.*

This time hearing his thoughts actually comforted me. Knowing he was afraid as well somehow made him seem more human. More approachable.

"I'm not worried, Detective. I believe in you," I responded in an equally quiet whisper and felt him relax. I could feel his confidence, which is exactly what I needed as the door creaked open.

"Freeze!" a feminine voice commanded.

"What the hell are you doing?" a male voice hissed. "I said to wait for me. Do you ever listen to anyone?"

"Jaz?" I sputtered.

"Detective Matheson?" Nik boomed at the same time.

The blinding beam from a flashlight shot straight into our eyes. "Kalliope Ballas, what in the world are you doing in my storage room? I could have shot your head off."

"How? Your gun is supposedly missing, or is there something you want to tell me?" Boomer countered in a snarky voice, earning the beam of light to be leveled on him now.

I blinked the stars out of my eyes and considered the pair. Jaz's hair hung long and loose in thick honey-brown curls. She had on a cute designer dress in several shades of purple, with matching heels, full makeup, and jewelry to boot. She'd said that morning that if she dressed like she normally would, then maybe her life would get back to normal quicker. Boomer wore jeans like Nik, but he opted for a brown leather jacket rather than a sport coat, bringing out the lighter tones in his russet hair. Unlike Nik, who towered over me, Boomer stood eye to eye with Jaz.

"Last time I checked *you* still had a gun," Jaz responded. "Keep messing with me and I might just shoot your head off."

He let his hands hover over his weapon as he leaned into her. “Is that a threat?”

“I don’t make threats, darlin’.” She thrust her face even closer to his. “I make promises, and I’m nothing if not true to my word.”

“Hey, Pebbles and BamBam, you’re giving me a headache. Can you play nice in the sandbox for two seconds so we can figure this thing out?” Nik let go of me and rolled to his feet.

“I agree. Let’s all call a truce and get out of here; we can talk out in the shop. I’m getting claustrophobic.” I stood as well, smoothing the dust and Lord knew what else off my skirt, then made a beeline for the center of the store before anyone could change their minds.

My skin was most definitely crawling now.

Jaz was the first person to reach me, followed quickly by Boomer, and then Nik bringing up the rear. It was still light outside, but Jaz turned the power back on and reset her alarm. We sat on the two sofas near the fitting rooms. For a moment, we all just stared at each other like we didn’t have a clue where to start.

I finally broke the silence. “Jaz, how did you know I was here? Even more confusing is how you ended up here with Detective Matheson? And why on earth did you cut the power?”

“I cut the power so my alarm would stop and no one else would show up. Besides, I wanted the advantage with you two in the dark. You know I keep my treasures in that room. I can’t risk anyone finding my steals and launching them first, so when my secret alarm went off, I tried to call you. I couldn’t reach you, so I called Detective Stevens. When I couldn’t reach him, I had no other choice. So please answer me this: What on earth are *you* doing here, and with Detective Stevens no less?"

"You're not going to like this," Detective Stevens interjected. "You have a mole."

"I have several, thanks to my mother's side of the family, but thanks for noticing." Jaz covered her cheek. "Gee, Detective, way to make a lady self-conscious."

"Trust me, Ms. Alvarez, you have nothing to be self-conscious about. I was talking about the other kind of mole."

"Ewww, the kind that burrow into the ground?" She shuddered and lifted her feet off the floor to curl her legs beneath her as she began to nervously eye every nook and cranny in the store. "I knew I shouldn't have bought such an old building."

"Jaz, this is not one of your finer moments," Boomer said with a snort while shaking his head.

"Pipe down, Beefcake," she snapped at him, then turned to me. "What the hell are you all talking about?"

"Jaz, honey," I said carefully. "I was here making sure your treasures were still in place, and verifying what I feared most." I paused and took a fortifying breath before blurting, "Anastasia launched the exact same outfits you were going to."

"Wait, what? When? How?" We all just stared at her, and then she smacked her forehead with the palm of her hand. "Oh my God, I have a mole."

"Really? What gave you the clue?" Boomer asked sarcastically, and Jaz lunged at him, falling off the sofa.

"Detective Matheson, can I have a word with you in private?" Detective Stevens pulled him to his feet and they walked off to the side just in time while I intercepted Jaz before she tried to strike again.

"That man makes me crazy," she said as I helped her to her feet, but then I heard, *Dammit, why do I let him get to me? Why do I care? Why the hell do I still miss the idiot?*

"I know the feeling. But if we don't all work together, we're never going to get anywhere in solving this case. Put your feelings aside and call a truce already."

"Easier said than done," she huffed, shrugging my hand off her shoulder as she sat back down. "And quit reading my mind. That's not fair." She blew out a breath. "All right. I'll try, that's all I can promise."

"Thank you." I took my seat once more.

The men rejoined us in the cozy seating area next to the dressing rooms, with Boomer appearing flushed as though he'd just had a stern talking to. He shot a quick look at Detective Stevens, who hardened his jaw and nodded. Boomer refused to look at Jaz, but he managed to mumble, "Sorry," and then took the seat by me on the burgundy microfiber sofa.

Detective Stevens removed a decorative pinstriped pillow, joined Jaz on the matching loveseat and said, "Can you think of anyone who could possibly be the mole?"

"Well, it could be one of my employees. I have a girl who is majoring in fashion design that works around her college classes. There's also my cleaning crew. They are here alone after hours. They all would have access to my treasures, I suppose. I just can't see any of them as traitors."

"What about the UPS guy?" I asked. "He delivers to both Full Disclosure and Vixen. He might not be able to see inside the boxes, but he would for sure be able to see where your boxes come from."

"I never thought of that. He's always flirted with me, but I've always blown him off."

"Shocker," Boomer muttered. After Nik glared at him, he added, "It's a shocker you never thought of that."

"This is a nightmare," Jaz said more to herself than any of them, sounding stressed and genuinely upset.

Boomer hesitated, then sighed. "I talked to the widow, and from what she told me, we just might be looking in the wrong direction."

"What do you mean?" Nik asked.

"I mean Darrin aka Scott had quite the past."

"And what exactly does that mean?" Jaz asked.

"That the killer might not have been after you at all, princess. It's very possible that the killer could have been one of Scott's enemies. We don't just have a mole, we could very well have a dangerous outsider in our midst."

Thursday morning I drove all over Clearview looking for the widow Wilma Parks. Detective Stevens and Jaz had agreed to work together, trying to come up with leads on the mole angle, while Detective Matheson and I were supposed to concentrate on Darrin's possible enemies. Boomer had said to start with the widow, so that's what I did. Nik had taken one for the team to keep the peace, leaving me to deal with Boy Wonder. Boomer had told me to wait for him. That he needed to do some work at the station and then he would call me. Not one to sit idle, I had ventured out on my own, but to no avail. I did learn one thing, though…

My car got lousy gas mileage.

I was just about to head home when I rounded the corner and saw Wilma coming out of Newcomer Funeral Home. I pulled over and parked at the curb, then waited a moment. No one else came out to join her. She turned toward my car, and I gasped over what she held in her hands.

An urn.

I knew for a fact this cavernous funeral home held a crematorium in the back. What I hadn't realized was the coroner must have finished his autopsy and released the body to the next of kin, aka his wife. Why have him cremated here with no friends or family around? Why not take him home? Granted, it was cheaper to carry an urn on a plane or train, rather than pay to ship the body, but what about her daddy? She had said he had plenty of money. Nothing was making sense.

I got out of my car and slowly approached her. The last thing I wanted was to startle her and have her drop Scott all over the sidewalk. "Mrs. Parks, how nice to see you doing better," I said as I approached her.

She stopped and blinked at me. "I just cremated my husband, and you call that better?"

"Oh, well, I mean…I just meant…your color looks better."

"Extreme heat tends to do that to a person," she said dryly, looking and sounding much less mousy than the first time I'd met her.

The question was, who was the real Wilma?

"I really meant no offense, and I truly am terribly sorry for your loss."

She seemed a bit pacified after that. "Thank you," was all she said.

"I couldn't help notice you're alone," I said quietly with real sympathy in my voice.

She glanced at the funeral home, and then back at me. "I was married for five years, but sadly, felt more alone then. At least now Scott will be with me all the time."

Creepy. "If you don't mind me saying so, why not wait to cremate him until you got home, surrounded by family and friends?"

The stiffness in her slight shoulders was evident beneath her drab gray dress. "My personal affairs and how I choose to grieve are my business, Ms. Ballas. But if you must know, I wanted Scott's cremation to be private, just between the two of us. It felt more personal and special that way, but I will have a ceremony once I return."

"Once again, I meant no offense." I was really awful at this whole investigating thing. "When do you plan to return home?"

She raised her eyebrow at me like she couldn't believe my gall.

"I mean, in case you need anything at all. I am at your disposal."

"I'm not leaving until tomorrow, but don't call me…I'll call you," she said with an edge to her tone, her message loud and clear.

Conversation over.

"Alrighty then. I'll be on my way." I waved, but she didn't budge.

I got in my car and drove away, but parked down the street around the corner. Then I doubled back to hide in the bushes, as close as I dared without being seen. Wilma was still there. She just stood there, standing alone on the sidewalk, holding the urn. I was close enough to see her frown down at the urn, looking like anything except a grieving widow. She looked angry and a little crazed.

Maybe she was waiting for a cab. I should have offered her a ride, but somehow I doubted she would have taken me up on it. She kept checking her watch and looking back at the doors to the funeral home. Finally, a man walked out and down the steps to join her on the street with his back to me. She didn't look surprised, like maybe she knew him, but she didn't look happy either. They started talking and it was evident by their gestures they were arguing. I studied him closer, but couldn't see his face, though his body looked familiar. When the man turned around, I opened my mouth to let out a scream.

But the scream never came.

A large hand clapped over my lips and yanked me out of the bushes on the other side so we stayed hidden. My body immediately revolted, squirming and tingling with the heebie jeebies. Not that this man was dirty. He smelled quite nice, in fact, of a spicy aftershave. But he wasn't Nik, and that was the problem. If I had any doubts before, I didn't now. Touching Detective Stevens was most definitely a unique experience for me, because obviously with everyone else I still had an issue.

What the hell is it with these two? Damn woman doesn't listen any better than her roommate.

"Boy Wonder?" I mumbled from behind his hand.

"Excuse me?"

"I mean boy, Boomer, you found me," I amended, calming myself so he would let me go.

It worked.

"Don't scream and I'll let you go. Can you handle that?" he asked in a low voice.

I nodded furiously. He let me go and I lurched forward, inhaling a huge breath and biting my tongue at the urge to ask him when the last time he washed his hands was. Pressing my lips together, I turned around to face him.

"I thought I told you to wait for me?" he asked with exasperation. "I get Jaz not listening because, well, Jaz is Jaz. A hot-headed, stubborn woman. You, however, are supposed to be the cool, level-headed one. What were you thinking?"

"That I would try to get some information and save time while you were doing your thing at work. I'm sorry, but I—"

"My *thing* at work?" he sputtered. "It's called police work, and I'm damned good at it." He crossed his arms.

I held up my hands in a passive gesture. "I know, I'm not saying you're not. I'm just saying I . . . "

He started to pace before me. "If you had waited, I would have told you that Scott Parks' body was released to his widow. The coroner has finished his autopsy, and—"

"He's not dead!" I cut him off this time with a swipe of my hand.

He stopped and gaped at me. "Come again?"

"That's why I almost screamed. It's what I've been trying to tell you." I rubbed my temples, feeling a whopper of a headache coming on, and then tried again. "I saw Wilma come out of the funeral home with an urn. I talked to her briefly, and then I left. Only, I didn't really. I doubled back and was spying on her. She kept standing there, so I thought she was waiting for a cab."

"I'm guessing she wasn't?"

"No, she was waiting for a man, but not just any man."

"Then who pray tell did you see?"

"Her dead husband. He's either a ghost, or Scott Parks is still alive."

Chapter 11

Boomer and I ran around the bush to the front of the funeral home, but Wilma Parks and her ghost of a husband were no longer there. The streets were empty, the sun shining bright in clear blue skies, a slight cool spring breeze in the air. A typical spring day, only it was anything but.

"You sure you weren't seeing things?" Boomer asked, scratching his head.

"Positive. My vision is 20/15. Better than average. I'd know Darrin aka Scott anywhere. They've gone, but Wilma said she wasn't leaving until tomorrow. Maybe we can still catch them at the hotel."

"Come on. I'll drive, but this had better not be a wild goose chase, Cat Girl." He gave me a knowing look. "That's right, I heard the Boy Wonder crack. For the record, I'm not Detective Stevens' sidekick any more than you are his leading lady."

I gasped. "Yeah, well Jaz will never be your Bat Girl either, so there!" I spat, then gritted my teeth, frustrated I let him get to me. But unlike Jaz, I wouldn't miss him one bit if I never saw him again. "Look, let's call a truce, okay?"

"Fine," he said with a shrug of his shoulder as though my words hadn't gotten to him, but I could tell he was as frustrated as I was.

"What about my car," I asked, happy to change the subject.

"We'll pick it up later. Let's go. We're burnin' daylight."

I followed him to his car, pulled out a tissue, and opened the passenger door. Inspecting the interior and deciding it looked decently clean, I spread the tissue out over the seat and sat down. He eyed me warily.

"Problem, Cat Girl?"

"What? These seats are leather. I can only imagine the chemicals they were treated with and what that can do to a person's body over time. I'm not taking any chances."

His brows shot sky high, and his look said it all: *You can't be serious, and if you are, then you're seriously crazy*. If he told me not to worry because I had nine lives, I'd have to *holy hit him, Batman* and not think twice about it. Thankfully, he didn't say a word. He just put the car in gear, and took off toward the Clearview Motel.

A few minutes later we pulled into the parking lot and cut the engine. "You ready?" Boomer asked.

"As I'll ever be," I responded, reaching for the door.

"Remember," he warned. "Let me take the lead."

"Aye-aye, Captain." I saluted him.

"It's Detective, but whatever. Just remember who wears the badge." He climbed out of the car.

Badge of arrogance, I thought. But I didn't say anything as I quickly followed his lead.

We walked inside the two-story motel to the small lobby that was in dire need of remodeling. Peeling white paint disgraced the walls, worn carpet covered the floor, and faded lumpy chairs sat in the lounge beneath a TV that had to be from the eighties. But the town of Clearview was small and didn't have many other options: a quaint bed and breakfast place on the lake, some cabins in the campground, and Larry Miller's motel.

“Detective Matheson, what can I do for you?” Miller asked, his thinning combed-over hair just as much in need of a makeover as well. His small round spectacles sat perched on the end of his bulbous nose, and his too-small eyes squinted jovially.

“Hey, Larry. How’ve you been?” Boomer shook his hand and then leaned against the counter in an open, friendly way that invited conversation.

“Oh, I’m gettin’ by, same as the rest of us, I suppose. My gout’s been acting up a bit. Must be we’re due for a storm.” He winced and rubbed his leg. Larry loved attention and reminiscing about the old days, but once he got started, it was nearly impossible to get him to stop. “Why, did I ever tell you about the time—”

“Oh, my goodness, would you look at that?” I said, pointing out the front window.

Both men looked outside, then back at me with startled expressions.

“Silly me, I thought I saw Elvis.”

Boomer frowned.

Larry puckered his brow.

And I laughed nervously.

“I once saw Big Foot, you know. On a hunting trip. And I know lots of people have seen Elvis, but never here in Clearview,” Larry said in wonder.

“Stranger things have happened.” I shrugged, then winked at Boomer, but his Boy Wonder Catdar must be off, because he wasn’t reading me loud and clear. In fact, he didn’t seem to be reading me at all. “Isn’t that right, Detective? Haven’t we seen stranger things right here in Clearview just recently? I’m sure Larry would love to hear all about it. He loves a good story, don’t you, Larry?”

Boomer narrowed his eyes at me, clearly not happy with my interfering. But if I hadn't interrupted, we would have been here all day with Larry telling stories from his past. If Boomer ever wanted to become Batman, he needed to step up and take the lead. And now would be a good time.

"The floor's all yours, Boy—Boomer." I smiled sweetly and, embracing my inner Jaz, threw in an eyelash flutter for good measure.

He just shook his head. His expression morphed from one of relaxed conversation to that of stern disbelief. And suddenly, Boomer didn't look so boyish. He looked like a big, intimidating man. My smile vanished, and his turned smug. The vibrating undercurrent from his stare warned me payback would be coming.

He put on his professional face and focused on Larry. "What Ms. Ballas is getting at, Mr. Miller, is that Elvis isn't the only one she thinks has returned from the dead."

"Oh, my word, you don't say," Mr. Miller said in awe. "Please, go on."

"I'm sure by now you've heard about poor Scott Parks."

"Who?"

"Darrin Wilcox," I interjected, earning myself another scowl. I pursed my lips, looking down and inspecting my nails.

"Darrin Wilcox is an alias Scott used while in town. His real name was Scott Parks. I believe he stayed at your motel."

"Oh, yes, I know him. He was the man that was found dead in Ms. Alvarez's shop, right?"

I nodded. Boomer snapped his gaze in my direction, and I pointed to my lips, making the locking sign and throwing away the key.

"Yes, Larry, he was. The thing is, Ms. Ballas swears she saw him with the widow Wilma Parks earlier today outside of the funeral home. Do you know if either of them are here? We'd like to ask them some questions. If he is Scott Parks, then who is the widow carrying around in the urn?"

"The widow isn't staying here. She's out at the bed and breakfast. I guess this place isn't fancy enough for her." Larry smoothed his comb-over before adding, "But the other guy is."

"Who, Mr. Parks?" Boomer asked.

"No, he's dead."

"Are you sure?" Boomer took out his notebook.

"I'd bet my motel on it. The feller you probably saw was the other guy?"

"What do you mean other guy?" I asked, not caring if I got another dirty look.

Larry looked at Boomer for the okay before answering.

"What she said," Boomer repeated, not caring that it had come from me at the moment. We were both too captivated with this new piece of information.

"When Darrin checked in, I gave him his key, and he went to his room and then stepped out again. A while later, he came back in and asked for another room. I thought he was a little slow in the head, if you know what I mean. So I asked him if something was wrong with the room I already gave him. That's when the other one walked in. I sure as shoot thought I was smack dab in the middle of a Doublemint Gum commercial."

"Wait, what are you saying?" Boomer asked.

"That wasn't Scott Parks we saw with Wilma. It was his brother," I said in shock. "Scott Parks had a twin."

"You never call, you never write, you never visit..."

"Ma, we live in the same town," I said through my cell phone, regretting answering the stupid thing in the first place. Especially since Detective Matheson sat beside me as we drove to Flannigan's Pub that evening.

He stared straight ahead at the road, but I saw his lips twitch ever so slightly.

"Are you eating? You're too thin, you know. Your cousin, Yanni, could blow you away with his leaf blower. It can happen. I know these things. Or maybe it was his power washer. Yiayia Dido said she saw it on TV. The Discovery Channel, I think. Anyway, the point is you're not taking care of yourself."

"It was the Weather Channel and it was a tsunami, Ma, not Yanni." I took a calming breath. "I promise I am taking good care of myself."

A smothered chuckle came from the other side of the car, but when I glared in that direction, Boomer's face was expressionless and he still stared straight ahead, eyes on the road.

"I'm really worried about you, Kalliope. Your Aunt Tasoula said she heard from Mrs. Flannigan's daughter's friend while cutting her hair that someone trashed your car and robbed your house."

"It was Jaz's car, and no one took anything from the house, so it technically wasn't a burglary." That earned me a sharp frown from Boomer. I rubbed my temple. "And Jaz never reported that, Ma, so how...never mind. The point is, we really are fine."

"You might be fine, but *she* isn't. Eleni said she saw you at Vixen's. Now there's a classy lady, that Anastasia. It's about time you switched teams. I bet Ana would let you design wedding dresses in her shop. She—"

"I did not switch sides, and I am not designing wedding dresses." This conversation was giving me a headache. "I gotta go, Ma. I got a date with a mystery man." I hung up, knowing I was going to pay for that one later. At least it would keep her busy for a while, so I could focus on solving this murder and getting my life back.

"Wow."

"Don't say a word, Matheson, or I'll tell my mother my date was with you."

That shut him up and made his fair skin grow even paler. He didn't speak again until we pulled into the parking lot of Flannigan's Pub. Boomer and I had decided to retrace the victim's last steps before he died. We knew he had checked into the Clearview Motel, and we knew he had a twin who had also checked in on the same day. We also knew he'd gone to Flannigan's and argued with Johnny Hogan, who had threatened him, before meeting Jaz for dinner. Twins were a lot alike, so we were banking on Scott's twin having the same tastes and habits.

We walked inside of the Irish pub and struck gold. Sitting at the empty bar was the man I had seen earlier with Wilma. Scott's twin. Even from this distance I could see they were so nearly identical, it was uncanny. If Scott were here, I wouldn't be able to tell them apart. It dawned on me that if I couldn't tell them apart, then the odds were that the citizens of Clearview couldn't tell them apart either. Which begged the question what kinds of misunderstandings had taken place before Scott's death. This mystery man just might hold the key to answering a lot of our questions. If only we could get him to cooperate.

Boomer and I started to walk over to him when I stopped short. Boy Wonder stopped beside me and gave me a curious look. "Let me take the lead on this one. Something tells me he responds better to a feminine touch."

Boomer opened his mouth, and I knew he was about to make a snarky remark over the word *touch*, but at the last second he must have changed his mind. Or remembered our truce and his promise to Detective Stevens. He fell back and gestured for me to take the lead.

I undid the top button of my blouse and pulled the clip out of my hair, shaking the strands loose. Taking the seat right next to the man, I smiled up at the bartender, Mr. Michael Flannigan himself. He grinned back in surprise, his gaze shooting between the two of us with curiosity, devouring every detail to spread to the gossip mill as soon as I walked out the door, no doubt.

Oh the joys of living in a small town.

"What can I get for ya, lass?"

It was a bit early and not even the weekend, but I was willing to play the game. "A glass of chardonnay, please." I turned to the man next to me. "Hi, my name is Kalli." I held out my hand without so much as a wince this time.

"Bobby," he said, eyeing me carefully. He shook my hand, and I knew without a shadow of a doubt he wasn't Scott. Scott had oozed heat and sexuality, while this guy didn't have to think anything for me to know the only thing on his mind was hatred and revenge.

I quickly let go with a nervous laugh, discreetly rubbing my hand on my lap. "Okay, good. I'm not seeing a ghost. You must be Scott Parks' brother," I said and then wiped off the edge of my glass before taking a sip. "I'm sorry for your loss."

"Thank you." He relaxed a bit and held up his mug of beer. "To Scott," he said. "May he rest in peace."

"To Scott," I seconded and clinked glasses with him, then casually turned mine around to sip from the side that hadn't touched his. He didn't notice, thank goodness.

"I didn't realize Mr. Parks had any family, other than his poor widow." I swirled the contents in my glass, watching the way the soft amber lighting reflected off the golden liquid.

"He was a hard man to track down." Bobby grunted softly as though reliving some private memory. "I came in yesterday as soon as I heard."

"That's an outright lie," said a deep voice from behind us.

I nearly let out loud on a groan. What was Boomer doing? He had no room to criticize Jaz and me. He had no patience at all.

Bobby's head whipped up, and he looked sharply between the two of us. "I knew you looked familiar," he said to me. "You're friends with the woman who killed my brother, aren't you?"

"Allegedly," I said, refastening my top button and scooping my hair back into its twist.

"We'll ask the questions." Boomer flashed his badge.

"What is this: good cop bad cop?" Bobby asked warily.

"More like sidekick central," I muttered.

"What do you want from me?"

"How about the truth?" Boomer demanded. "Larry Miller said you checked into the Clearview Motel the same day as your brother. So why lie about it? And why didn't you come forward when we were looking for his next of kin?"

"My brother and I didn't exactly get along. Scott was a big gambler. He owed the wrong people a lot of money. It was ruining his life. I found out about his alias and went after him. I wanted to make amends and help him, but he wouldn't listen. So I waited at the hotel for him to get back from his date with another woman, except he never came back. I panicked and hid out, hoping the killer would be caught. Then Wilma showed up and saw me. She's never liked me. I was with her today to try to explain why I didn't come forward. She didn't believe me. That's why I'm here now." He lifted his beer and took a long swig.

"Maybe she's onto something. Why didn't you and your brother get along?" Boomer asked. "Did you hate him enough to kill him? Who doesn't come forward when his own flesh and blood has been murdered?"

The blond giant stared us down. "I told you I was trying to make amends and help my brother, that was all. I did not kill him."

"What I want to know is if Wilma didn't like you, then why didn't she rat you out when I confronted her in front of the funeral home earlier today?" I asked, earning an impressed look from Boomer. "You were inside, completely oblivious to our presence. We would have had you trapped."

"Probably because she has a secret of her own," Bobby said with pure venom, and it was obvious he disliked her as much as she did him.

"Interesting," I responded. "Care to enlighten us?"

"Wilma is pregnant," Bobby said.

"Shocking." Detective Matheson put his notebook away. "Don't waste our time."

"Hear me out," Bobby hastily added. "Wilma's pregnancy might not be shocking, but I have a piece of information that is full of shock value."

We waited not so patiently while Bobby drew out the drama, rivaling the best of the Ballas clan, and that was saying something. When Boomer reached for his cuffs, Bobby dropped the bomb.

"My brother Scott was sterile."

Chapter 12

Saturday evening Jaz and I invited both detectives to a spaghetti dinner at our house so we could compare notes. Jaz was a great cook. She had even used whole-wheat pasta for me, yet made it taste amazing. And I had to admit, both men *looked* amazing. Boomer wore dark-blue dress jeans and a soft cotton T-shirt in burnt orange, while Nik had on fawn Dockers and a baby-blue Polo shirt. I wore a pair of beige dress slacks with a mauve silk shirt, and I had even relented to Jaz's insistence that I leave my hair down.

"I can't believe Wilma took a life insurance policy out on Scott right before he died and didn't think it would look suspicious," Jaz said to Detective Matheson, looking pretty as a petunia in her yellow spring dress.

"After we intercepted Wilma at the train station, thanks to Bobby cooperating, we ordered her not to leave town," I replied, having a hard time stopping myself from always taking the lead, much to Boomer's displeasure based on the way he was looking at me. I quickly added, "Then Detective Matheson used his impressive connections, while I used the Internet, and we did some digging all day yesterday." I cut my salad into tiny pieces, garnering me a strange look from him. I couldn't win, so I gave up trying and put my fork down.

"I guess Wilma knew about Scott's gambling problem," I went on, "but she was willing to forgive him even though she was lonely. In a moment of weakness, she got pregnant and hoped that would save their marriage, but it turns out he was sterile and never told her. She asked for a divorce, but he threatened to expose her if she left him. Turns out he only married her because of her father's money. She didn't want the scandal, but she was heard vowing to find a way to make him pay." I picked up my water glass.

"Any idea who the father is?" Detective Stevens asked before taking a sip of his red wine.

"No, but she's not the only one with more to her story," Detective Matheson interjected around a mouthful of pasta. This time I gave him a judgmental look that didn't go unnoticed. He finished chewing, wiped his mouth, and continued. "Scott and Bobby were raised by their grandfather. I guess the old man had a lot of money. All their lives, Scott was the one who kept getting into trouble and screwing up, until their grandfather disowned him when he was eighteen. Scott got a job selling used cars, becoming a pro at wheeling and dealing, while Bobby remained the golden boy. Some kind of scandal happened years ago, but no one knows the details. Just that suddenly Scott was the favorite, and Bobby disappeared for several months. The grandfather died and left all of his money to Scott, and Bobby suddenly reappeared. That's when the rift between them occurred."

"I'm guessing Scott gambled away his inheritance, and that's when he found Wilma," Jaz said in disgust. "With his looks and charm, I'm sure he swept her off her feet before she had a clue what his real motivation was: her money."

"Exactly. Now we just need to find out where Bobby disappeared to and why he was no longer the favorite, then we'll have some answers," I said. "There are still so many questions, like who is the father of Wilma's baby, and does he have a connection to Scott? Also, did she take out that life insurance policy because she knew Scott was going to die?"

"I'm impressed, Ms. Ballas," Nik said, locking eyes with me. "Not bad for a rookie."

"Thanks," I said, feeling heat creep into my cheeks, yet finding great pleasure in his words.

Boomer grunted, and Jaz kicked him under the table. Nik flashed a look that said, *Really*? and Boomer asked, "How about you guys? Any more luck with figuring out who the mole is?"

"Sully Anderson, the UPS guy, wasn't around to question because he conveniently went away on vacation as of yesterday," Nik said after checking his notes. "He should be back in a few days, so I'll question him then."

"Yeah, and my student employee, Amy Fisher, is smarter than she looks," Jaz said, talking with her hands like she always did. Except she had her fork in her hand, with food still attached. My eyes never left the fork, terrified the half-eaten meatball was going to fly off. "Amy quit," Jaz continued, "and is now working for Vixen, claiming she can't wait around for my store to reopen. That she has to think of her career first, and with the recent scandal, Vixen is a better fit as an internship for her resume. Ha!" Swipe went her hand, and the meatball went sailing across the room. Prissy pounced and ate it, I gagged, and Jaz stabbed another meatball and started in again. "Anastasia was only too happy to give Amy a job, of course. Meanwhile, Amy claims innocence about any knowledge regarding my treasures and suggested we speak with her boyfriend who's a lawyer if we have any further questions..."

"So basically we got nowhere," Nik cut her off, bless the man.

"What about your cleaning crew?" I asked, knowing we needed answers but terrified she would pick up the fork she had finally, *thankfully*, dropped.

"They barely speak English and don't seem to have a clue about the fashion industry, not that they need to, to do their jobs." She picked up a piece of bread this time, absentmindedly ripping off chunks and sending crumbs flying all about, which wasn't much better. "They apparently moved on as well. Why can't I hire loyal people? At this point, I won't have a staff to reopen with anyway. Thank God for my online business, or I would seriously start to get worried."

My phone chose that moment to ring, thank the Lord. I glanced at the caller ID, and lost my appetite altogether. I excused myself and went into the kitchen for privacy. "Natasha, great to hear from you," I lied.

"I thought I would check in and see how your book of designs is coming along," she said pleasantly enough, but I couldn't help but think there was an underlying meaning.

"Oh, it's coming," I lied again, thinking going to church twice tomorrow might not be a bad idea.

"You do know what today is, don't you?"

And there was that edge I was getting more and more familiar with, I thought. I responded as innocently as I could, "Saturday?"

"Exactly. Don't forget, your deadline is one week away."

"Is that what Mr. Erickson says?"

"I told you. I am in charge of promotion. He might have hired you, but I can make or break you. I'm only being so tough on you because I know how hard it is for a woman to succeed."

"I'll do my best."

"No, Ms. Ballas, you need to be better than your best. You need to be perfect, and it better be worth my time. One week. No excuses." The line went dead.

No pressure.

Another Sunday brunch after church with my family. And shock of all shockers, Nikos and his Ma, Chloe, were invited. Her visit had turned into a full week now. The woman was retired, and I was terrified her "visit" would turn into a permanent stay.

Where was Frona when I needed her?

I glanced around and noticed the full gang was here this week. Ma and Pop, Dido and Yiayia. My aunts and uncles and too many Ballases to name. Lights were strung all over the gazebo, with statues and fountains gracing the yard and enough food to feed a small army.

My gaze settled on Jaz, who was flirting outrageously with my cousins Kosmos and Silas. I frowned. First of all, she was here, which was surprising enough. And second, she knew the rules. But then I realized the reason for the flirting. Boomer Matheson. What on earth had my mother been thinking?

The deeper we got into spring, the crazier my mother became. It didn't take a full moon to bring out her wild side. All it took was mating season, and she became possessed with spring fever. She had babies on the brain. There wasn't a single person she didn't set her sights on when it came to matchmaking. It was like a disease with her.

And there wasn't enough sanitizer in sight.

That was the only reason Jaz was here. Even Ma could see there was something between Boomer and Jaz. It didn't matter that Ma disliked Jaz. Ma couldn't resist the challenge of matching them up. She just hadn't counted on Jaz messing with her plans by flirting with her nephews. Eleni intercepted Ma before she had a chance to give Jaz a piece of her mind, and I made a beeline for my best friend.

"What, pray tell, are you doing here…trying to start World War III?" I hissed.

"What can I say, I'm bored. And your cousins are fun. And there's great food."

"And Boomer's here," I pointed out.

She rolled her eyes. "Oh, please. I don't care what you think you heard, I'm not into him. I broke up with him, remember?"

"And we both know why, because you liked him *too* much."

"You're out of your mind."

"And you're out of your league. You're surrounded by an army of Ballases. You're outnumbered big-time, sweetie. You do the math."

"Fine. I'll behave. Now quit worrying about me. You might want to worry about yourself because you're the one who's going to need rescuing soon."

I followed her gaze and saw my mother falling all over Nikos, trying to feed him, of course. He accepted more food on his already heaping plate without hesitation. He knew exactly how to hold his own with a Greek mama. He wasn't the one who needed saving. I was. I swallowed hard and watched with great trepidation as his ma headed in my direction, but she wasn't carrying food. What she carried was far more dangerous, and she didn't hold it in her hands. She held in her eyes.

A look of stubborn determination.

"Kalliope Ballas, as I live and breathe, you look beautiful today," she said, coming to a stop way too close, with no regard to personal space.

I resisted the urge to lean back. Instead, I smiled gracefully. "Thank you, Mrs. Stevens. I always wear my Sunday best to church."

"Your mama raised you right, and please, call me Chloe. I haven't been a Mrs. in quite some time." She looked wistful, and I didn't have to touch her to feel her longing. "That man was a stallion in the bedroom," her face turned sour, "but a stubborn mule in the rest of his life." She winked. "My Nikos got the best of both of us. My dark good looks, his Pop's stunning blue eyes and body, and my fun-loving ways. He loves to fool and have fun and eat." She looked me over carefully. "You look like you could use a good dose of all of those." She grabbed my hand. "Don't worry, honey, he'll fix you right up."

Oh, love is so grand, I miss it so. Everyone deserves to find happiness, especially my Niki. And you, my dear, are adorable. A mystery, yet stubborn and strong and independent. Exactly what my Niki needs. The things my baby boy could do to you. He could teach you so much. He is his father's son, after all. He could fix you. Darling, you're wound up so tight, what hot-blooded man wouldn't want to unwind your coils, pop your springs, and—

"Ma, what are you doing to the poor woman? She looks like she's about to faint," Nik's voice said from somewhere close by as Chloe was pulled away from me and let go of my hand. "For that matter, so do you. Are you feeling okay?"

We both blinked at each other like we'd been lost in a fantasy together and had been oblivious to the world. For once in my life, I actually hadn't wanted to let go, and that scared me even more than the germs that must be crawling all over my palm now.

"Opa, I need a drink!" She cleared her throat and walked away on wobbly legs.

I stared after her, reaching into my purse and absently pulling out my hand sanitizer to scrub my hands, my gaze still glued to her retreating back in wonder.

"Earth to Kalli, I said are *you* okay?" Nik touched my shoulder then dropped his hand immediately, but I'd felt the tingle in places I had no business feeling anything.

"I-I'm fine," I said and faced him, knowing my cheeks were bright red. "I see you finally escaped my mother." We started walking together, away from everyone to the edge of our yard under a big tree where it was less noisy and there was less chance of getting cornered by the mamas again.

"She's harmless," he said, his face softening. "I actually find her charming."

"That's one word for her."

"My mother on the other hand is—"

"Sweet," I said and meant it. "She loves you and only wants you to be happy." We came to a stop and faced each other.

"I could say the same about your mother. What exactly did my ma say to you?"

"Um, it wasn't exactly what she said, but I could tell she has spring fever same as my ma. It must be a Greek mama thing."

"Spring fever?" he asked, his lips tipping up in a mixture of amusement and curiosity.

"Yeah, you know," I said in a teasing voice, "the birds and the bees and all that."

"All that would be?" His thick brow crept up, his lopsided grin speaking volumes.

He was toying with me, pushing me to say it. I was a big girl. I could play along. "All that talk about spring being the season of rebirth."

"Ah, the mating season," he said.

"That would be the one. I guess the idea of reproduction and making babies ignites a fever in our mamas. Hence the term *spring fever*. It makes them all hot and bothered, and then they bother everyone else."

His Adam's apple bobbed as his gaze dropped to my lips. "Good thing we're not each other's types." He took a step toward me.

"Yeah, good thing," I replied, standing my ground even though my knees were shaking, "because neither of us wants that kind of distraction right now."

"True," he whispered, his face a few inches from mine now, "distraction would be really bad right now." He cupped my face and leaned in, *But I bet it would feel so damn good*, he thought seconds before his lips pressed against mine.

I froze, but I didn't move. Part of me squirmed with the thought of the exchange of germs that kissing involved. Before I could read minds, kissing wouldn't have been an option. But now that I could hear his every thought, my mind was so full of his seduction, it couldn't hear the part of me screaming to pull away and gargle with...

You smell so good, baby. Like wildflowers in a meadow. And your taste...my God, it's like pure spun honey. Your lips are so soft, and your skin is like silk. Oh, baby, your body fits so perfectly against mine, I can't take much more. I want to—

"Nik and Kalli standing under a tree, K I S S I N G. First comes love, then comes marriage, then comes baby in a baby carriage," sang a feminine voice as it circled around us, followed quickly by peels of giggles. "Or maybe the baby comes first." More giggling ensued as she skipped circles around us.

Sure, *now* Frona shows up. We broke apart and noticed that all eyes were on us.

"Kalli?" came a familiar male voice. "I thought you said you didn't date."

I turned to the side and couldn't believe my mother had invited Max of all people. "I don't," I said weakly.

"Could have fooled me," he said and then stormed out.

I looked back at Nik, and we just stared at each other in shock and awe and wonder. Part of me was glad I never got to hear what he wanted to do to my body. I was still shocked over the fact that his thoughts could seduce me, allowing his body to do things to mine that once would have never been possible. I was terrified. What was I supposed to do with that? He might want me physically, and it might actually be a possibility now, but he'd made it clear he didn't want a relationship or a distraction right now. Would that be enough for me?

I suddenly realized the answer was a resounding, *Hell yes*!

What if I woke up and my gift went away? I might not ever have the chance to satisfy my urges. Oh, good Lord in heaven, I just realized I wasn't so different from my mother after all, because one thing had just become perfectly clear...

I had spring fever too!

Episode 5

CHAPTER 13

Monday morning I made my excuses and slipped out before Detective Stevens could see me. After that kiss, I needed to think of him as a detective rather than Nik the sweet sexy Greek who had swept me off my feet just one day ago. Don't get me wrong, I still had spring fever in a big way. I just had no clue how to go about taking care of it. And even though he wasn't the one who could read minds, I was mortified to think everything I was feeling might be written plain as day across my face. While his charming smile and gentle touch made me think anything was possible, that little voice in the back of my head warned me that Detective Stevens might be far more than I could handle. So my answer for now...

Avoid him at all costs!

Rumor had it Sully Anderson—aka Jaz's UPS guy—was back in town. My cousin Eleni's boyfriend's sister Marigold—the one who put the voodoo curse on Jaz—was friends with Sully's sister Val. Turns out Marigold likes Sully and was jealous of Jaz, even though Jaz had made it perfectly clear that Sully wasn't her type.

Clearview wasn't that big. I was bound to run into the UPS delivery truck at some point. I drove around for the next hour in the rain until finally I got lucky. I was stopped at a stop sign when the truck drove right by me. I ducked and then popped my head up just enough to see what was going on. The truck pulled over and the driver got out.

He made several trips to deliver packages to my yiayia and papou's dry cleaning business. Then my aunt's hair salon next door, followed by my cousin's bakery down the street. By the time the driver—who was most definitely the curly caramel-haired Sully—climbed back into his vehicle, I had nearly fallen to sleep. The soft pitter-patter of rain on the roof of my car tended to do that to me. And the sleepless night of tossing and turning hadn't helped.

Most UPS drivers were quick, delivering their packages promptly and efficiently. Not Sully. He loved to talk. Mix that with my family, and he could spend half a day on just one block. Lucky for him the citizens of Clearview loved him, or he'd probably get fired. Finally, he pulled away from the curb and headed to a different part of town. I followed, careful to maintain enough distance without losing him as I squinted through the swipe swipe swipe of my windshield wipers.

He made a stop by Sinfully Delicious. Once again, he chatted forever with Maria, then he stepped back outside. He stared across the street at Full Disclosure for what seemed like forever. Finally, he got back in his truck and drove away. Again I followed. This time he pulled up at Vixen's, but he didn't park out front like he had at all the other places. He pulled out back. I waited for a while, but when he took even longer than at any other place, I parked down the street out front and then ran out back, minus an umbrella. I peeked around the corner, but he had already gone inside. I briefly wondered what the ever-worsening ozone could have done to the rain and what long-term side effects might be occurring within my body at this very second.

Pushing down the panic attack that was threatening to take over at any second, I thought about what I was supposed to do. If he came back outside right now, he would see me. There were no bushes to hide in like there had been at the funeral home. I couldn't risk him seeing me, but I needed to hear what was going on, if anything. I spied a dumpster and knew in my gut this was going to send me straight to therapy. I took a deep breath and reminded myself that Jaz was worth it.

I slowly made my way over, swallowing hard and feeling my stomach churn with every step. I came to a stop by the edge and felt my pulse. Yup, racing like the first-place car in the Indy 500. Slipping on the rubber gloves I carried in my purse before I could freak myself out even further and change my mind, I opened the top of the dumpster. Grabbing onto anything I could, I climbed to the top.

Oh, God, the trash hadn't come yet!

Rain, rotting garbage, and Lord knew what else...I was going to be sick. There was no way I could do this, I thought and started to back my way down when I heard the unmistakable sound of a door being opened. With nowhere to go, I squeezed my eyes shut and jumped. I tried to catch my breath as dumpster materials squished around me and rationalized how doing things that terrified me would only make me stronger. And getting stronger was exactly what I needed if I was ever going to do something about my spring fever.

Stifling my gag reflex, I pushed through the rancid trash and peeked through a crack in the corner of the dumpster but didn't see anyone yet. It finally stopped raining and the sun broke through the clouds, causing a brilliant rainbow to arch across the sky. I couldn't even enjoy it because the stench of my surroundings turned even the most beautiful things vile. Something crawled across my shoe and I screamed, then I slapped a hand across my mouth. The smell of latex was a welcome distraction.

The back door of Vixen swung open.

"What was that?" Ana asked, her sharp gaze darting about the back lot of her store.

"Probably just a cat," Sully responded with a shrug as they both faced the dumpster, providing me with a perfect view. "You'd be surprised the things I encounter on my route."

"Darling, I can only imagine." Ana reached out and squeezed his hand. "Why don't you quit and come work for me? You're so good at servicing people. My customers would love you."

"You drive a tempting bargain, Ana, but alas I can't." He pulled his hand from hers and rested it on his heart. "Your customers already love me, as I probably have serviced most at least a time or two."

"That's my point. You're so popular."

"I do what I can."

"And you do it so well." Her laugh trilled through the air.

He bowed gallantly and then winked. "Well, duty calls. Guess I better head out."

"Oh, here." She looked around suspiciously, then handed him a note. "I trust you know what to do."

"Honey, I always know what to do." He took the note and slid it into his back pocket.

She laughed again, waved, and then went back inside. He walked to his truck, whistling along the way. The note slipped out of his back pocket, but he never noticed. I stayed in the dumpster until I heard the unmistakable sound of his truck start up and then drive away.

Hoisting myself up, I scrambled out of the dumpster, stripped off my gloves and tossed them back over the edge. Thank goodness the heaping mound of trash had made it possible to escape relatively easily. If I had gotten stuck in there, I would never have survived. The thought of that alone caused perspiration to dot my forehead. There wasn't enough hand sanitizer on the planet to rid me of the filth covering me. It would take three hot showers, minimum. But first, I had a note to fetch.

Using stealth moves like I'd seen on TV, I skirted over to the side of the building, snatched up the note, and then sprinted to my car, not stopping until I was safely ensconced inside—which took a bit of time, considering I had to cover the seat with the paper towels I had conveniently in the trunk. Like my yiayia says, you never know when there's going to be a big mess to clean up and I didn't want a single speck of dumpster doo-doo touching anything else that belonged to me. Finally, I opened the note and read it.

Meet me at the same time same place: Lakeshore Heights, tonight at ten pm. Ask for Stacy Walsh.

Lakeshore Heights was a small motel just across the line in the next town over. Bits of Ana and Sully's conversation came back to me: *so good at servicing people, drive a tempting bargain, so popular, do what I can, you do it so well...* Sully had pulled his truck around back, instead of the front. He'd spent the most time in Ana's store. They'd flirted and then she'd acted all shady, looking around and giving him a note. It didn't take a genius to figure out what was going on.

Anastasia Stewart was having a secret affair she didn't want anyone to know about, and her lover was Sully Anderson.

"You did what?" Jaz asked as we sat around the dining room table having lunch. More like Jaz was having lunch. I didn't have an appetite. I'd taken three hot showers, scrubbing my skin nearly raw, and I still felt dirty. Not to mention, the smell seemed to be permanently adhered to my nose hairs and no amount of blowing cleared it out. I might need to see a doctor.

I set down a crystal dish filled with only the best tuna for Prissy, before I answered Jaz. "I tailed Sully to see if he was up to anything suspicious and then dove in the dumpster to spy on him."

"I heard that, I just can't believe it." Jaz stared at me in shock and awe, crossing her arms over her warm-up suit and leaning back in her chair. "You're changing. *He's* changing you."

"I don't know what you're talking about." I dusted an imaginary piece of lint off my yoga pants and then pushed my bowl of salad away. "Can you smell it? I think I can still smell it." I extended my arm toward her face.

She set the legs of her chair back on the ceramic tile with a resounding thud and pushed my arm away. "You know exactly what I'm talking about. Nikypoo is the kind of man you need, just like I'd hoped he would be." She grinned.

"He's not changing me. My *gift* is."

"True, but it's *his* thoughts that are working their magic."

I tossed my hands in the air. "Yeah, well, none of that matters if I don't have a clue what to do about it. I've had issues my whole life, so needless to say, I'm not exactly experienced in the art of seduction." I picked up my bowl and carried it to the sink, rinsing it out thoroughly with soap and hot water before putting it in the dishwasher.

"No worries, babe," Jaz said as she followed me. "That's what you have me for."

"No offense, but that terrifies me." I laughed, then frowned as I leaned against the counter, facing her. "Speaking of seduction. Sully is a good-looking guy and highly respected around town. Why would Ana act all secretive if she were dating him?"

"Good question," Jaz said in all seriousness as she wiped down the counter. She'd learned to spray it three times with a disinfectant because she knew if she didn't, I'd follow right behind her and do it anyway. "Who knows with that woman? She's so uppity. Maybe she thinks he's beneath her or something. Their affair does surprise me, though."

"Why's that?"

Jaz waved the sponge about as she talked, nearly giving me a heart attack when it almost came in contact with me. The last thing I wanted to do was take another shower. I preferred paper towels, but Jaz refused to cave on that one. She had no idea I threw the sponges out daily, replacing them with brand new ones when she wasn't looking. "Sully was just flirting with *me* right before he left."

"But you always turn him down," I replied, taking a big step back, well away from the deadly sponge. Lord only knew what germs it harbored. I could practically see the multiplying bacteria. “Maybe Ana’s easy.”

Jaz tossed the sponge beneath the sink, then popped her head up, her eyes going wide. “Or maybe he’s the mole.”

Her words made me forget the sponge. “He does deliver to both of you. If you kept turning him down, maybe Ana said yes on purpose. If he delivered your trade secrets to her, she would agree to sleep with him, but only if he kept the affair a secret. That way you’d never make the connection.”

“Exactly. They just didn’t count on you going all Veronica Mars on them. Man, I can’t wait to see Ana’s face when we blow her little secret right out of the water. I’ll show her what happens when someone messes with me.”

“There is no *we*, Jaz. I agree with Detective Matheson on this one. You need to stay out of this. You’re not helping the situation any by getting all up in Ana’s business. You’re just going to make yourself look crazy and capable of killing someone.”

“Detective Matheson is the one I’d like to kill,” Jaz grumbled.

“All in due time. But first, we have a murder to solve.”

“I thought there wasn’t a *we*?” she threw my words back at me, sarcasm dripping from each syllable and a big ole pout spread across her face.

“We’re still a team, it’s just I will be the one to check out the motel while you hold down the fort here.”

“And do what?” she sputtered. “There’s nothing more I can do.”

“Then do something else, like spring cleaning or something.”

"Puh-lease. Like this place isn't already spring cleaned 24/7."

I rolled my eyes. "Then do some spring planting."

"Um, you've already planted, pruned, and picked just about every spec of this yard already. There's not a single spring anything I can contribute to." Suddenly she got a look in her eyes that could only mean trouble.

"Oh, no. What are you up to?"

"Just coming up with a new recipe."

"A new recipe for what?" asked a familiar male voice from the doorway.

Jaz and I both jumped. Prissy looked up and hissed, then pranced away with her nose in the air.

"Sorry, door was open," Nik said through the screen. He had on his typical work attire of jeans, sport jacket, and tie. "May I come in?"

"The door's always open for you, Detective," Jaz fairly purred. "Isn't that right, Kalli?"

"Sure thing." I smiled stiffly, feeling my ears burn as my face flushed fire red.

He stepped inside and shoved his hands in his pockets, looking a little nervous. Was he reliving our kiss from yesterday afternoon as well? I'd made the excuse I felt sick last night, took off early from the party, and hadn't spoken to him since.

"I hope you're feeling better today. You took off so early this morning, I didn't have a chance to check on you. I had some time on my lunch break, so, well, here I am."

"To answer your question, Detective," Jaz looked right at me as she finished with, "I'm working on a new recipe for a cure. A homeopathic cure. It involves oysters, among other things."

His brow puckered, and he scratched his head. "For what?"

"Oh, just a little something that's ailing Kalli these days. She has a fever."

I gasped, and my eyes shot to Jaz. She wouldn't dare, would she?

"I thought she looked a little flushed," Nik said, his gaze running over me with worry. "I hope it's not anything serious."

"I'm fine," I quickly interjected, feeling my cheeks grow even warmer, which wasn't helping my case one bit. "Jaz is just—"

"Concerned," she cut me off. "But it's nothing a little TLC—you know, tender lovin' care—won't cure."

I covered my eyes and groaned.

"You sound like my ma," he said to Jaz, and I could hear the humor in his voice. I opened my eyes to see his lips twist into a lopsided grin, and he suddenly looked much more relaxed as he studied me with blazing curiosity and definite interest in his eyes. Good Lord, was he catching on to what she was talking about? If so, then I truly was in danger of dying of mortification.

"So does this ailment have a name?" he asked as his eyes settled on me.

I fanned my cheeks. "It's not an ailment, really, it's—"

"A little known thing called *spring fever*," Jaz finished with relish, then added, "No worries, Detective. I know just what to do."

Chapter 14

Kill . . . me . . . now!

The rest of Monday passed with Nik checking in with me constantly. He might have been curious after Jaz's ramblings, but I wasn't sure if he had clued into what spring fever really meant. We'd had the whole teasing conversation about our mothers and spring fever, but he wasn't giving anything away. And he didn't trust Jaz to have the "cure," so he'd told his mother, who promptly told my mother, who then told half the town, which consisted of most of my family. Thanks to Jaz I'd spent the rest of the day in bed, being fussed over and fed more chicken soup than anyone should ever have to eat. And Ma was over the moon that Detective Dreamy was so concerned about me.

Twenty-four hours was all I could take.

"For the last time, Ma, I said I'm fine. I don't know what came over me, but I'm sure it won't happen again. I need to get out of this house. I'm going someplace quiet to work on my book of designs."

"Come to the restaurant. We'll find a nice quiet spot for you to work. You gotta eat, right?"

I shook my head even though she couldn't see me through the phone. "I ate enough for a week yesterday. No offense, but I'm not setting foot near that restaurant or any of the family."

"Okay okay, but bring a sweater and make sure you keep an eye on your temperature. Your Uncle Phelix had the fever once. Remember what happened to him?"

"Ma, I keep telling you the fever didn't give Uncle Phelix rabies, the raccoon out back in his shed did. The fever was just a side effect."

"Fine, don't listen to your mother, but when you get the rabies, don't come crawling back to me."

"No worries there, Ma."

"What, now you don't want to be near me? What has the world come to when my only child doesn't want to be near her mother? Wait until your father hears this one. It's that Jaz, I tell you. She's turning you against your own family."

"There's my doorbell. I've got to go. I'll call you later." I hung up to her yelling for me to look through the peephole and not open the door to strangers.

There wasn't really anyone at the door; I just couldn't take any more of that conversation. It was early, and Jaz was still in bed. She was another person I didn't want to face after what she'd put me through. Besides, I wasn't so sure I wanted to do anything about my spring fever anymore. I'd given up on the idea of love and romance long ago, but then Nik had come along, and my gift had made everything possible. He was the only one who had ever physically affected me this strongly, and my gift made me stop thinking altogether as his thoughts seduced me. But I wasn't sure what to do or even how to be intimate, and that embarrassed me greatly.

The only thing I knew for sure that I wanted to do at this point was follow up on Ana and Sully and their motel rendezvous on the outskirts of town, so that's exactly what I did.

I slipped outside and drove across Clearview's town line straight into Lakeshore. Lakeshore Heights was a quaint little hotel that sat on the shores of a small lake, tucked into the woods. Most people wouldn't know about the place, as it pretty much catered to the overflow of outsiders who came to the lake in the summer when the cottages and campgrounds were full.

It was the perfect little getaway for someone who didn't want the locals to find them.

Someone like Anastasia Stewart. She would never stay at a dive like the Clearview Motel. Lakeshore Heights might be small, but it was picturesque and modern, right up Ana's alley. She just hadn't counted on this local finding her note to Sully.

I headed inside and took in the charming rustic interior as I approached the desk. The animal heads on the wall kind of creeped me out, but the wooden accents and scenic paintings throughout the lobby added a warm and cozy feel.

"Good morning, ma'am. Welcome to Lakeshore Heights. Our cabins down at the Oasis don't open until after Memorial Day, but we have several rooms here at the Heights open during this time of year if you're interested," said a pretty young blonde girl.

"Actually, I was looking for a friend of mine. I was supposed to meet her here yesterday for her birthday, but I got held up out of town. I was hoping to catch her this morning."

"What's the name, and I'll see if I can find her for you."

"Stacy Walsh."

The girl didn't even have to look through the registry book. Her face got all flushed, her eyes going dreamy.

"I remember her. She came in late last night just before the end of my shift."

"Wow, she must have really stood out."

"Not her, but the guy who was with her sure did."

"You mean she had a man with her?" I asked, feigning surprise. "Are you sure?"

"Positive. I wouldn't forget a guy like him. Guess she found someone else to celebrate with."

"Good for her," I said. "I don't want to disturb them, but if you don't mind, I'd like to wait around until they check out."

"That's not possible."

"I promise I won't loiter or disturb your other guests. I'd really just like to wish her a happy birthday myself."

"It's not that. I mean, you can't wait for them because they've already checked out."

I blinked. "This early?"

She shrugged, and then leaned in close, looking left and right to make sure we were alone. "Can I tell you a secret?"

I met her half way with an encouraging expression on my face as I whispered, "I love secrets."

"They checked out separately and left alone and... he winked at me on his way out. If you ask me, her birthday wasn't that happy. Poor thing. He was hot, but I'm thinking he wasn't that good. What a shame. She looked like she could use a little excitement in her life."

"No worries. I know exactly what to do to put a whole lot of excitement back into her life. And there's no time like the present," I said, heading out the door on a mission.

"Where's the fire?" Detective Stevens asked as he leaned against his car in the parking lot of Lakeshore Heights.

"Excuse me?" I stopped short, and my cheeks flooded with heat at the mere sight of him.

"I see your fever's back," he said, eyeing me suspiciously.

"Yup, that's right. In fact, that's why I'm here. I didn't want to contaminate anyone. But I'm feeling a little better now, so I decided to go home. See ya." I walked around him and headed to my car.

"Not so fast," he said, falling into step beside me. "I talked to Jaz, who woke up and had no clue where you were. Then I talked to your mother who thinks you're working on your book. So I checked out all the possible *quiet* places you might be with no success. Finally, I went back to Jaz. When she told me about the latest you had found out, we put two and two together. I took a chance and came here. Imagine my surprise to see you investigating alone when we had specifically agreed to share information and work together." He grabbed my arm to stop me until I faced him. "Why are you avoiding me, Kalli?" *Especially after what we shared. You can't tell me you didn't feel anything.*

"That's why," I said on a shaky breath, pulling away from his hand.

"What's why?" He arched a brow. "I don't understand."

Ugh, it was so frustrating not being able to tell him that I could hear his thoughts, but the last thing I needed was for him to think I was even more of a freak. "I know you don't. I just . . ."

"Is it because we kissed?" he asked quietly.

I met his gaze. "No. Yes." My shoulders slumped, and I looked down. "I don't know."

"Hey," he waited until I looked at him, "I'm not sorry for kissing you."

I took a minute to trace his features with my gaze before admitting, "I'm not either."

"Then what's the problem?"

"You wouldn't understand." The men I'd dated in the past never did.

"Try me."

"It's just hard for me."

He paused for a minute and then said, "Because of your quirks?"

"Bingo," I laughed harshly. "Scared yet? Ready to run for the hills?" I folded my arms in front of me.

"Not at all," he said without hesitation. "It was just a kiss, Kalli. It doesn't have to be anything more. We both agreed we didn't want a relationship, but sometimes the most unexpected surprises happen. Let's just take this one day at a time and see what happens, okay?"

It felt like a huge weight lifted off my shoulders. "Okay."

Until he added, "As long as we're honest with each other, it will all work out."

"Right." I sighed, knowing total honesty at this point was out of the question, unless I wanted him to think I was crazy. Jaz was counting on me. I didn't know a lot about the law, but I was pretty sure crazy people weren't allowed to help out with an ongoing murder investigation.

"In the meantime, we have a case to solve, and you seem to have a head for this," he said, solidifying my point. "Since you appear to be on to something, how about you fill me in on what you just found out while I drive." We started walking back to his car, which reminded me of mine.

"But what about my car?"

"I'll send someone to pick it up and drive it back to your place."

"Okay. In that case, let's go find Sully Anderson."

While Nik drove all over Clearview looking for Sully's UPS truck, I filled him in on what I had found out so far.

"Wait, back up a step. You climbed into a filthy dumpster yet you have a problem kissing me?" He arched his eyebrows and gave me a disbelieving look.

"Neither snow nor rain nor a stinky dumpster will keep me from seeking justice." I fluttered my lashes at him.

"Cute," he smirked, "but you aren't helping the post office, you're helping a police officer, and you didn't answer my question."

"Speaking of the post office, did you know the U.S. Post Office doesn't actually have a motto? 'Neither snow nor rain nor heat nor gloom of night stays these couriers from the swift completion of their appointed rounds' is really just an inscription the architects put on the General Post Office in New York City. Most people think it's their creed."

"This isn't a game of Trivial Pursuit, Kalli, this is real life. And you, my dear, are avoiding giving me a straight answer. Classic evasion. Why is that?"

"A woman can't tell all her secrets, Detective. Then there would be no mystery, and what would be the fun in that?" I gave him a Mona Lisa smile, trying to act like Jaz, but then my stupid cheeks heated again." I studied the road as if it were the most fascinating thing I'd ever seen—anything to avoid direct eye contact—as I added, "Besides, I thought we had a case to solve. Don't you think we should focus on that?"

"You're a mystery, all right," he said with a sigh.

"That's me, a regular enigma," I muttered, and then I noticed Sully's truck parked in front of the construction company that Johnny Hogan worked for, Banks Construction. "Look, there's Sully's truck." I pointed.

Nik pulled into the parking lot. "Remember, you're not a cop, but I am, so let me take the lead. Okay?" I nodded, and we went inside the main office. Sully was chatting away with Ronald Banks, the owner of Banks Construction. Ron was a short, stocky man with a bald head and glasses. He looked much older than a man in his fifties, like all the years spent working in the sun had finally caught up to him, which reminded me to reapply the sunscreen I always carried in my purse and used year round.

They had just finished talking, and Sully headed in our direction. Sully was tanned and toned, with brown curly hair with model good looks. Jaz had just never been into him. He wasn't big enough for her tastes, but he wasn't a blonde. Boomer had been the only exception, which I still believe made him special, no matter how many times she denied it.

Sully stopped short when he saw us. "Hey, Detective Stevens." He nodded at him and Nik nodded back. Then Sully looked at me. "Ms. Ballas. How y' all doing? How's Ms. Alvarez these days?"

"Hi yourself, Mr Anderson." I smiled pleasantly, trying to keep him at ease.

He held up his hand to stop me. "Please, call me Sully."

"Only if you call me Kalli."

"Done," he said while wearing a charming smile. It was easy to see why he had the entire town under his spell.

Nik frowned and cleared his throat.

"Jaz is hanging in there," I continued. "Not an easy task after being accused of murder and missing out on her spring launch."

"I heard about that. It must be hard for a woman like her. I know she takes her work very seriously."

"Yes she does," I said. "That's why it's killing her that there is still a murderer on the loose while she is innocent."

"Speaking of suspects," Detective Stevens interjected with a serious tone as he took the lead. "I've been meaning to talk to you since you got back from your convenient vacation."

"What do you mean convenient?" Sully's charming smile faded, and he eyed us both carefully. "My sister and I surprised my parents with a cruise for their fiftieth wedding anniversary."

"That just happened to take place right after the first murder Clearview has seen in decades," the detective added.

"I couldn't have predicted that guy would die in Jaz's shop right before my trip. What does any of that have to do with me?"

"You could have planned the murder," I jumped in, trying to help, even though the detective gave me a warning look, which I promptly ignored. "It's no secret you had a thing for Jaz. Maybe since she kept turning you down, you turned to her competition out of spite. You delivered Jaz's new secret spring line, so you could have easily found out where she ordered it from. Then you gave it to her competition, killed Jaz's date to frame her for murder and have her shop closed down just before the launch so Ana could beat her to it, then you conveniently took off out of town."

His face registered a mix of shock and horror. “You’re both crazy.”

“Where were you on the night of the murder?” Detective Stevens asked, pulling out his notebook and pen.

“With my sister, going over last-minute details for our trip. Ask her.”

“All night long? Because the murder happened in the middle of the night just before dawn. Was your sister awake then to verify you were still at her place?”

Sully’s jaw hardened. “I didn’t kill anyone, and I would certainly never do something like that to Jaz.”

“You would if you were sleeping with Anastasia Stewart,” I blurted, and Nik just shook his head.

“You son of bitch!” a deep voice boomed, and before we knew what was happening, Johnny Hogan launched himself at Sully Anderson, hitting him square in the jaw.

The men fell to the floor, landing blows and rolling about on the ground. I jumped out of the way, making sure no drops of blood landed on me. I searched my skin for any cuts, shuddering to think of what would happen if someone else’s blood mixed with my own. God forbid I ever needed a blood transfusion. I seriously don’t think I could handle it.

“Break it up, you two,” Nik bellowed, stepping between them and pulling the big blonde giant off of Sully.

They slowly rolled to their feet, battered and bruised and panting heavily.

“What the hell gave you the idea I was sleeping with Ms. Stewart?” Sully asked.

“First of all, you flirt with her all the time,” I said, pointing out the obvious. Nik just tossed his hands in the air and gave up trying to stop me.

Sully shrugged. "Truthfully, I flirt with everyone. It's just my nature."

"Well, I saw you Monday morning at the *back* of her store, when for every other store you pulled up out front."

"You followed me?" he asked, looking stunned.

"Never mind that. She's working with me," Detective Stevens covered for me. "Why pull into the back of Vixen?"

"Because Ana—I mean Ms. Stewart—had a private delivery she didn't want anyone to know about." Sully looked at me to drive his point home. "Same as Ms. Alvarez has had me do in the past. You of all people should know that."

"Then why did Ana give you this?" I asked, thrusting the note that had fallen out of his pocket that day at her shop. Nik gaped at me like he couldn't believe I'd kept it instead of turning it over to him. *Whoops*, I mouthed, realizing at that moment I really didn't know much when it came to investigating.

Sully remained oblivious to our exchange as he took the note and read it. "I was wondering where that went," he said, not looking surprised in the least. "This isn't mine."

"But I saw her give it to you when I was in the dum—"

"When she was with me," Nik amended. "We know it's yours, so cut the act."

"It's not his," Johnny said, taking the note from Sully. "It's mine." He looked at Sully apologetically. "Sorry, man."

The detective and I looked at each other in surprise. Sully Anderson wasn't the one who was having the affair with Anastasia Stewart. Johnny Hogan was.

Chapter 15

"Freeze!" Detective Boomer Matheson yelled as he barged into Banks Construction.

"Boomer, what the hell are you doing here?" Detective Nik Stevens ground out.

"I called the police," Ronald Banks said, adjusting his glasses.

"I *am* the police," Nik growled.

"Looked like you needed backup to me." Ron shrugged, then gestured to Sully and Johnny. "I didn't need these two gorillas messing up my office."

"Put your gun away, Boomer," Nik said with a sigh. "I've got everything under control."

Jaz poked her head around Boomer's back, her honey-brown curls bouncing as she spoke. "What on earth is going on?"

Boomer did a double take, then slid his gun in its holster. "Jazlyn Alvarez, I thought I told you to stay in the car. Are you ever going to listen to me?"

"Probably not." She patted his shoulder and then stepped around him. "Kalli, what's going on?"

He shoved a hand through his russet hair and then dropped his palms to his hips as he looked at Nik, who raised his own hands helplessly, looking as though he felt his pain.

Ignoring them both, I filled Jaz in on what had just happened. And that's when World War III happened.

"You're sleeping with Ana?" Jaz shrieked, launching herself at Johnny.

He caught her mid-air and pinned her arms to her sides. "You're the one who broke it off with me."

"I don't want you back, you big buffoon. I just can't believe you fed that bottom sucker my spring collection. It was bad enough you trashed my car."

"Easy, there, Hogan."

"Me? Talk to your girlfriend. She's the psycho."

"I'm not his girlfriend, you traitor," Jaz spat and hit him again.

Boomer pulled Jaz away from Johnny and kept a firm grip on her so she wouldn't attack again.

"I didn't feed Ana anything, and I didn't trash your car," Johnny said to her. "You're delusional. I'm glad I'm in a relationship with her and not you."

"Relationship? Ha! She's using you, and you can't even see it. It's kind of sad actually."

"Kind of like you used me? I'd say you're the sad one."

This time Sully launched himself at Johnny. "That's no way to talk to a lady," he said, as his fist connected.

"She's no lady, and you're downright pathetic if you think you stand a chance with her. You're probably the one who leaked her spring collection to Ana, but she turned you down too. How's it feel to know nobody wants you?" Johnny replied, following his words up with a punch of his own.

They tumbled to the floor once more and rolled around, each one trying to get the upper hand. Johnny was bigger, but Sully was faster.

"For the love of God," Nik said, this time pulling Sully off of Johnny.

"You're all nuts," Johnny said, backing up a step like he might make a run for it.

I reacted without really even thinking about what I was doing or how much trouble I was going to get in or how mad Detective Stevens was going to be as I pulled his gun from its holster and shot the ceiling. "You're not going anywhere, Mr. Hogan."

Everyone froze as little particles of sheetrock floated down from the ceiling.

Then chaos erupted as their shock turned to shouts and reprimands and lectures and arguments and accusations. Boomer tried to calm everyone down, while Nik tried to convince me to give up the gun. Everyone talked over each other, and I couldn't take it anymore. I did the unthinkable and pulled the trigger again, this time taking out a ceiling light.

"I'll tell you where you're all going," Ron thundered, running into the room with a shotgun. "Straight to jail." And then he picked up the phone.

A couple hours later, Jaz and I sat in a holding cell at the police station. Her for inciting a riot, and me for discharging a police officer's weapon. One cell over, Sully and Johnny were in for disturbing the peace. Meanwhile, Boomer and Nik were in their captain's office, getting a stern talking to by the sound of the raised voices down the hall behind closed doors.

I'd take the cell any day, although I wasn't about to sit on the moth-eaten cot or touch anything within the small space.

The detectives finally emerged from the room down the hall, and I was thankful for the bars between us. That was a thought I never imagined having. They stopped in front of our cell and just stared at Jaz and me, clearly furious with us both. We both took a step back and exercised our right to wisely remain silent.

Sully and Johnny weren't so smart.

"Hey, let me out of here," Johnny yelled. "I didn't do anything wrong. I am an innocent victim in all of this."

"You're a lot of things, Hogan, but innocent isn't one of them," Sully replied. "I'm the one who didn't do a thing wrong. This whole thing is ridiculous."

"Yeah, well, you weren't the one who had a gun pointed at him. I should sue you all for the emotional damage you've given me."

"You big overgrown baby. I still don't get how any woman could possibly find you appealing."

"Keep it up, you two, and neither one of you is going anywhere," Nik said.

That finally shut them up.

Boomer pulled out a key and unlocked the door to our cell.

"What are you doing?" Jaz asked.

"You're free to go," he said, a muscle in his jaw bulging.

"Both of us?" I asked hopefully.

Quiet grumbles came from the cell next door, but the occupants didn't say a word.

"Apparently so." Nik nailed me with a hard stare. "Ron Banks decided not to press charges, so long as you pay for the damages to his ceiling and replace the overhead light."

"Done," I said, stepping forward and walking out of the cell before anyone could change their minds. Jaz quickly followed, and we both stayed as far away from the detectives as we could.

"You took the word right out of my mouth, Ms. Ballas," Nik said with a controlled but obviously angry tone. "We are definitely done."

Well, that didn't sound good.

"That's right, ladies," Boomer added, a lot less controlled than Nik. "There is no more *we*. Not if *we* want to keep our jobs. If *we* see either of you anywhere near this investigation, you'll find yourselves right back in here for obstructing justice. Do *we* make ourselves clear?"

"Crystal," Jaz said, barely suppressing an eye roll as she took my arm and pulled me toward the door. I could hear she had a comeback that was dying to slip out, but the woman wasn't stupid. She knew when to shut up and get the heck out of Dodge.

"I can't believe we got off without any punishment," I whispered to Jaz on our way out.

Apparently, not quietly enough.

"Oh, I wouldn't go that far, Annie Oakley," Nik said from behind me, sounding more than satisfied. Even a little pleased, if I wasn't mistaken.

My steps faltered, but I didn't turn around as I asked, "And why's that, Detective?" fearing the words I suspected were coming.

He didn't disappoint as he uttered with unmistakable delight, "Your mother's right outside."

My stomach dropped. "What about Sully and Johnny?" I asked, desperately stalling, not wanting to face the music.

"Yeah, what about us?" Johnny asked, sounding much meeker this time.

"I have a route to finish," Sully said earnestly.

"We still have some questions for them both before we release them," Boomer said.

"But—" Johnny started.

"Shhh," Sully hissed.

A minor scuffle ensued, and then they were quiet.

"I suggest you worry about yourself," Nik said to me, "and what's on the other side of that door," he added, and with that, they were gone.

"Well, kiddo, have fun with that." Jaz patted my arm and turned around.

"Where are you going?" I sputtered.

"My mama didn't raise no fool. I'm heading out the back." Her high heels clickety clacked as she disappeared down the hall.

I contemplated following her, but knew my family wouldn't rest until they tracked me down. Knowing Nik, he'd probably called her out of spite. Taking a deep breath, I turned around and walked out the front door with my head held high. Dark clouds had rolled in, looking gloomy and ominous, threatening a doozy of a storm.

"You see?" Ma pounced on me immediately, her polyester pantsuit making a swishing noise with her every movement. "Even God is unhappy with you." She pointed toward the sky. Her beehive of hair swayed about as she inspected every inch of me. She knew better than to touch me, but she had no qualms about invading my personal space. Her face was literally an inch from my body.

"I'm fine, Ma." I stepped back a foot, and her face fell a little. I knew it bothered her, but she understood I couldn't help it. If only I had been more like the child she so wanted and needed. "How did you hear I was in jail?" I asked, trying to distract her from my actions.

"That's not important," she said confirming my suspicions. "Mamas know everything, you know that. And you don't fool me. You're not fine. First with the fever, and now with the rabies. I told you this would happen."

Thunder rolled off in the distance, making me nervous. Lightning could be nearby. The odds of surviving a hit by lightning weren't good.

"I don't have rabies, Ma, but I am tired. I'd like to go home."

"See, you're sick." She looked at me knowingly as she tsked. "Why else would you shoot up poor Mr. Bank's construction office? Only the rabies would make you do something so crazy. I know these things. It's only a matter of time before you lose your mind, just like cousin Phelix."

"Ma, I didn't shoot up the office. It was only two shots, but mostly I was pointing the gun at Mr. Hogan to stop him from leaving." Whoops. I regretted the words the second they slipped out.

My mother made the sign of the cross and said a quick prayer, looking ready to faint. "My baby's a criminal. This is going to send Yiayia right to the hospital with heart palpitations.

"Yiayia is going to outlive us all, and you know it."

"That's it. You're coming home with me. We'll stuff you good, then smother you in aloe and wrap you in duct tape. That will cure this fever of yours."

No worries there. Nik had already cured it by turning into Nikos and calling my mother. "You're supposed to feed a cold and starve a fever. Not the other way around, Ma."

"You already starve yourself, and look where it's gotten you. Skinny and sick."

"I'm not skinny, and I'm not sick."

A streak of lightning lit up the sky, making me jump. My heart raced, and my breathing picked up, and I was pretty sure my face had grown pale.

"Mmm, hmmm. I'm not taking any chances. Let's go." She grabbed my arm and pulled me toward the parking lot. My car was home, and the lightning worried me. Having no other choice, I let her drag me along. *I hope they keep that awful woman behind bars. First murder and now this. I bet she's the one who gave my baby girl the rabies in the first place. Someone needs to put that looneybin out of her misery.*

There was no point in arguing with my mother. She was too stubborn to listen to reason, and I knew from a lifetime of experience that she wouldn't leave me alone until she got her way. So with lead in my feet, I stumbled along to her waiting car, trying to block out her thoughts. It wasn't hard to do because my thoughts wouldn't stop reminding me of exactly what the rest of my evening would entail…

A date with a jar of aloe, a roll of duct tape, and a stomach ache from consuming way too much food.

"Hang on a sec, Ma." I pulled away. Two could play at this game. "Everyone who's in jail is allowed one phone call. I never got mine," I said, as an idea came to me.

"But you're out now, and I'm here to take care of you. What do you need a phone call for?"

"Oh, I don't, but trust me, someone else does. And you're so right. Everyone needs their mama in times like this," I said, opening my cell phone and dialing a number that had been added to my contacts whether I'd wanted it there or not.

"Hi, Kalli, I'm so glad you called. I've been meaning to catch up with you, but you've been so busy lately," said a female voice through the earpiece of my phone. "How are you feeling?"

"I've been better, Chloe," I said, trying to keep the smile out of my voice and sound grave. "Thank you for asking. I must say your son has been better too."

My mother's whole face brightened when she realized whom I was talking to. She nodded, patting my head in total approval of what I was doing. She just had no idea about the real motivation behind my call: payback.

I continued with my own amount of satisfaction as I said, "Did you hear the news . . . your son is in big trouble?"

Episode 6

Chapter 16

Wednesday morning Nikos the Greek burst into Jaz's and my side of the house, looking three sheets to the wind and out of breath. His thick, wavy, black hair stood out in all directions, and he still wore the same clothes he'd had on the day before when we all did "time."

"*Why* would you call my mother?" he blurted, all wide-eyed and possessed, sending Prissy bolting down the hall to Jaz's bedroom. Little good that would do her since Jaz didn't stir before noon unless she was headed into work.

I calmly finished eating my Wheaties—the breakfast of champions, because that's what I was, of course—and dabbed the corners of my mouth with a napkin. I was showered, fully dressed in a cute lavender spring suit, and ready for my day as I glanced at my watch. I'd been expecting him, and quite frankly, I'd thought it would be sooner than now. That meant I owed Jaz twenty bucks. I pursed my lips. Just another reason to be angry with the detective.

"Get a clue, Detective. It's a little thing called payback," I said with a smug smile as I inspected my perfectly clipped, filed, and buffed nails.

"What are you, five?" he sputtered.

"As I recall, you tattled first." I slapped my palms down on the table and stood, glaring daggers at him. "You want to know what I am, Detective? I'm itchy! See these hives?

I spent my evening smothered in aloe and wrapped in Duct Tape, while the relatives' relatives came to view poor little Kalliope's rabies and consulted with yet again even *more* relatives, who then proceeded to try out further home remedies that date back to the Stone Age. Good times, Detective." I narrowed my eyes and repeated with a hiss, "Good times!"

Nikos's eyes lost their dazed crazy look only to open wide as his eyebrows arched sky high, then he burst out laughing. When he finally recovered, he said, "You win!"

I crossed my arms and looked down my nose at him and sniffed sharply, then frowned, lifting my wrist to my nose—careful not to touch it, of course. "I still smell from dumpster diving."

He rolled his eyes. "You don't smell, Ballas. It's all in your head."

I nearly snorted as I thought, *If you only knew*. But then I sniffed again and winced. "I'm telling you, I smell. See?" I thrust my wrist up beneath his nose, definitely careful not to touch it. Lord only knew when the last time he used a neti pot to thoroughly clean out his sinus cavities. I shuddered.

He took a big sniff and then shook his head no.

I puckered my brow. "Why don't you smell this?" I smelled a third time and was ready to face the dreaded inevitable. "That's it. I need to see a doctor. I hate doctors, but I don't want to die. Something could be seriously wrong with me. What if the odor seeped into my pores permanently?"

He grabbed my arm before I could avoid him and inhaled deeply. *I think your brain has permanently left your skull and you need to see a shrink*.

I gasped and yanked my arm away.

He gave me a funny look. "What? I didn't say anything?"

"You didn't have to." I pointed my finger at him. "It's written all over your face, which isn't that attractive at the moment, I might add. You think I'm crazy."

He blinked. "Wait, you think I'm attractive?"

"Ah, men! Who needs them?" I threw my hands up in the air and started to pace. "And you think *I'm* the crazy one."

"I don't think you're crazy," Nik the nice guy said in a much calmer, more pacifying tone before adding, "I think you're a little paranoid. You smell fine."

I gaped at him. "Fine? You think I smell just fine?" *Not good or amazing, after I'd let the comment about him being attractive slip? Hmph!* Good thing he couldn't read my thoughts, because I'd show him exactly what I was: aka royally peeved!

He rubbed his forehead. "Women really are from another planet," he muttered.

"So, how *is* your mother these days?" I smirked. "Did you enjoy your quality time together?"

"Funny," he snarled as I thought, *Look who's laughing now, Hot Shot*! "You know perfectly well there was nothing *quality* about our time together after you got her all worked up," he added.

"Awww, what's the matter? A big guy like you is afraid of a small, little woman like your ma?"

He scowled. "In this case, size *doesn't* matter! Do you know what I had to endure? She barged into the station, dragged me out of there by my ear, and then put me in a time-out in my own damn kitchen. One minute per year. I had to sit for thirty-four minutes! All while listening to her lecture me about the use of guns and violence and bad guys and putting you in danger."

"Oh my," I snickered, trying to maintain a straight face. I could picture the whole scene perfectly.

"After my time-out, I tried to tell her that was my job. Then I had to listen to another rant on how maybe it was time I changed my occupation and became a nice accountant like my cousin Apollo. My ears still hurt. Then when she saw my scrapes and bruises, she called in reinforcements and nearly hauled me into the emergency room. She only allowed me to stay home if I agreed to let her take care of me all night long. I've been poked and prodded more than any human being should ever have to endure in an entire lifetime, especially by their ma."

I couldn't stop giggling. "Okay, okay. I'd say that was a tie. You're a grown man. Why did you go along with everything?"

"You of all people should know the answer to that. For the same reason you let your mother take you home. When it comes to Greek mamas, sometimes it's easier just to let them have their way. Defying them is *not* worth the price you'd have to pay."

"Touché." Once I got my giggles under control, I said, "What do you say we call a truce and get back to work?"

"Uh, I don't think so," Detective Stevens said, back on duty. "Working together is what got us in trouble in the first place. And my captain will have my badge if I break protocol again."

"Okay," I said, but that didn't mean I would stop investigating on my own. I would just operate on a need-to-know basis. And he most definitely didn't need to know.

He stood with his hands on his hips and studied me. "I don't like it."

"You don't like what?" I asked innocently and sniffed, wondering if maybe he smelled something after all.

"You agreed with me way too quickly."

"Just trying to keep the peace, officer." I relaxed in relief.

"Mmm hmm. I catch you anywhere near this case, you're going to be in the middle of World War III. Understood?"

"War. Hmm. Good Lord, ya'all." I waved my hand at him, then placed my palm on my chest, trying to look as sincere as I could. "Why on earth would I want to start World War III with you?"

"Beats the hell out of me." He scrubbed his hands over his face. "I'm probably the one who smells. I've got to go home and shower before I'm late for work."

"Good idea. You do that." I batted my eyelashes at him, and he gave me a look that said, *You call that a truce*? "Sorry, I've got something in my lashes." I rubbed my eye. "It's better now. I promise."

"Riiight," he said, pointing his finger at me. "Stay out of trouble. I mean it. Don't make me call both our mamas. They'll fix you right up."

I saluted him, and he just shook his head, leaving me to finish my coffee with glee. The sun wasn't shining today, yet my morning had never looked brighter.

Later Wednesday afternoon, I decided to make my move. I'd waited until Detective Stevens had left for work and had given him enough time to visit Vixen. I was sure after Johnny had made it clear that he was the man Ana was having the affair with and not Sully, the detective would want to talk to Ana. He was the cop, not me, and yet even I knew that was the next logical step.

"Where are you going?" Jaz asked, finally getting up and fixing herself coffee. She set Prissy down. "And why was Miss Priss in bed with me? She never turns to me unless something scares her and you're indisposed. So tell me, darling, what happened while I was sleeping?"

"Nothing really, just a little visit from our neighbor. Let's just say his night was as rough as mine was." I handed her a twenty-dollar bill. "You won."

"Nice." Jaz laughed, taking the money and tucking it into her bra. "Serves him right after what he did to you. If only Boomer was Greek, all would be right in my world."

"Trust me, dating a Greek is not worth everything that goes along with it."

She shrugged. "Yeah, but I'm not the one who would have to live with it because we're not dating. I just meant I'd love to sic that kind of punishment on him."

"If you say so." I grabbed my purse.

"Don't even start with that again." She stabbed her cereal spoon in my direction.

"I'm not starting with anything." I glanced at my watch. "And I really do have to go."

"You still haven't told me where."

Need-to-know basis, Kalli, need to know, I reminded myself. For her own protection, I said, "To the grocery store. We're out of a few things."

"Like replacement sponges for the ones you keep throwing out?" Jaz said with a knowing tone.

I gasped.

"That's right, chica. I know everything. Not to mention I haven't had to replace that sponge in six months, and it looks like new. It doesn't take Sherlock Holmes to figure out what you've been up to, missy. Just try not to get caught today. We don't need to be in any more trouble with Starsky and Hutch than we already are. And if you buy anything from *her*, you're dead to me."

"Jaz, you know I would never—"

"I know." She sighed. "I just feel better ordering you about since I know I can't go with you."

"You'll be with me in spirit," I said.

"Good, because something tells me you're going to need me."

I left the house, wondering why I had this odd feeling in my gut. Almost like indigestion. Like my food hadn't digested right, souring my stomach big-time. I popped a couple of antacids, hoping my mother's aloe and Duct Tape hadn't given me stomach cancer. I made a mental note to have that checked out at the doctor's as well. Maybe I could just see Pop's friend the animal doctor. Ma could arrange it in no time. I had to do something. For now, I put everything out of my mind and focused on the task at hand: solving this blasted murder case so I could get my life back.

I pulled into the parking lot of Vixen and couldn't believe my eyes. The place was packed for a Wednesday. Then I read the sign: Super Spring Sale. All of Jaz's fabulous finds were displayed front and center in the storefront window for all to see. But what I saw was my cousin Eleni's car, Mrs. Flannigan's car, Jaz's former employee Amy Fisher, and Jaz's spring collection. Ana had taken everything from Jaz, including her ex-lover Johnny. It was a good thing Jaz wasn't here, or no telling what she would do.

I climbed out of my car and slipped inside the busy store to scope the situation out. See just how bad things had really gotten. No one noticed me as I stood in the corner, observing. Jaz's finds were flying off the shelves. It was bittersweet knowing she'd been spot on in her eye for finding bestsellers, yet the sales were going straight into Ana's cash register.

I saw Johnny Hogan walk in and head straight for Ana. She pulled him aside, and they got into a heated argument, drawing a few stares. She shot him a menacing look and then promptly ignored him. He balled his fists and then walked off toward the back. Glancing around, he slipped into a room when no one was looking.

No one except me, that is.

Guess the honeymoon was over already. And what could he want from that back room? I started to walk in that direction when something made me freeze in my tracks. Max Rolland crossed my line of sight. What on earth was he doing here? We'd been friends for as long as I could remember, but I didn't ever remember him so much as giving Ana or her shop a second look. He stunned me further when he came to a stop right beside her with a smile I'd only ever seen directed at me before. Ana's whole face softened as they chatted intimately. I didn't know what to do, feeling like a kid with her hand caught in the cookie jar.

Suddenly Ana's gaze landed on me, yet she didn't look surprised to see me. Her lips tipped up ever so slightly, but then she masked all emotion except pure adoration for Max, which he seemed to be eating right up. Until he noticed me, that is. He blinked as though surprised and then excused himself from her side. He walked straight toward me and didn't stop until he stood directly in front of me.

"What are you doing here, Kalli?" he asked, his jaw tightening and a muscle in his cheek pulsing.

"Shopping. I've got to say her spring finds are fabulous, yet familiar. Gee, I wonder why." I crossed my arms over my chest and smirked.

"Ana told me you were out to get her."

I threw my hands up in the air. "Are you kidding me?"

"Nope. I'm dead serious, Ms. Ballas."

"Come on, Max. You've known me since we were both in diapers."

"And yet I feel I don't know you at all." He shook his head. "The Kalli I knew didn't date."

"I still don't."

He leaned in, thrusting his face in mine, making me hop back a step. God forbid his spittle made contact with my pores. I might not make it out alive. "You could have fooled me based on what I saw at your parents' house on Sunday," he ground out.

I bobbed and weaved, barely avoiding a drop of saliva and earning an odd look as he asked, "Is that a new quirk? I think they're getting worse."

"I'm fine, just a little crick in my neck," I said as his words finally registered. I replied, "That wasn't a date. That was just a kiss."

"Which I would have thought was worse. Guess it would only be worse if it had been with me."

"Max, I—"

"You're armed and dangerous, is what you are, Annie Oakley. I heard the gossip. My mama always told me to avoid situations where I might get hurt."

"So you turn to Ana of all people? You honestly think she isn't playing you for a fool?"

"Can't be any worse than what you've done since we hit puberty."

I rubbed my temples. "I can see this isn't a good time."

"No, Kalli, it isn't. And something tells me it will never be a good time for you and me."

I dropped my hands and stared at him, pleading, "Max, please don't be like this. You're one of my closest friends."

"That's the problem. I guess I always thought the issue was with your quirks and being with *any* man, but now I know it was really about being with me."

"I'm sorry. I don't know what's going on with me. I never meant to hurt you." I tried hard not to, but my eyes welled up with tears.

He sighed, and his face softened. "I'll get over it. I just need some time. And I think it's time you left."

"Okay," I said, feeling helpless as I watched him walk away, back to Ana—and out of my life for good, I was afraid.

That also meant spying on Johnny was out.

Ana kissed Max's cheek, whispered something in his ear that sent him on an errand for her. I saw Johnny slip out of the room while shoving something in his back pocket, then look around, but no one noticed him again except for me. Ana headed toward him with a suspicious look on her face, but Mrs. Flannigan intercepted her and started up a conversation. Johnny's expression read total satisfaction as Max walked back in, carrying a cup of coffee for Ana, none the wiser. I would have to find out what Jonny was up to some other way, and soon. Not to mention what kind of game Ana was playing. Max was too important to me, and I was terrified that if I didn't do something quick, Max would be headed for his biggest heartache yet.

Chapter 17

By the time I got home, it was just before dinner. I walked inside our half of the house and called for Jaz. No answer. She must have gone somewhere. I set my purse down and took off my lavender suit coat, rolling up the sleeves of my white silk blouse. Slipping off my heels, I finally began to relax. I poured myself a glass of white wine and ran into Prissy. She turned up her nose at me and pranced away. Clearly she hadn't forgiven me for this morning when I'd let the detective inside our sanctuary.

"Awww, don't be that way, Prissy," I said. "Come see me, and I'll give you some milk."

She refused to look at me as she stretched out lazily on the windowsill overlooking the back yard. She purred in the sun that had finally graced us with its presence, shining its rays of hope on a bleak day. Until she looked outside. Then she hissed and turned her back against the window.

I glanced out into the yard to see the source of her displeasure.

Wolfgang!

Earlier today I'd watched the detective let the dog out and then put him back inside before leaving for work. If the dog was outside now, then it meant the detective had come home. Maybe if I got him talking, he would reveal what he'd found out earlier about Johnny and Ana. Carrying my glass of wine and grabbing one of Jaz's beers, I headed next door under the guise of a peace offering.

I knocked with my elbow, but no one answered. I knocked again, and this time the door opened. I called out Nik's name, but he didn't answer. There's no way he would have left without locking his door. I studied the doorknob, and it was still locked. Must be he hadn't closed the door fully. I was no detective, but given that he hadn't fully closed his door and he'd left his dog outside, I'd deduced he was called away in a hurry.

I bit my bottom lip with a smile. My day was most definitely getting brighter. I didn't have to break or enter anything. The beast was outside. And the detective was long gone. Even Jaz wasn't home to pass judgment on me. I was completely alone, and that never happened to me.

It was a sign!

I stepped inside and used my bare foot to close the door fully. Unlike the detective, my mama didn't raise no fool, and I didn't like surprises. Taking a fortifying sip of my wine, I wandered around, checking out his place and admittedly looking for clues to what he'd found. The layout of his half of the house was set up exactly the same as Jaz's and mine, but that's where the similarity ended. Jaz had put her stylish flair for decorating all over our side of the house. Modern elegance and class. Whereas the detective was a bachelor with a capital B. Bare minimum and nothing matched.

Walking down the hall, I made my way into the detective's bedroom. My stomach did a weird little flip when I saw his rumpled king-size bed. I attributed it to indigestion and not the fact that I still longed to do something about my spring fever. Things were just so complicated right now. What was I doing here, anyway? This was crazy.

I turned away from the bed and was about to sneak back to my place before anyone was the wiser, when Nik's desk caught my attention. I don't know why but I tiptoed over, as though that would somehow make a difference and keep me from being discovered. Or maybe I was just subconsciously worried about the microscopic dirt from his carpet touching my bare feet. I kept Jaz's half of the house so clean you could eat off the floor, so I didn't worry about going barefoot over there. This just showed how rattled Nik made me that I'd actually ventured into parts unknown with my feet in the buff.

I curled my toes and kept moving, refusing to be deterred.

Stopping at his desk, I looked down and my jaw unhinged. Bingo! I'd struck gold. The security tapes from Ana's store Vixen on the night of the murder. Beside that sat a file. I set my wine and his beer down on the desk. Glancing around, I spotted a box of tissues and grabbed one. I carefully opened the file and started to read. Johnny Hogan stated that on the night of Darrin aka Scott's murder, he didn't actually go home from Flannigan's Pub. He had been angry at Jaz and had gotten in an argument with Scott, then proceeded to get drunk and walk it off, but he never made it home.

Ana confessed that she picked him up and took him back to her store. She knew he was in a vulnerable state, and she used that to seduce him. She made him keep the affair secret because she didn't want Maria to know. She wanted Maria to continue hating Jaz and not her. Meanwhile, she tried to seduce Jaz's secrets out of him, figuring

Jaz had let her spring line slip over pillow talk. But Jaz was smarter than that. She never mixed business with pleasure and certainly wouldn't let something that important slip. Once Ana realized that, Johnny had become useless to her. She didn't want Jaz's sloppy seconds, so she'd tried to break things off with Johnny, but he wouldn't take no for an answer.

She'd arranged for Sully to deliver the note for Johnny to meet her at Lakeshore Heights. Other than their first time together in her store the night of the murder, Ana and Johnny had started meeting at the small hotel in Lakeshore. She'd broken things off with Johnny once and for all that night; that's why they had left separately and the clerk hadn't thought things went well. And that's why Johnny was so angry at Sully. He'd thought Ana had dumped him for another man. He hadn't looked any happier today after obviously finding out she'd only used him.

Kalli tried to process everything. So Ana had been having the affair with Johnny, not Sully, but Johnny wasn't the mole. And neither was Sully. Sully said he wasn't the killer, either, because he was planning his parents' anniversary party with his sister, but she couldn't be sure he didn't sneak out during the night. And Maria was still a suspect because she had no alibi and the Full Disclosure security tapes did show her peeking in the windows. But what about Ana and Johnny? She refused to say who gave her the information about Jaz's spring collection, but she did confirm she and Johnny were each other's alibis for the night of the murder, and she could prove it.

The security tapes had a sticky note taped to them that said, *Proof.*

I picked up the tape, played it, and nearly threw up. That could *not* be good for my esophagus. Gasping for air, I slapped a hand over my eyes and groped about with my other hand until I switched the tape off. The image of Ana and Johnny going at it in her office at Vixen would forever be burned into my retinas. I refused to call it making love because there was nothing lovely about what I'd just seen. I briefly wondered if something like that could ruin a person's vision and was about to go buy the strongest eye drops I could find, but then I heard the sound of the front door being unlocked.

There was no way out!

My burning eyes would have to wait. Nik would be by the front door, and I wasn't going to attempt the back door with the beast in the yard. So that left hiding somewhere. Footsteps grew louder as he made his way toward the bedroom. Figured, my luck would run out. Had I said my day was getting brighter? That was a joke.

I had no choice. I quickly closed the file, picked up my wine and his beer, and then hid in his closet. I had barely closed the door when he walked inside while talking on his cell phone.

"Ma, this is ridiculous." I peeked out through the slatted door and saw him put his phone on his bed, hit the speaker button, and then pull off his shirt and tie. His bronzed muscles rippled as he moved, and my mouth went dry. Who knew all that had been hidden beneath his clothes? I mean, I could tell he was built through his clothes, but I had no clue he was built like *that*. Broad shoulders, huge biceps, bulging pecs, and rippled abs, all covered with a thin layer of hair that tapered to a fine line and disappeared into...

Oh, yeah. I most definitely still had the fever.

"I told you I'm fine," he said out loud, and I couldn't agree more as I tried to focus, realizing he wasn't talking to me, he was talking to his mother.

"What's happening? Did you put the speaker on me?" Chloe said.

"No, I didn't put the speaker on you, Ma. I put *you* on speaker phone."

"Well, I don't like it, Nikos. You sound all hollow. Or maybe that's your voice, and I'm right. I just knew you were going to get the rabies. I saw how you looked at that girl. I like her, but she's not full Greek, you know. That makes her susceptible to things like rabies."

"She's not Greek at all, Ma, and I'm not full either." He scrubbed his hands over his face and then stared up at the ceiling as though he was counting to ten. I couldn't blame him. His mother sounded exactly like mine, and they'd obviously been talking. "I'm not getting rabies, and Kalli doesn't have rabies either, and being full Greek wouldn't make a bit of difference anyway."

"She's got something, I tell you. I've seen the way she looks at you too, and I'm not alone. We've all seen it."

He stopped moving and gaped at his bed. "We? Who's we?"

"The mamas, of course. You can't fool the mamas, you know."

He undid his belt, button and zipper, then dropped his pants. *Be still my beating heart,* I thought, taking a hearty sip of wine. My temperature had risen a few degrees, and I was pretty sure I had a fever of some kind. Pausing at her words, he just stood there in his boxer briefs with his pants pooled around his ankles, staring at his phone like he was processing her words.

"You're crazy, you know that? You're all crazy." He stepped out of his pants, but left his boxers on, and I let out the breath I hadn't realized I'd been holding. He looked around for a minute at the noise, but I'd frozen and held my breath once more. Just when I thought I'd pass out, he grabbed a towel off a hook and started to move, allowing me to quietly breathe once more.

"You've been bitten by the bug," his mother said through the phone.

"What bug?"

"The love bug." He snorted with laughter, until she added with certainty, "You'll see. You don't realize it yet, but you will."

"Next time don't call me while I'm working unless it's an emergency. I gotta go, Ma."

"Enjoy your cold shower," she said knowingly and then hung up.

He stared at his towel and then frowned, heading down the hall and out of sight. I heard a commotion and then finally the water in the shower turned on. I downed the rest of my wine, grabbed his beer, and then slid the closet door open to make my escape.

I'd only crept halfway down the hall when an unmistakable whine pierced my ears. My head snapped up, and I locked eyes with the beast. He stood massive and strong, his tail wagging furiously, as he blocked my path to freedom. I froze, afraid to so much as breathe and clue him in to the fact that I was not just a figment of his imagination or doggy daydreams. I glanced at the front door, then I looked at the back door, then I peeked at the bathroom door. It was just enough movement to send the canine into ecstatic motion.

Every ounce of his fur quivered and his entire being wiggled in glee as he launched his body into motion. I screamed to the top of my lungs and started to run to the closest door to me.

The bathroom door.

Muscles bunched as they flexed and then lengthened and then flexed once more, over and over as the massive creature lumbered toward me. His humongous pink tongue hung long and loose with doggy drool flinging about nilly willy, splattering everything within a four foot radius. It was like a horror scene being played out in slow motion, and I was his next victim.

I truly was in jeopardy of dying.

I did the only thing I could. I whipped open the bathroom door, ran inside, and slammed it shut.

"What the hell?" Nik said, poking his soaking wet head out from behind the shower curtain, obviously naked as his boxer briefs lay in a wadded up heap at my bare feet.

I smiled wide, thrust my hand out in front of me as if it was the most natural thing to do, and said the only thing I could think of. "Care for a beer?"

Chapter 18

The bathroom door burst open, and the steam in the room swirled around my head.

"We heard the scream and came as quickly as we could!" Jaz blurted, then jerked to a stop. "Whoa...." She gaped at the sight of me standing in the bathroom, wrinkled and disheveled. My hair was falling out of its chignon as I held an empty glass of wine in one hand, a full beer in the other, and unattractive beads of perspiration dotted my face.

I opened my mouth to speak, but my mind proceeded to go blank.

"You're a hot mess if ever I saw one." Her gaze dropped to the boxers on the floor, and her eyebrows arched higher.

I slid the boxers behind me with my toe and then pressed my lips together before I said or did anything to make me look even guiltier. I hadn't done anything...well, okay, I guess I had...but certainly not what she was thinking, judging by the expression on her perfectly made-up, non-disheveled face.

Nik had already shut the water off and finally opened the shower curtain with a towel wrapped around his waist, thank goodness. He hadn't dried off. Drops of watered dripped from his hair as though he'd quickly shaken it, streaming down his bronzed body in small rivulets. Great! That made me guilty as charged.

Boomer came to a stop right behind Jaz, wearing the same expression she had worn a moment ago, with a firm grip on Wolfgang. The beast whined harder when he spotted me. His massive body started his usual shake and quiver, and I knew what was about to happen before he'd so much as twitched. My eyes zeroed into tunnel vision, and everything happened so fast. The St. Bernard lunged, and I yelped, hopping into the tub right behind Nik. I wrapped my arms around his slippery wet torso, which thoroughly soaked my white silk blouse, as I tried to climb his back, which felt like the Rocky Mountains.

Not an easy task in a pencil skirt, mind you.

"What are you waiting for? Save me," I shrieked, scratching him with my nails as I tried to get a better grip. Panic tended to push a normally sane person to near hysteria, and right now I was teetering on the edge of lunacy.

Save you? More like save me. He grunted. *First Ma and now Kalli. Full Greek, half Greek, non-Greek… it doesn't matter. These women are crazy!* "He's not going to get you, but you're going to get a big surprise if you don't quit wiggling," Nik replied in exasperation, holding his towel in place before I kicked it off, which I was dangerously close to doing as I dug my toes into anything that might give me a better foothold. He stilled my progress with his other hand, by gripping my ankle. "Boomer, for Pete's sake, take Wolf outside! Some backup you are, *partner*."

Boomer cursed under his breath. "At least someone's getting lucky," he muttered as he walked away to do Nik's bidding.

Lucky? I'll pass. If this is lucky, then I'd rather be shot after the day I've had, Nik thought, and then said, "You can get down now, Ballas. The big bad wolf is gone. You're safe."

"Good. I don't much care for *crazy* men and their insane dogs," I replied in a huff and shimmied down his back, then stepped out of the tub, smoothing my skirt as I tried to regain my dignity.

He gave me an odd and definitely suspicious look over my choice of words, and I didn't even care if he found out about my gift, which did not feel like a gift at this point. He made me so mad. He pushed my buttons even further when his gaze dropped to my breasts. I glanced down and gasped, crossing my arms over my shirt as I realized I looked like the winner of a wet t-shirt contest. There was literally nothing left to the imagination when a white silk shirt and lace bra got wet.

I cringed. "Do you mind?"

"Sorry." He looked away, flushing slightly. "Call it a reflex."

Ugh, men!

"Would someone please tell me what's going on?" Jaz asked. "And why is it I always seem to be the last one to find out?"

"Yeah," Boomer said as he joined her in the hallway. His eyes bugged, making me acutely aware that my crossed arms didn't cover much.

I grabbed the hand towel by the sink and held it in front of me. "Seriously?" I snapped. "What is it with you guys?"

"Sorry. Call it—"

"A reflex," I cut him off with an eye roll. "So I've heard."

"I was going to say call it a libido thing, but a reflex works too when you put all that on display."

"I did not put anything on display, thank you very much," I ground out.

"And why the hell are you two drinking in the bathroom?" he said with a puckered brow as if I hadn't uttered a word. "Doesn't washing each other's backs work better if you're *both* in the shower?"

"You're such an animal." Jaz rolled her eyes.

"If I recall, you're the one with claws," he replied, leaning over her menacingly, "and they definitely came out tonight."

"Wait, when?" I asked, for the first time noticing she didn't look as put together as I thought. Her makeup was a bit smudged, her clothes a tad rumpled, and her hair ever so slightly out of place. The average person might not notice, but I knew Jaz. She didn't go anywhere without looking picture perfect in every way.

"You first." Jaz shot me a sharp look that said, *Don't change the subject, missy, you're not getting off that easy.*

"Yeah." Boomer focused his frustration with Jaz on Nik and me. "I want to know why you two were playing spin the bottle in the bathroom while I was out playing cops and robbers."

"Oh, for the love of Zeus, that's not what we were doing," I said.

"Then what exactly *were* you doing?" Jaz asked.

"Great question," Nik said, teaming up with them and staring me down.

"Which I will gladly answer if the lynch mob will allow me to change," I replied.

"I don't know. I kind of like the view," Boomer smirked.

"I'll take that beer now," Nik said, glaring at Boomer as he added, "and meet this knucklehead and you ladies at your place in five after I do the same. The sun's long gone." He glanced at my wet blouse again as he said, "It's starting to rain." At first I thought he was making some comment about my blouse being wet and him being in the towel, but then he lifted his gaze to my eyes as he finished with, "I need to let Wolf back in."

That was all I needed to hear.

Five minutes later after we were all dry, fully clothed, and safe, the four of us sat at Jaz's kitchen table. The guys each had a *cold* beer, while Jaz and I were on glass number two from the rest of the bottle of wine.

I had on my yoga pants, a warm fleece pullover, fuzzy socks, and the thickest bra I could find. Nik had on an old pair of police academy sweats and a worn out T-shirt that somehow looked sexy. Or maybe it was the way he had towel dried his hair, which curled up at the ends in the most adorable way. Or the fact that he smelled amazing. How could he make me mad at him one minute and yet want him the next? Maybe I really did have something wrong with me—other than the usual, that is. My eyes locked with his, and his crinkled at the corners until I looked away.

"I'll go first since I have a feeling our story is much shorter and less interesting than yours," Boomer said, eyeing Nik and me like we were unwrapped Christmas presents, and he had the itch to sneak a peek.

"Fire away," Nik said, and then took a sip of his longneck before adding, "This ought to be good. Let me guess, your story involves one Jazlyn Alvarez."

"It's a free country." She inspected her perfectly manicured nails. "I have a right to go shopping like anyone else."

"Yes, but you don't have a right to disturb the peace," Boomer replied, his tone turning bitter as he rolled up the sleeves of his work shirt and loosened his tie. "I have a job to do, which involves trying to save your pretty little hide, but you won't let anyone do that. You're so damn stubborn you just have to try to do everything yourself, don't you?"

"I knew you still thought I was pretty," Jaz said teasingly, then took a dainty sip of her wine.

"Not gonna work this time, Alvarez," Boomer growled.

"You two done?" Nik asked dryly.

"Jaz, I told you to stay away from Vixen," I chimed in.

"And I did... at first, anyway." She looked down in a guilty fashion. "But you were gone so long. I can't help it I got worried. I went to get my nails done and tried to stay out of it, but then I saw Ana's front window display with *my* fabulous finds, and well, I kind of sort of lost it."

"That's putting it mildly, considering you caused a big scene and would have trashed her window if it wasn't for Max." Boomer shook his head, then looked at Nik. "She's lucky she's friends with Max Rolland. He somehow talked Ana out of pressing charges, or Jaz here would have found herself behind bars again. That's all we would need for the captain to see."

Nik scrubbed his face and muttered a curse behind his hand.

"I didn't ask for your help," Jaz said quietly, then looked us each in the eye one by one before raising her chin and adding, "Any of you."

"No, you didn't," Boomer replied in a serious tone. "But sometimes you need it, whether or not you want to admit it. We all do." He reached out and squeezed her hand. "You need to start letting us help you before it's too late."

"Okay," she said, staring down at their joined hands and nodding her head, then she sat up straight, pulled her hand away, and took a deep breath. "But enough about me."

"I agree. Enough about Jaz," Nik said, nailing me with a hard look. "What I want to know is what Kalli was doing at Vixen when I specifically told *her* to stay out of our way and away from this case."

"What she said," I gestured to Jaz. "It's a free country, and I was just doing some shopping."

"I knew you agreeing so quickly with me to behave was too good to be true."

"All I did was look around. I wanted to see how Jaz's finds were doing, which they rocked by the way. But I was surprised to see Johnny slip into Ana's back room. He didn't look too happy. Now I know why. She used him to get at Jaz's collection, and then discarded him like a broken zipper. I just can't believe they're each other's alibis." I shuddered, trying not to relive in mind what I'd seen.

Nik had just taken a sip of his beer, which he promptly spit all over as he sputtered, "You watched the tape?" He used the back of his hand to wipe his gaping mouth as the judge's gavel slammed "guilty" in my head, and I resisted the urge to run and grab the mop or sanitary wipes.

I jerked back from the table to avoid the drops, and my chair tipped over. Jaz jumped up and wiped down the table with disinfectant as though it had become second nature, bless the woman. "What do you mean, they're each other's alibis?"

"Wait, what tape?" Boomer asked. "And what the hell were you doing in his bathroom?"

"I was bringing a peace offering after our argument, when his beast scared me."

"His beast, huh..."

Nik ignored that comment and explained everything we'd found out about Ana and Johnny. And while Ana might be Jaz's arch nemesis and Johnny might be out for revenge, neither one had done anything illegal. The time stamp on the surveillance tape proved neither one could be the killer. And While Ana beat Jaz to the punch in showcasing the fabulous finds, she hadn't actually stolen anything. She'd simply been tipped off on what and where to order, but she refused to tell who the real mole was. I'd kind of suspected that anyway because Johnny wasn't smart enough to be the mole.

"So where does that leave us?" I asked.

"Back to there is no us," Nik said firmly. "You stay out of trouble for real this time," he said to me, then gave Jaz a stern look as he added, "and you let us help you by doing our jobs."

"You get that, Alvarez?" Boomer asked.

"Oh, I get it, Matheson. And I promise you this. You won't be getting any from me anytime soon."

My jaw fell open.

Nik's eyebrows shot up.

Boomer's eyes narrowed.

"Any more *trouble* from me, that is." Jaz scowled, but I could see the sparkle in her eyes. "Geez, people, get your minds out of the gutter. Apparently Kalli isn't the only one with spring fever."

"Did you hear the news?" my mother said through the phone on Thursday morning.

"Ma, I have two days until my deadline to get my book of designs done. I haven't heard anything but the pounding in my head."

"I'm sure that's what that poor widow said this morning." My mother tsked.

"What do mean?" I took a sip of strong coffee, knowing I was going to need it to get through this conversation with my mother. Actually, *any* conversation with my mother.

"That outsider, Wilma Parks."

"I pretty much figured out *the who* by the word widow. It's *the what* I'm asking about."

"The what? What are *you* talking about?"

"The news, Ma! You're the one who called me. Are you ever going to tell me or just keep torturing me?"

"You're so touchy. Are you sure you're over the rabies?"

"Don't start on that again, or I'm seriously going to lose it." I dumped my cup in the sink, my stomach turning sour.

"Hmph! If I didn't know better, I'd swear you were going through your change."

"I'm twenty-nine, Ma, not forty-nine." I popped a couple of tums, hoping the lining of my stomach wall hadn't burned off from all the acid churning about in there. Then I reached for the bottle to scan the label and make sure I hadn't gone over the maximum dosage per time period.

"Then start acting it and give me some grandbabies."

"Ma! Can we get back to the news please? The widow, her headache, what happened?"

"Oh, yeah. The news. Now I remember," she said, and I slapped my forehead, ready to hang up. "She fell down the stairs of The Bistro. If she had gone to Aphrodite, that never would have happened." Ma sniffed sharply.

"Was she hurt?" I asked more calmly as I strove for patience.

"She hit her head, but the baby is fine, thank goodness. At least she's giving her mama a grandbaby."

"That's nice," I said, trying not to groan and quickly changing the subject. "Did she say what happened?"

"That's the juicy part of the news. She says someone pushed her. No one was around her at the time, and she didn't see who it was, but someone is out to get her. Poor thing, as if she hasn't gone through enough."

Maybe the killer was after her for some reason. Maybe she knew something about Scott that none of us did. Or maybe she was the killer and faked her own accident to take suspicion off herself. That was a whole lot of maybes...

Maybe it was time I started asking some serious questions.

I made my excuses and hung up with my mother, then headed to the hospital to pay Wilma Parks a visit. Hopefully the detective hadn't heard the news yet, and I'd slip in and out before he arrived. The last thing I needed was to get into more trouble with him. A short while later I picked up flowers in the gift shop and made my way to her floor. I knocked, and she said to come in without even looking to see who it was, making me wonder if she was expecting someone. There was a pastry box next to the bed. Obviously Maria had been there.

"Did you forget something?" Wilma's gaze made contact with mine, and she blinked. "How did you know I was in here?"

"Small towns and Greek mamas." I shrugged.

She smiled slightly. "Enough said." Her smile faded, replaced by a wary look as she glanced behind me. "No sidekick today?"

"It's just me," I said and handed her the flowers. "These are for you."

She slowly took them, sniffed, and then set them on the table beside her. "Thank you. They're lovely, though I'm not exactly sure what prompted them."

"Putting our differences aside, no one deserves to be pushed down the stairs, especially someone who is expecting a baby." I went for sympathy and compassion, letting on that I believed she had really been pushed. I was alone so I would have to play good cop bad cop by myself. Maybe if I got her to let down her guard, she would slip up when I pounced. With Ana and Johnny ruled out as suspects, that only left Wilma, Bobby, and Maria. I was running out of time, and frankly, I was getting worried about Jaz.

She relaxed. "It *was* traumatic, I must say. First I lost Scott, and now I nearly lost the baby. I don't know what I would have done if that had happened." Her words said one thing, but once again, her expression told a different story. She was hiding something, I was sure of it.

"Well, it didn't. You were lucky. Just focus on that. And maybe try to remember what exactly *did* happen."

"I was pushed, just like I said."

Her statement sounded rehearsed to me. "And that must have been so scary," I replied carefully. "Do you have any idea who would want you dead?"

"Scott had a lot of enemies," she stated with an almost bitter tone. "It could have been anyone."

"Do you think maybe it could have been someone who was after you?"

Her sharp gaze focused on me, making her look like anything but a victim. "What on earth for?"

"Well, you did just come into a lot of money from that big life insurance policy you took out right before Scott died."

Her guard came back up, and she stiffened. "I did that because I had just found out I was pregnant. I wanted protection for myself and the baby because I knew Scott had lots of enemies. His days were numbered a long time ago, unfortunately. And while I loved my husband, I wasn't about to go down with his sinking ship."

"Or maybe you sank his ship permanently to cash in on the life insurance policy since he gambled away all of your money, especially after he found out your baby wasn't his. He refused to let you divorce him by threatening to ruin your reputation. Somehow I doubt love is what you felt for him at the end."

"How dare you!"

I jabbed my finger in her direction. "How dare *you* try to pin this on my best friend."

"How dare you obstruct justice," said a familiar male voice from behind me, and I felt something cold and hard clamp around my wrist.

"What are you doing?"

"Something I should have done from the start," Detective Nik Stevens said from beside me. "Locking you up for your own good."

"What?" I gulped, feeling the blood drain from my face.

"Looks like Jaz won't be the one to find herself back behind bars these days."

"You wouldn't dare," I said, terrified of what his thoughts might be.

Wouldn't dare? How about you, sneaking into my house? Now there's a dare I never thought would happen. "You can't say you weren't warned."

"And you know what they say about payback," I stammered, the familiar frazzle from knowing his thoughts doing all sorts of crazy things to my insides. "I would have thought you'd learned your lesson from the last time."

Oh, there's some lessons I'd like to teach you, but I'm not sure you could handle them. And at the moment, I'm not sure I want to teach you them. But no matter how hard I try, I can't get that kiss off my mind. "Care to add threatening an officer to your list of crimes?" He leaned in until our faces were about an inch apart and added in a dead serious voice, "You have the right to remain silent, Ms. Ballas. If I were you, I would."

Episode 7

Chapter 19

"Kalliope Ballas, as I live and breathe," my mother said a couple hours later after paying my bail and escorting me out of the police station by my ear. *I don't know what I did to deserve this. First, I can't have children. Then the gods give me a daughter like her. I don't know what I did wrong, but I obviously made someone upstairs very angry.*

"Ow, Ma. Stop pulling. That hurts." *In more ways than one*, I thought.

"I'll stop hurting when you stop misbehaving," she said sharply. *Honestly, is it too much to ask that she find a respectable job and stop embarrassing the family? And what's so wrong with finding a good Greek man, settling down, and having some babies? I'm not going to live forever.*

"For crying out loud, Ma, I'm a grown woman. If I make mistakes, they're my mistakes to make. And not everyone is meant to get married and have babies."

"Blasphemy!" She let go, thank God, and faced me in the parking lot, crossing her polyester-covered arms, her beehive tilting slightly askew. "You no think you need your mama anymore. I see how it is." She frowned. "And I didn't say anything about getting married and having babies."

"You didn't have to," I said, rubbing my ear. "I can read you like a book." I sighed. "Look, I'm not saying I don't need you anymore, but I certainly don't need to be hurt."

"You need to feel pain so you will come to your senses. Not getting married and having babies is unnatural. Not to mention designing trashy clothes and getting arrested is outright scandalous! What are the neighbors going to think? I'll never be able to show my face again. My baby girl has a rap sheet. You put your Nikos in a very awkward position by making him arrest you, you know. Oh, the horror of it all. Chloe is going to be shamed." She fanned her face as though she were about to faint.

"Detective Stevens is not my anything." I threw my hands up and began to pace. "I wish you'd all stop trying to make something more out of our relationship."

"We're not the ones making a spectacle of ourselves. You're the one kissing the man in public and getting arrested twice. What do you have to say for yourself, young lady?"

"I say you make me crazy."

"Well, you're no saint. I say I'm taking you straight home. And by home I mean back where you belong, under my roof."

"Ma, I'm not going—"

"To cause any more trouble. Wonderful. That's just what I thought you were going to say." She glanced behind me and then looked at her watch. "Oh, would you look at the time. We'll finish this conversation later. Something just came up. And look, there's Jaz. I'm sure she'll give you a lift to your car." She pushed me uncharacteristically toward Jaz's car, which had just pulled up to the curb, not even questioning why Jaz was conveniently there. "Gotta go." She whirled around and bustled away quickly. I stood there scratching my head and realizing this must be how she felt every time I cut her off. But my mother *never* cut me off. What on earth was going on?

A movement caught my eye, and I noticed a tall, muscular, caramel-skinned bald man in his thirties heading in the same direction as my mother, who was far away from me by now. If I didn't know better, I'd swear he was following her. Was he who she had been looking at over my shoulder? Did she know him? If so, then why was she avoiding him? He looked familiar. I was pretty sure I had seen him around recently. Maybe it had something to do with the family restaurant, and she didn't want to deal with it right now. I hoped she wasn't in any trouble and made a mental note to ask her about it later. But right now I had more important things to worry about, like escaping before Nik realized Boomer had let me out.

I looked at Jaz and sighed in relief. My getaway driver. The window rolled down. "Get in," said Jaz. "Girl, you get into more trouble than I do." She shook her head and then laughed. "I love it!"

"Well, I don't," I said as I slid inside and slammed the door.

"Thelma and Louise, baby." The tires screeched as we roared away from the curb.

"If you remember right, that didn't end too well for either of them." I held onto the bar above my head for dear life.

"Technicalities." She giggled. "Besides, I'm a better driver."

I mentally pleaded the fifth on that one. "How did you know I was here?"

"You're mother's not the only one who has eyes and ears everywhere. Which way?"

"The train station," I replied with something I could safely answer, adding, "A little birdie sang while I was in the cage and told me Bobby Parks was on the lam."

"Interesting." Jaz turned serious, and I could see her sleuth wheels spinning in her brain. "And why would someone need to be on the lam unless they did something wrong?"

"My thoughts exactly. I think we just found out who pushed Wilma down the stairs. The question is, why?"

My source had been right. Bobby was indeed at the train station. Gary Bolin was a regular at Flannigan's pub every evening and had spent last night in a cell to sober up. By the time Nik had locked me up, Gary was rambling on and on about how it wasn't his fault he'd gotten into the fight. That Bobby had been mad as hell and looking to give someone a good beating. Gary was just glad that Bobby was leaving on a train to anywhere today. The second I'd heard that, I'd known what I had to do.

Call my mother.

I'd wanted her to drop me off at my car at the hospital, but Ma had a mind of her own. Things couldn't have worked out better as my mother had gotten distracted and my getaway girl had shown up in the nick of time, which was even better because now I had backup. The universe was finally cooperating. So long as Detective Stickler-for-the-Rules didn't show up, we might just have a chance at making some headway in this case.

He made me so angry. He kept insisting I back off and let Boomer and him do their jobs. It wasn't my fault they weren't doing their jobs very well. I was Jaz's best friend. Who better than me to defend her from this insane murder wrap? It only made me more determined than ever to beat

Detective Dreamy to the last clue and save the day. Then maybe I'd finally get the respect I deserved, and Jaz would get her life back.

Now that we were here, the train station was dead for a Thursday afternoon. Or rather, late afternoon. The sun was sinking low quickly this time of year. Jaz, swaying her hips with every step, sauntered over to Bobby, who sat like a big blonde giant on a bench by his suitcase, while I hid behind the corner. I clicked on the mini-cassette recorder I always carried in my purse in case inspiration struck for one of my designs. It would come in perfect for recording a confession right now. We had worked out a plan on the rest of the drive over. I'd show the detective once and for all that I could actually be a help if he'd just let me.

"Wow, you really do look like Darrin. I mean, Scott," Jaz said as she sat down beside Bobby.

He tensed, eyeing her warily as though he might bolt at any second, but I wasn't worried. Jaz had a way with men. "How'd you find me?" he asked suspiciously, scooting an inch away.

"I didn't, silly." She shrugged, scooting closer to him in the process. "I'm here to catch a train to anywhere."

"I thought you weren't supposed to leave town."

"Oh please. Last time I checked neither were you. I guess we're both making a run for it."

"I don't know about you, but I'm innocent."

"They tell me that's what they all say."

"Won't your boyfriend be mad at you?"

"Boyfriend?" Her eyebrows disappeared into her hairline. "Detective Boomer Matheson is *not* my boyfriend. You should talk. You seem pretty chummy with your brother's wife."

"Trust me, she's not my girlfriend either."

"Who needs love anyway, right?"

He grunted. "I can't take it anymore. I don't care if they throw the book at me, I've got to get the hell out of here before I go insane."

And that was my cue. I got down on my hands and knees, cringing all the way as I thought about what micro-germs were trying to make their way through my pores at this very moment. Breathing deeply three times, I tried to block out that image and focus on the task at hand—catching Bobby's every word—as I came to a stop directly behind the bench and sank as low as I could.

"Looks like we have something in common." Jaz leaned back and sighed in dramatic fashion, flopping her arm over the bench and discreetly tapping my head.

Gotta love Jaz, there was no getting anything by her.

"This whole case is ridiculous," she went on. "I have no motive for killing Scott, yet I'm still a 'person of interest'." She made a set of air quotes with her fingers. "It's stupid if you ask me." She faced him, curling her legs up beside her on the bench, looking anything but threatening. "Look, I know Scott was your brother, but he was an idiot. I had no idea he was married, or I never would have agreed to our date. I wish I had never met the man."

Bobby relaxed completely. "Finally someone who doesn't think the sun rises and sets with him. Scott has always been a screw-up. Do you know how many people he has pissed off? He has a lot of enemies. Any one of them could have come after him. We were raised by my grandfather, and for years Gramps and I were on the same page and Scott was the outcast. I make one stupid mistake and suddenly

Scott's the golden boy, and *I'm* on the outside. Talk about no loyalty."

"Don't even get me started on family, and I know all about being an outcast. It's not easy being me in a town like this. No one appreciates my originality, my creativity, my sense of self." She reached out and touched his arm. "I can't help it; I'm very expressive." His gaze fell to her hand and then locked on her face. She had his full attention—right where she wanted him. She threw in a little pout for good measure as she added, "I've had to work hard to make something of myself."

"Exactly." Bobby slapped the back of the bench and I flattened myself like a pancake on the nasty ground a mere millimeter from getting whacked by his meaty palm. If the powers that be didn't throw the book at him, then I would.

"Scott has been handed his life on a silver platter," Bobby went on. "First by Gramps when he died and left him all of his money, cutting me right out of the will. Then second by Wilma when Scott married her for her daddy's money because he'd gambled away Gramp's life's worth. Of course Scott used Wilma's money to pay off the loan sharks, but then gambled himself right back into trouble. Cheating, drinking, and gambling is his life, yet Wilma refused to see any of it, except for the one time. I thought she would listen to me that night."

"What night?" Jaz asked all breathy-like as though he were a god. I'd have to congratulate her on her Oscar-worthy performance if I got out of this horrible predicament in one piece, I thought, seconds before Bobby dropped the bomb.

"The night I got her pregnant."

Jaz sucked in a breath. "You're the father of Wilma's baby?"

He laughed harshly. "A lot of good it did me. Since Scott and I are identical, she thought he'd never find out he wasn't the father. She never knew he was sterile. At first I just wanted to pay Scott back, but to think I fell in love with her. I was the twin who actually wanted her and would have stayed true to her. Only, she didn't want me over Scott any more than my grandfather did."

"What happened?" Jaz asked, sounding as though she were weakening and now falling under *his* spell. She was such a sucker for an underdog.

"Scott refused to give her a divorce," Bobby said. "He didn't even care that he wasn't the father, because he didn't love her. But he *did* love her father's money and was trying to find a way to tap into more. He threatened to expose her infidelity if she tried to fight him, and frankly, he was pleased his child might look like him, and he wouldn't be forced to sleep with boring ole her. Basically, my payback failed because he didn't give a crap about anything but himself."

"I am sorry for that." Jaz squeezed his hand. If she caved after all of this, I would smack her. She was always the one doing the dumping and using, not the other way around, because she was terrified a man would hurt her first like her mother had. Boomer had been the first man ever to get under her skin. Even though he didn't look anything like Bobby, I could tell Jaz was thinking of him. I poked her back through a slot in the bench. This was *not* the time to go soft on me.

She sat up straight and let go of his hand. "You were saying?"

"In the end, we both hated him, yet Wilma still didn't want me."

"Is that why you pushed her down the stairs?"

Atta girl, I thought.

"Yes," he said before thinking, and then looked startled as he blurted, "No! I mean, I don't know. It wasn't like that."

"Too late," I said, having rolled to a crouched position behind their bench as I clicked the handcuffs around his wrist and fastened him to the metal.

"What the hell are you doing?" He surged to his feet but the handcuffs—courtesy of Jaz's purse and her words, *you just never know when a pair might come in handy*—yanked him back in place. Handy for what I didn't dare ask. At this moment I was grateful she had her own quirks.

"I'm making a citizen's arrest, Mr. Parks," I said, as I stood.

"For what? I didn't kill my brother."

"Which you can't prove, but that's not what I'm arresting you for. You just admitted to attempted murder of Wilma Parks and her unborn child."

"I did no such thing." He frowned. "Wait, have you been there the whole time?" he asked.

"Yup, and I heard everything." I held up my cassette recorder, clicked it off, and slipped it back into my purse.

Mission accomplished.

"You're gonna regret this," he ground out through his teeth.

"You don't scare me," I said, clamping my shaking knees together and hoisting my chin high.

"Well, I sure as hell better," Detective Stevens said from behind me. "Unbelievable, Ballas!"

I whirled around and took a step back from the intimidating presence of the seething detective and his sidekick, Boomer, who looked like he was about to go ballistic.

"They set me up," Bobby blurted.

"Save it for the jury," Jaz said, stepping around him in a wide berth, because even with handcuffs on, he looked like he was ready to strangle her. She turned to Nik and Boomer as she said, "Bobby just confessed to pushing Wilma down the stairs, and we have a tape of the confession."

"You bi—"

"Watch it, pal," Detective Matheson boomed.

"Yeah?" Bobby said with relish, locking his eyes on Jaz as he said with glee, "Wait until you listen to the tapes. Something tells me you'll agree with me."

Detective Matheson glared at Jaz, who waved at him nervously, as he briefly unlocked the handcuffs before grabbing Bobby roughly and hauling him away to the squad car.

When he disappeared inside the car and drove away, Jaz turned on me. "Thanks, *pal*." She huffed off toward her car and disappeared inside to drive away as well.

I bit my bottom lip and looked around to no avail.

"That's right, Ballas. It's just you and me. Please don't tell me I have to arrest you again." he groaned.

I held out my wrists on a sigh and said, "All in the name of justice."

Chapter 20

"You mean you're not going to take me back to jail?" I sputtered later that evening when Detective Stevens pulled into our adjoined driveway instead of heading to the station.

"You have no idea what I had to endure from my mother the last time I arrested you," he muttered. "It's easier just to punish you myself."

Even from inside his car I could hear Wolfgang whining and scratching to get out. I swallowed hard, terrified of what his idea of punishment would involve.

Nik followed my gaze. "I'm mad enough to do what you're thinking, but even I'm not that cruel."

"No, but you are definitely unusual. I'm even more afraid to hear what you have in mind."

"Relax, Ballas. I'm not Boomer, so rest assured you won't be chained to my bedframe if that's what you're worried about."

I almost laughed hysterically. He had no idea how the sound of his words made me feel, and terrified wasn't even close. Excited was more like it. What was wrong with me? I was nearly thirty and I hadn't had sex in way too long to remember, and the memories I had were anything but good. But Nik was different, and my gift shed a whole new light on the idea of intimacy. I guess I was more worried he wouldn't make a move. Or he would, and it wouldn't work, and then he'd *really* think I was a freak.

"You okay? You look a little flushed," he broke the silence.

I flinched. "Huh? Oh, yeah. I'm fine." I cleared my throat. "About that punishment...?"

He sighed. "You and I both know I'm not going to do anything."

"That's what I thought," I muttered, trying to hide my disappointment.

"Excuse me?"

"That's what I hoped," I said louder.

"I just wish you'd trust me. I'm trying to do the right thing by keeping both you and Jaz safe while solving this murder. You taking matters into your own hands behind my back is only hindering that process."

"But you heard what Jaz said. Bobby admitted to pushing Wilma, the mother of his child. He's capable of anything. And he tried to flee when he was strictly ordered not to leave town. That has to mean something. He's probably the one who broke into our house and Jaz's car. It probably never was Johnny. He's pathetic but not a killer. Bobby, on the other hand, we don't know anything about. And from what I've seen so far, I don't trust him one bit."

"And that's why he's locked up right now until we get to the bottom of this whole mess."

"Which I'm grateful for. So you can relax, Detective. I'm safe." Safe from killers and apparently safe from a night of pleasure as well. I mentally sighed, but on the outside I gave him my best I'll-be-a-good-girl smile.

"I'm not sure about anything yet."

"Well, I am, so can you take me to bed?"

He blinked. "Come again?"

I flushed to the root of my hair, turning my blonde hair a flaming red in my mind's eye. "I meant, I want you to take me to bed. Or to the door, I mean, you know to keep me safe so I can go to bed. Alone. Not that you're not appealing because you are. Very much so in fact, but you must hear that all the time, or not. I don't know what you hear. How could I, right? And then you can leave, or not, I mean you don't have to tuck me in or anything. Oh God, I'm really tired after today's events. Ignore me. I'm being stupid."

"Kalli," he said with a soft, husky voice. "You're not stupid, you're unusual. Look at that. We have something in common. You just need to learn to relax."

He studied me curiously until I squirmed, and then he went for it. He moved in before I could think twice and locked his lips to mine. Heat. Intense heat infused my every cell as his mouth worked its magic. My lips parted ever so slightly, and his tongue didn't hesitate to slip between them. Little zings of pleasure spread throughout my body as his tongue touched and tasted and...spread germs. I started to stiffen, but then his arms wrapped around me and his big hands caressed every inch of my body that they could reach.

Oh, God, you feel like heaven, I heard, and instantly I relaxed. *Your skin is like silk, and you taste so sweet.* My anxiety faded away, the voices pointing out everything that could go wrong from kissing him were dwarfed by his thoughts, allowing the feelings he was creating inside me to build. *Baby, you're so beautiful you take my breath away. The things I want to do to you all night long.* I didn't even worry that they might cause some serious internal damage to my organs. At least I didn't worry *too* much. I was too busy basking in pleasure. *If only you weren't so pig-headed.*

You're gonna get yourself killed, and Jaz is going to go to jail for life if you're not careful.

"Stop thinking like that," I muttered around his lips. "Keep thinking sexy."

He pulled his head away from mine and arched a thick black brow. "What are you talking about?"

It was like someone dumped a bucket of ice water on me. I suddenly was acutely aware of his hands on my body, and couldn't stop wondering where they had been and when he had washed them last. Not to mention he'd had coffee recently. When was the last time he brushed his teeth, and did he floss daily? Maybe I should ask him. What was I doing? Oh, Lordy, the moment was ruined. I pushed him away and sat up, adjusting my clothing and moving closer to the car door.

"Oh, nothing. I could just tell you have a lot on your mind, and like I said, I really am tired. I'll see myself to the door." I quickly climbed out of his car and bolted up the walk. Risking one last peek over my shoulder, I could see by the expression on his face he was confused. It clearly said, *What the hell did I do this time*? Meanwhile I was giddy as a schoolgirl. For a little while there, things had been working. His thoughts overrode my brain's resistance, urging my body to seek what it craved. It wasn't until reality intruded on his end. For once I wasn't the one who needed to stop overthinking things. He was. And I knew just what to do. I had a plan. I would seduce him. That would get him thinking sexy for sure.

Who would have thought I would ever want a guy with a one-track mind?

In the wee hours of Friday morning, I was in bed dreaming of ways I would seduce Detective Dreamy now that I knew intimacy was a probability and not just a possibility anymore. Jaz was sound asleep in her room. I was tempted to run some ideas by her, but she slept like the dead. Nothing would wake her short of an earthquake, which we didn't often get in Connecticut, and when we did, they were mild. So for now it looked like I was alone with my thoughts.

Or maybe I wasn't...

A noise sounded in the living room. I bolted straight up in bed. It was faint, but I could definitely hear something. Maybe it was Prissy. I crept out of bed and eased my door open. It was still so dark out I couldn't see a thing, and I didn't dare turn on a light for fear of what I might find.

Had Bobby broken out of jail and come after me for ruining his life? Or maybe he was still in jail, and Wilma was coming after me. Though, last I talked to her, she was in the hospital. Or maybe it was one of Scott's enemies: a pissed-off husband or a jilted ex-lover or someone he owed money to. I was starting to freak myself out, so I took three deep breaths and tried to calm myself as I looked for Prissy.

"Prissy," I whispered, feeling my way into the living room. "Here kitty kitty. Come to Mama."

Prissy brushed up against my leg, and I jumped higher than Frona on a pogo stick. When my heart finally returned to normal, I flicked on a light and blinked rapidly until my vision adjusted. Glancing around, I didn't see anything, so I let out an explosion of air and gave my cat a scolding look. "That was very naughty, young lady. You nearly gave me a—"

Something hit me in the back of the head, and pain shot through my skull. I stumbled forward but caught myself before I fell. Opening my mouth to scream, I tried to turn around to look at my attacker, but gloved hands wrapped around my throat before I had a chance. My windpipe was cut off, and I couldn't breathe. I briefly wondered if my vocal chords would be damaged and I wouldn't be able to speak again. But then I realized I might die, and it wouldn't matter anyway.

That sent adrenaline surging through me. I tried hard to read my attacker's thoughts, hoping to gain the person's identity, but the thick gloves prevented it. I could feel intense animosity and hear faint gurgling, but the actual thoughts were muffled. Bare skin on skin worked best, or even thin clothing worked okay. But the thicker the clothing, the less clear the words were.

And thick leather gloves were nearly impossible.

Air. I needed air. I clawed at the gloves to no avail. I tried to twist and turn, but that didn't work either. I felt so helpless. My eyes blinked over and over, and the world around me started to close in with a dark inky black. My limbs tingled, and I could feel myself losing consciousness. I glanced at Prissy, realizing it was the last time I would see her, which brought on the realization that as much as my family might annoy me, I would miss them terribly. And Detective Dreamy…I couldn't even think about him. The pain in my chest intensified, and the last thing I heard before the world around me faded to darkness was a high-pitched shriek of a meow.

I woke up a couple minutes later and blinked my eyes open, gasping for air. My neck ached, my lungs burned, and my body felt like it had been sat on by the beast. Memories of what had happened came flooding back to me. I grabbed my throat and wilted in relief that the gloves were gone. The gloves. I surged to a sitting position, then grabbed my head as the blood rush made me dizzy. Once the room stopped spinning, I looked around but didn't see anything.

Not even Miss Priss.

Panic seized me. I crawled over to the phone, trying not to make too much noise, and dialed 911. Then I sat back and waited. It was only a matter of minutes before I heard the ambulance. Boomer burst through the door in full cop mode, looking like he was on the set of the latest detective movie. He glanced once at me, all business like, and then proceeded to do a sweep of the house, Sherlock Holmes style. I didn't have the heart to point out he looked more like Watson.

Max charged through the door next with his equipment in tow and gray eyes looking terrified. He came to a stop by my side, breathing heavy, his perfect body shaking. "Oh, my God, Kalli, are you okay? Are you hurt? What happened?" he blurted, rapid-firing questions at me as he rubbed a hand over and over the top of his sandy-brown flattop.

Usually he was the calm, cool, and collected one in emergencies, but he looked frazzled and on the verge of a breakdown right now. He felt my pulse. *I'm such an idiot. I should never have talked to her the way I did. I don't even like Ana. How could I have been so stupid to shut her out and now almost lose her? I would never forgive myself if anything bad happened to her.*

"It's okay, Max." I squeezed his hand. "I'm okay." I pulled my wrist away and patted his hand, trying not to show my discomfort at his touch.

"What the hell happened?" He sat back on his heels, studying me intently but looking more relaxed.

"Honestly, I'm not sure. I woke up early this morning, dreaming about... well, just dreaming. And then I heard a noise from the living room. I don't know why, but it felt like something was wrong. I can't really explain it, but something wasn't right. So I went out to see where Prissy was, and she startled me. I turned on the light and scolded her, when suddenly someone hit me from behind."

"What did they hit you with?" He inspected the back of my head, then broke an ice pack and had me hold it over the bump.

"I don't know, but it was really hard." Oh, my goodness, what if I had a concussion? Or what if the blow had literally dislodged my brain. It could be floating about freestyle in my skull, giving a whole new meaning to scatterbrained. What if little pieces fell off and actually scattered about willy-nilly? I might never be the same again. Another thought dawned on me...

What if it ruined my gift?

I started panting for breath, my limbs tingling and knees feeling like jelly. Grabbing Max's hand, I stared at him and looked deep into his eyes, waiting for something. Anything. But nothing happened. He just looked back at me. I was about to hyperventilate and pass out from a full-blown panic attack when I suddenly heard, *Well, now, maybe I have a chance with her after all.*

"Oh, thank God... and no!" I quickly let go of his hand.

He frowned and looked at me like I'd completely lost my marbles.

"I meant no, don't hurt me. Post-traumatic stress, I guess," I said by way of explanation. "I forgot to mention my attacker strangled me."

His body language registered alarm once more as he inspected my neck with a worried expression on his face, then he shined his little flashlight in my eyes and studied my pupils. "Are you feeling dizzy or nauseated? Headache? Between the blow to the head and the loss of oxygen, you may have a concussion."

"I would have died if it wasn't for Prissy." I blinked. "Oh, my gosh, where is Miss Priss?"

I tried to get up, but Max blocked me. "We'll find her. Don't worry."

Boomer came from down the hall with Jaz in tow, carrying Miss Priss, whose calico fur still stood on end. Prissy leapt from Jaz's arms the second she saw me. She pranced over to me in a dignified fashion even though I could tell she was worried by her stiff gait. She was so like me. She gingerly sat on my lap, not daring to lick my arm. She knew better, bless her little heart. She kept everyone at bay, protecting me like my sweet little hero. I stroked her fur so she would know it was okay.

"The coast is clear. No one is in the house except you two," Detective Matheson said.

"Why would someone be in the house? Nothing looks tampered with or stolen?" Jaz said, all rumpled and looking half asleep still.

"Because I stopped them first," I replied with a hoarse voice. I rubbed my neck and tried to swallow through the pain.

Max helped me to my unsteady feet.

"Holy crap, are you okay?" Jaz asked, sounding fully alert now.

"I've been better." I looked at Boomer. "Is Bobby still in jail?"

He nodded. "And Wilma is still in the hospital, if that's what you're thinking."

"So what does that mean?" Jaz asked, looking a little concerned.

"That the killer is still out there, and they're not going to stop until they get what they want."

"Which is?" Jaz asked, looking downright scared for the first time.

"You dead or behind bars is my guess," Boomer answered with a serious tone. "Now are you going to listen to me?"

"What's going on?" Nik asked, still in his wrinkled pajamas and bare feet with dark messy hair sticking out in every direction as he burst through the door and took in the scene before him. He looked like he'd just rolled out of bed. I guess Jaz wasn't the only sound sleeper.

"Someone broke in, but Kalli stopped them, and then they tried to kill her, but Miss Priss saved the day," Jaz blurted, sounding like a chipmunk near hysteria.

Boomer patted her back, and she launched herself into his arms. He didn't even hesitate, wrapping his strong arms around her securely until she stopped shaking.

Nik's piercing blue eyes settled on me, and I wished he'd do the same. I wouldn't be so lucky based on the hard angry look he was nailing me with. I swayed. Max quickly caught me, leaving his arms securely locked around me, only his touch did nothing to settle my nerves. I didn't have the strength or energy to move away, so I just stood there, which did not help my situation any.

"Let me get this straight. Someone tried to kill you, and you called him, even though I was right next door?" he asked accusingly.

"Um, hello. I didn't call him, I called 911. The number one is supposed to call in an emergency. If you would just listen to reason and quit being ridiculous, I would explain," I said.

"No need. A picture's worth a thousand words. I'll just take my ridiculous self and go, since I'm obviously not needed here," he responded and then walked out my door—and, I was afraid, out of my life for good.

That's right, pal. She's finally mine.

"Never gonna happen, Max," I said and found the strength to step out of the obviously confused EMT's arms. So much for being safe and so much for my seduction. I had a feeling after today, it was *never gonna happen* with Detective Dreamy either, and at this rate, I wasn't sure I wanted it to now anyway. So there.

Stubborn mule!

CHAPTER 21

A couple hours later, I sat waiting for my walking papers in the hospital, hoping they would release me soon. Most people hated the smells and sounds of a hospital, but the smells of cleaning chemicals and antiseptics and monitoring devices actually comforted me. I just didn't like doctors and nurses who poked and prodded and invaded my personal space way too many times. This time I didn't have a choice.

Turns out I did have a concussion and a bruised neck, but other than that, I was going to live. You'd never know it according to my mother. She'd literally rallied the family, and they had shown up at the hospital before the ambulance had even arrived. It was uncanny how she knew what was happening all over the town, virtually seconds after it happened.

"She doesn't look good, Ophelia," my yiayia Dido said. My pop and papou were down in the cafeteria, no doubt giving advice on how to improve the food, but the women had refused to leave my side. "I don't like her color." Yiayia shook her head, and her gray bun slipped a bit. She pulled some aloe out of her apron pocket.

"Don't put that stuff on me, Yiayia. I'm fine. People are going to think we're even weirder than we are," I said, looking around. A couple of nurses and doctors walked by in the hall, but no one so much as glanced inside the room.

"Oh, posh. Who gives a whoopty whoo what anyone thinks? Besides, I've changed the diapers of most of these people from back in the day when I ran my daycare service. No one would dare say a word against me. They know better."

"Whoopty whoo, whoopty whoo, I give a whoopty whoo," Frona chanted while bouncing on my bed.

"Her color's fine, Ma," my mother said to Yiayia as she grabbed Frona's arm to still her.

"Thank you," I said, shocked that my mother finally agreed with me on something.

"It's her head I worry about." She reached into her polyester pocket and pulled out her roll of Duct tape. "Here, let me cover that bump."

I knew I had spoken too soon. "Good Lord, you two." I slid off the bed before either of them could touch me, feeling much stronger than earlier so long as I didn't move too quickly. "I'm the one who's fine. You're the one I'm worried about," I said to my mother, pointing my finger in her face.

She froze and looked alarmingly guilty, which was *never* a good thing. Patting her black beehive, she asked, "Why?"

"You know why." Eleni snorted, then gave her a whoops-I'm-sorry look.

"What aren't you telling me?" I stated suspiciously, crossing my arms over my hospital gown. "I saw that man follow you yesterday from the steps of the jailhouse. He's not from around here, yet I've seen him in town lately."

"Kalli's got a boyfriend, Kalli's got a boyfriend," Frona sang, spinning in circles while sitting on the chair with wheels.

"I told you all. Detective Stevens is not my boyfriend," I replied in exasperation.

"Not McDreamy," Frona continued, "Mr. Cleany. Cheater cheater pumpkin eater."

"Mr. Cleany?" I rubbed my temple, my headache threatening to come back.

"Squeaky clean, baldy bean," Frona kept singing and spinning, her lopsided pigtails twirling away.

"For the love of Zeus." Eleni stopped the chair, and Frona fell on the floor giggling. "Frona, stop it. You're confusing poor Kalli."

"Wait a minute," I said, almost afraid to hear the answer to my next question. "You mean the bald man I saw wasn't after Ma?"

"I knew this would happen," my mother said, wringing her hands and pacing about the room. "That floozy has you mixed up in that awful online dating. I've always said no good can come from the Twitter. Imagine people twitting about. It's just wrong, I tell you. Wrong!"

"Highly improper," Yiayia agreed, tsking and shaking her head.

"Twitter, Twitter, twitting about," Frona jumped back on the bed. "Whee, I want to twit."

"You are a twit," Eleni snapped, and Frona stuck out her tongue.

"Look what it did to Jazlyn," Ma continued. "Landed her floozy fanny in jail. You've already wound up in jail twice. I don't want to see you wind up a floozy too, or worse, dead. That man looks downright scary if you ask me."

"It's not the Twitter, it's the Internet, and it's called tweeting, but never mind that." I swept my hand through the air, my energy sapped already. "And stop pacing. You're making me dizzy." My mother stopped walking and faced me. "What makes you think I met this man through online dating?" I asked warily.

"Because he's been asking for you all over town. It's a good thing we have Ballases everywhere. He knows you're Greek, and he knows your name is Ballas, but he obviously doesn't know what you look like. At least you were smart enough not to post your picture. We've been running inference and sending him on wild goose chases all over town. He said he tried your number, but it's disconnected."

"I changed my phone carrier, remember?" I had told my family and work, but no one else yet.

"Of course I remember. How could I not?" My mother harrumphed. "First you leave me and now you cut me off. I can tell when I'm not wanted. My only daughter is trying to obliterate me right out of her life."

My yiayia patted my mother's hand and gave me a disapproving look.

"Ma, come on. You know I don't want you out of my life. I didn't cut you off. I just got on my own phone plan. I'm almost thirty. I figured it was time I got a life of my own." Forget failure to launch. In my family you were condemned if you failed to stay.

The scary part of this whole ordeal was trying to figure out who this guy was and how he had gotten my old cell phone number. Thank goodness I had changed it and he didn't know what I looked like. I could work with that. I didn't want to worry my mother by making her think there was a virtual stranger scary guy on the loose who was after me. He could be one of Scott's enemies and out to stop me from looking into the case further. Or he could be one of Bobby's enemies and maybe Bobby had been the real target all along. Or he could be the father of Wilma's baby and trying to stop me from finding out. He could very well be the guy who broke into my house and attacked me last night.

Oh my gosh, he could be the killer!

In the meantime, I had to keep my mother from locking me up. If she knew the truth, she wouldn't ask anymore. She would insist I go home with her, and she had enough backup to enforce her wishes. Not to mention Detective Dreamy was mad enough not to stop her from kidnapping me. Nope, for all our sakes, I would stick with the online dating angle and deal with the consequences that bit of information would bring.

"You're right, Ma. Bad idea on the whole online dating thing. I should have been more careful. But I don't need Baldy anymore because now I have Detective Dreamy. Do me a favor and keep the bald man off my trail, would you? The last thing we both want is for him to interfere with my relationship with a nice Greek boy."

She was thrilled to have something to do. To have a purpose. To feel needed. I could tell she was on a mission. "Don't worry about a thing. I'm on it," she said to me, then turned to Dido. "Let's rally the troops, Ma. It's time to get to work. You know what to do."

And I knew what I had to do. I hated to admit it, but Nik was right. I didn't feel safe one bit.

"You were right," I said, walking into Detective Steven's office in the police station. I hadn't been in there since he and

Detective Matheson had questioned Jaz the morning of the murder. The walls were still white and the desks still bare of any personal effects. This really was a place of all business, which made it hard to talk about anything personal. But I knew I had to set the record straight for both our sakes, even though I still felt he'd overreacted. I just hoped he could move past everything that had happened because I still hadn't given up on us.

"Excuse me, what was that?" Nik asked, sitting back and locking his hands behind his head, getting comfy. "I couldn't possibly have heard you. Could you repeat that?"

"Very funny." I walked inside and shut the door. Boomer wasn't there, so it was now or never. I took a breath and then sat in the chair across from Nik, folding my hands in my lap so I wouldn't fidget. I'd come straight from the hospital so I still had on my yoga pants and zip-up hoodie. Now I wished I had stopped home to don a suit. I would have felt much more confident saying, "You were right, and I was wrong, and I'm sorry."

He slowly lowered his arms and stared hard at me. He had showered and donned his typical jeans, dress shirt, tie, and sport coat, clearly giving him the advantage. I couldn't help it. I started to fidget until he finally made up his mind about something. He said, "Apology accepted."

I sighed, rubbing my temples.

His gaze turned soft and concerned. "How are you feeling?"

"A bit of a headache and a little sore throat, but I'll live. And for the record, you overreacted big time. I didn't call Max. I called 911. I wasn't thinking straight and 911 was about all I could handle. Besides, do you really think I have your cell phone memorized?"

"I'm an ass," he said, and I blinked in surprise. "I figured that out once I went home and cooled off. "I'm the sorry one for acting like a jerk. I got jealous. I admit it. Jealous people sometimes do stupid things." He cleared his throat, which suddenly sounded as hoarse as mine, before adding, "Truth is, I hated seeing you in another man's arms. It wouldn't have mattered who it was."

I read the sincerity in his eyes, and my body warmed with pleasure over his admission. I couldn't help smiling a little on the inside as things were most definitely looking up. "Apology accepted," I repeated his words softly and then bit my bottom lip.

His gaze dropped to my mouth as he said, "Guess my pride was a little stung after you bolted on me the night before. I thought things were going well. I thought we were on the same page in wanting to see where things could go between us. I apologize if I was wrong."

"You weren't wrong, and we were on the same page. We still are, I promise." How did I say this without giving away that I could read his mind? I stood and started to pace. I might be adopted, but there were some things I definitely got from my mother. "I could just tell you weren't totally focused on me," I went on, talking with my hands. "You had a lot on your mind, so to speak. And you know I have quirks. This whole romance thing is hard for me. So in the future," I paused to watch his intense gaze lock on mine, and then added, "make no mistake, Detective, there *will* be a future."

"I can live with that." His grin came slow and sweet. "You were saying?"

"In the future, do me a favor and don't think about anything but me." I could feel my face flush fire red but knew if we were going to have a chance at all, then I had to go for it. "And, um, think about *exactly* what you want to do to me. And don't leave out any details."

"Seriously?" he asked, his eyebrows shooting sky-high as he stood.

I backed up, but then shook off my embarrassment and conjured my inner Jaz as I added, "Definitely. Think you can handle that, big guy?"

"Um, gee, let me think about that." His gaze turned heated as he started walking around his desk, slowly stalking me. "When I kiss you next time, you want me to think in explicit detail about making love to you. About all the things I want to do to you. About every place I want to touch you, and kiss you, and—"

"Yup, that'll work!" I bumped into the wall behind me, trapped as I tried to calm my rapid heart rate and erratic breathing. "Trust me."

"Then trust me when I say, hell yeah I can handle that." A chuckle rumbled deep in his chest as he came to a stop mere inches before me.

I had to admit I liked this lighter, more playful sexy side of him. "Good." Feeling daring I said, "Care to give it a try right now?"

"You never cease to amaze me, Ms. Ballas."

"Remember, think sexy," I blurted breathlessly.

"No problem there." He braced his hands on the wall on both sides of my head and leaned in. His lips were a fraction of an inch from mine when someone knocked on the door.

He closed his eyes, and I could see his cheek pulse as he ground his teeth, struggling for control. After a moment, he said in a husky voice, "Hold that thought." Taking a step back, he barked, "Come in."

We just stood there by the wall, looking awkward and guilty of something even though nothing had happened yet as Boomer barged through the door. He looked at Nik and then at me and then raised his brows.

"What's up?" Nik asked. "What's the emergency? And there'd better be an emergency."

"Oh, right." Boomer shook off his confusion over us and refocused "Maria Danza has just been arrested."

"The hell you say," Detective Stevens said, looking floored.

"Why?" I asked in complete shock.

"They found the murder weapon in her pastry shop," Boomer explained, looking pleased to be the first one in the know.

"So what does that mean?" I asked, unable to process what I was hearing.

"It means, Jaz is a free woman," Nik said, "and we just caught our killer."

Episode 8

Chapter 22

"Maria wants to speak with me?" I sputtered Friday evening, staring at Detective Matheson in shock. He'd dropped the bomb that Maria Danza had been arrested for the murder of Darrin Wilcox aka Scott Parks. They'd found the murder weapon in her pastry store, Sinfully Delicious, shortly after I was attacked earlier this morning.

"That's what she said," Boomer replied, leaning against his desk in the office that he and Nik shared at the police station.

"Why me?" Today was turning out to be one of the worst days of my life.

"Don't know, she didn't say, but she does get one phone call. She didn't want her lawyer or anyone else. Just you."

"Then why didn't she call?" I asked, feeling light headed.

"She tried," he answered. "Seems no one knows your number these days."

"I do," Nik said with a frown, looking from Boomer to me then back to him again.

"My bad," Boomer said, smirking, reminding me he still owed me payback for the Boy Wonder crack. If he told Nik about Baldy and the online dating misunderstanding, I'd holy smoke his Docker-clad behind.

"You have my number, but most other people don't," I explained. "I recently switched to a new carrier and got on my own plan."

"I see." Only, he didn't look like he did. He still looked suspicious, and my glaring at Boomer was probably not helping.

"What if Maria was the one who attacked me? Maybe she broke into our house to kill Jaz or kill me because I was getting too close? She could have stashed the murder weapon in her shop after she left my house. What if she wants to see me to finish the job?" I swallowed hard, not too proud to admit I was terrified.

"It's okay, Kalli. Calm down before you give yourself a panic attack. I will be right there with you."

"Negative," Boomer said. "She wants to speak with her alone."

"You don't have to do this, you know," Nik said to me.

"No, it's okay," I replied, taking a deep breath and striving to remain calm. I was the only one who could find out for sure if she was lying or not. I knew what I had to do, even if every ounce of my flesh recoiled at the thought. "I need to put this case to rest once and for all. I need closure. I just want this whole thing to be over, and maybe after today, it finally will be."

"Just know we'll be right outside the door, and she'll be in handcuffs. You so much as raise your voice, I'm coming in."

"Okay, and thanks." I smiled at him. "For everything."

He nodded, and then Boomer led the way down the hall to the holding room with me in the middle and Nik bringing up the rear. Boomer knocked once and then went inside the room with Maria.

Nik turned to me and rubbed my shoulders before I could object, then dropped his hands to his hips. "You sure you're going to be okay?"

"Yes. I'm ready. I think I actually need this."

"Okay. Just remember, it will all be over with very soon. I for one am looking forward to putting this whole thing behind us and moving on to whatever the future might have in store."

There was that word *future* again. I smiled with a mixture of hope and anticipation. "Me too."

The door opened. "She's ready for you." Boomer stepped outside and held the door for me.

I took a moment to even my breathing, then held my head high and walked through the door. A resounding click sounded behind me, and I jolted, much to my frustration. The room was cold and white and empty except for a table and chairs. Maria sat at the table with her handcuffed hands in front of her, looking way more terrified than I felt. Somehow that put me instantly at ease. Something wasn't right here. My gut was screaming for me to get to the bottom of it. She glanced up at me and promptly burst into tears.

Something deep within pushed me forward and made me sit down across from her. "Maria, what's wrong?" I asked, my heart melting for the very real and sincere distress written across her plump rosy cheeks. Yes, I wanted this case to be over with. And yes, I wanted Jaz's name cleared. But not at the expense of another innocent victim taking the fall in her place. And every ounce of my being screamed this woman was innocent.

"Everything!" she wailed. "No one believes me. I admit I don't like Jaz, but come on. I'm a pissed-off jilted ex, not a murderer. And I think I'm even angrier at Johnny than I am at Jaz. I have no clue how that stupid gun wound up in my shop. I was just as surprised as the cops were when they got an anonymous tip. And of course I don't have an alibi for early this morning when you were attacked, which I am so sorry about, by the way. No one deserves that."

"What happened?"

"The truth of the matter is I live alone. I get up at the crack of dawn to bake, not attack people. Do they really think I am capable of that? The real attacker must have slipped the gun in my shop before I started baking this morning's pastries. Can I prove it? No. What do I have to do, install security cameras too? I really didn't think I needed them, but apparently every business is vulnerable in this town."

"Why did you ask to talk with me?"

"I don't know. Something I saw in your eyes the day we talked in my shop, I guess. You just seemed like you really wanted to get to the bottom of this case and find the truth. Jaz wants her freedom—which trust me, after today, I can't blame her—and the police want this case closed, but you seem like the only person who really cares about seeking justice. Oh, my God, what if justice never happens? What if I go to prison for the rest of my life? I'll die in there."

She started sobbing uncontrollably, so I did the unthinkable. I grabbed her hands and held on tight. *Oh, please, God in heaven, let someone believe me. I'm innocent. I've lost my boyfriend, now I'm going to lose my freedom, and then I'll lose my business. What did I do that was so wrong to deserve this? I'm a good person. Why don't I deserve happiness? It's not fair. None of this is fair.*

I felt her sincerity with every fiber of my being. I shuddered, then let go and stared at her with sheer determination. "It's going to be okay, Maria."

"I-It is?" She hiccupped.

"Yes. Because I believe you."

"B-But Jaz is your best friend."

"Yes, she is. But she too is innocent, and if I know Jaz, she would never stand for anyone being accused of something they didn't do."

"I misjudged her." Maria looked down, her face crumbling with shame. "Why is love so hard? I let a stupid guy cloud my judgment." She sniffed and looked up at me, holding her chin high. "Never again, I tell you." "If I get out of this mess in one piece, I will never again allow a man, of all things, to get in the way of the sisterhood and my common sense."

"Well said," I replied with a squeeze to her hands before I let go. "And trust me when I say Jaz shares your sentiments. You two are more alike than either of you realize. Something tells me when this is all over with, you're going to become fast friends."

She blinked, showing the first signs of hope. "You really think so? For some strange reason, you might be right."

"Yes, I do think so, and I know I'm right. This too shall pass, and we *will* prevail."

"What makes you so sure?"

I stared hard in her eyes, trying to give her enough hope to hang onto. "Because I won't stop until I find the real killer. I can promise you that."

She wiped her tears away and nodded, sitting a little straighter and looking a whole lot stronger. We said our goodbyes and I left the holding room. Nik went in to talk to Maria briefly and then rejoined me.

He smiled, studying me closely. "You look good. Your talk must have gone well. So, are we done now? Can we finally get on with our lives? You know, focus on the *future*?" His gaze held a sparkle that spoke volumes.

"Absolutely," I replied. "My talk went very well, and I am definitely ready to focus on the future, but we are so not done."

He blinked, and a look of wariness clouded his gaze. "What do you mean?"

"Maria Danza might be a lot of things, but guilty of murder she is not. She didn't do it, which means, dear detective . . . we still have a murderer in our midst."

"This has been the day from hell. I can't believe he did it to me again," I said to Jaz later that night while sitting out back on our deck, looking across the yard and over the new fence Nik had paid to have replaced. The sun was setting, but not as quickly these days, and the temperatures were growing warmer.

"Let me guess," Jaz said as she joined me with a glass of wine for each of us, "you must be referring to Detective Dreamy. What did he do this time?"

Nik's sliding door opened. He let Wolfgang out, who whined when he saw us, causing Prissy to hiss loudly and drawing Nik's gaze to our side of the yard. He smiled and waved. Jaz waved back, but I turned away, staring straight into our side of the yard. I heard his grunt, then I heard the door close.

"He insulted me again."

"I'm sure he didn't mean to. I do know from my conversations with Boomer that the chief wants this case wrapped up quickly. They are under a tremendous amount of pressure. Even if they have any nagging doubts or want to believe Maria didn't do it, they are being pushed into wrapping up this case."

"By putting an innocent person behind bars? Maria didn't kill anyone, and she's not the one who broke into our apartment."

"How did my gun get in her shop?"

"The real culprit must be trying to set her up. I'm thinking my attacker is probably the same person who broke into your car and the house the first time, and most likely, the same person who killed Scott. I'm telling you, I held Maria's hands and heard her thoughts. She really was home at the time, but no one will believe her. I know how she feels. No one wants to believe me either."

"Come on, Kalli, you know I believe you."

"Yeah, because you know about my gift. Detective Drive-Me-Crazy doesn't. Is it too much for him to go on blind faith? To trust my gut? He didn't say the words exactly, but it was pretty clear he would trust his own instincts and even Boomer's but not mine because I'm not a *real* cop. And he can't understand why I'm not dropping this and jeopardizing your freedom."

"Hey, don't worry about me. I'm a big girl and can take care of myself. The last thing I want is for anyone, even Maria, to fall on a sword for me. The truth always comes out. In the meantime, you keep digging. If anyone can figure this thing out, you can, from your sheer stubborn determination to prove Dreamy wrong." She held up her glass.

"Thanks, I think." I laughed, clinking my glass to hers.

"So, I take it your date night is off?"

"Um, yeah. You could say so. I'm keeping my head in the present, living for today, so to speak. I'm beginning to think the future is highly overrated." I took a sip of wine. "Let's back up a step. Tell me more about these conversations with Boomer that you've had lately. Dare I ask if you engaged in pillow talk?"

"Trust me when I say the past is anything but overrated, yet far too dangerous to relive. Let's just say based on experience if we were on the same pillow, we wouldn't be talking." She sighed wistfully. "Nope, these days our conversations are more of a factual nature."

"Really? And what facts did you discuss?"

"Turns out Scott wasn't the only twin with an addiction. Bobby was addicted to drugs. I guess his allowance from his grandfather wasn't enough to supply his habit, so he started dealing. After some kid overdosed on drugs he got from Bobby, their grandfather covered it up and sent Bobby away to rehab. By the time he got out, his grandfather had died, leaving all his money to Scott," Jaz said, looking pensive. "I think you might be right. Baldy could very well be after Bobby instead of Scott and have mistaken him when he killed him since they look so much alike. They both had enemies and people who might want revenge."

"I just thought of something else. The attack on me didn't start until the investigation turned toward outsiders. Baldy could have broken in, trying to discover what I'd found out, and then attacked me to try to stop me."

"What are you going to do?"

"Turn the tables and stop him first."

"You should tell Detective Stevens."

"I don't have proof. He won't believe me any more than he believed Maria."

A rumble of thunder sounded and it started to sprinkle. We gathered our drinks and Prissy, then headed inside. The phone rang, and Jaz checked the caller ID. "Speak of the devil..."

"Great. My day just keeps getting better and better," I said, taking the phone from her.

"On that note, I'm headed to bed. Big day tomorrow with the reopening of my shop. You better be there."

"I wouldn't miss it."

"Don't stay up too late." She saluted me, then took her wine and headed into her bedroom.

"Hello, Detective," I said through the phone. "This really isn't a good time."

"Why? Got a hot date?" he ground out. "It sure didn't take you long."

I frowned. "What are you talking about?"

"After all Jaz has been through, I can't believe you're getting involved in online dating."

"*Boomer*." I scowled.

"Worse! I had to hear about it from my mother. But hey, I have no say, right? You made it perfectly clear earlier there is no us. I wish you both the best of luck," he grumbled and then hung up.

I scoffed. He had some nerve. The next time I talked to him I was going to give him a piece of my mind.

The phone rang again, and I snatched it from its cradle without even looking. "You stubborn, hotheaded mule! You have *got* to stop jumping to conclusions and making false assumptions."

"I take it I can assume you have *not* finished your book of designs then, even though tomorrow is your deadline," Natasha Newlander said over the line with obvious displeasure.

I gasped. *Fantastic*. My life wasn't the only thing that was a mess. My career was in jeopardy of ending before it even had a chance to get started. "I am *so* sorry, Ms. Newlander. I thought you were someone else."

"I should hope so, Ms. Ballas, otherwise I would have no choice but to draw the conclusion that you are highly unprofessional."

"I can assure you, Ms. Newlander, I am as professional as they come."

"Wonderful. Then I can count on your book being finished tomorrow, right on schedule. No excuses." She hung up.

Don't stay up too late, Jaz had said? Ha! That was a joke. Looks like I wouldn't be getting sleep any time soon since the day from hell had just turned into a night in purgatory.

CHAPTER 23

"You stealing, conniving witch!" Anastasia Stewart screeched the next morning at Jaz's grand reopening of Full Disclosure. It was a bright sunny morning, and unusually warm outside, and Jaz's boutique had never looked better. Not to mention it was packed with patrons from Clearwater and several towns beyond.

"What?" Jaz feigned innocence, yet oozed confidence. "You don't like my fabulous finds?"

"Those are not meant for spring." Ana stabbed her finger in the direction of Jaz's front window display. "Now what am I supposed to do?"

"Not my problem." Jaz leaned forward and emphasized each word with a hard edge. "You should have thought of that before you messed with me."

"Those are *my* finds for summer, and you know it. Not to mention, it's not even summer yet. What kind of businesswoman are you?"

"I don't know any such thing, and take a look around, honey. I'd say I'm a great businesswoman judging by this lovely crowd. Besides, didn't you get the memo? Spring is so yesterday." Jaz turned to the growing number of people. "Step right up, everyone, and get your steamy summer steals. The heat is on, folks."

"You're right. The heat *is* on," Ana spat out, looking on the verge of hysteria. "And you're going to burn in hell for what you did."

"After you, darling." Jaz bowed gracefully, looking calm, cool, and collected. "Fortunately for me, I don't burn. In fact, I like it hot." She let her gaze run over Ana's fair skin. "Something tells me you're the one who's going to get burned."

Ana stomped her foot and let out a garbled yell, which drew several disapproving stares. She took a deep breath and composed herself, smoothing back her hair, and then turned and headed toward the door. Suddenly, she jerked to a stop before a gloating Johnny Hogan.

"You did this," she said to him on the verge of tears.

"You know what they say about payback," he replied with relish.

"It's over between us forever now."

"Babe, you weren't that good anyway," he said, then saluted Mrs. Flannigan and walked out the door with a jovial bounce to his step.

Ana gasped, losing her composure once more as she shrieked, "You mean you were in on this too?" She gaped at Lois in shock.

"What can I say? I'm on a fixed income, and Ms. Alvarez had a better offer." Lois shrugged and then went on to looking through the sale racks, turning her back on Ana.

I watched Ana leave Full Disclosure, looking disheveled, dazed, and confused. Then I turned to Jaz, who looked fabulous, sharp, and satisfied.

"What just happened here?" I asked.

"A little known thing called revenge."

"But how?"

"Remember when you saw Johnny sneak into the back room of Ana's shop and then emerge, shoving something in his back pocket?"

"Yeah."

"Well, early on I figured out that Mrs. Flannigan was the mole."

"Wait, what?" Now it was my turn to gape at her. "Mousy little old Mrs. Flannigan?"

"Michael Flannigan's pub does okay, but not well enough to support his wife's shopping addiction. Lois has been a regular since I opened my place. She knew the ins and the outs and was even privy to a lot of information I would never trust anyone else with. I knew she wouldn't jump ship without just cause. Meaning someone had paid her enough to make it worth her while."

"Talk about no loyalty. I can't believe she would do that to you."

Jaz shrugged. "I can. Fashion tends to make people a little crazy, if you haven't noticed by now. Anyway, I confronted her, and she crumbled. She's really not a bad person, she just can't resist a good sale. I knew Ana would figure it out if Lois tried to turn the tables on her, but I also knew Johnny was just as angry with me as he was with Ana. Whereas Lois can be very charming when she wants to."

"What did you do?"

"I got Fickle Flannigan to get Johnny to sneak into Ana's back room and discover her fabulous finds for the summer. Then he leaked them to her, which she in turn gave to me."

"I can't believe he agreed to that."

"Everyone has a price, chica. His was revenge and enough money to get the hell out of town."

"He's moving?"

"He's loading his moving van later today."

"Can't say I'm sorry to see him go," I said. "Maybe you and Maria can finally move on then."

"That's wishful thinking, doll."

"Stranger things have happened."

"Ain't that the truth?" Jaz snorted.

"There you are," a familiar female voice said from behind me.

I swallowed hard and turned around with dread. "Natasha, how wonderful to see you again," I lied.

"Likewise." She shook my hand. *If I have to stay in this godforsaken town one more day, I will lose my mind. I have a lot riding on this book. It had better be good.* She let go of my hand, thank goodness, because she was freaking me out. "Now that it's been two weeks, time's up. I am excited to see your book of designs."

My stomach turned over. What if she didn't like it? What if none of them did and they changed their minds? I'd stayed up all night working on my book until finally, blessedly, I'd finished. But now I was second-guessing myself. What if it wasn't any good? Lord knew I'd had enough distractions lately with trying to solve a murder and dealing with Detective Dreamy. I hadn't exactly been focused on work to say the least.

"Ms. Ballas, did you hear me? I asked where the book is." She looked at her watch.

Based on her thoughts, I was sure she'd already booked her ticket on the next train out of here.

"I'm sorry. My mind has been a bit scattered lately." I regretted the words immediately.

She frowned. "I hope that isn't reflected in your work. You only get one shot at this, Kalli. You can't afford to blow it."

Gee, no pressure! I smiled, hiding my fears and putting on my game face. "No worries, Natasha. I'm confident you'll like what I've come up with."

"It's Ms. Newlander," she said matter-of-factly, implying she was allowed to be informal but I hadn't earned that right yet. "When can I see it?"

"How about an hour from now? I can't just leave Jaz hanging. I'll meet you at my house."

"Your house. One hour. No later." She gave me a pointed stare. "Some of us have other things to do than wait around. Understood?"

"Perfectly." I waited until Natasha disappeared out of sight, and then decided I had to leave Full Disclosure and head for home, even if it disappointed Jaz. I needed that precious hour to put the finishing touches on my book. Yes, it was finished, but Lord only knew what I'd drawn in my delirium last night.

Thirty minutes later, I'd managed to sneak away from Jaz and head back to my house early. I went to my bedroom and pulled out the book from my hiding spot in a secret compartment beneath the floorboards of the old house. I'd grown up in a family of nosy Greeks, and the only way to truly keep things private was to find a hiding place. Some habits died hard. Even though I lived with Jaz, and I was pretty sure my designs were safe, I still continued to hide them. I was superstitious that way. Didn't want anyone to see the finished product before it was truly finished, for fear of jinxing it.

Sitting down, I was a little afraid to look at what I'd done. Opening the cover, I began to turn the pages with surprise and satisfaction. They were good. I could feel it in my gut. Just a few more tweaks, and it would be ready. I pulled out my pencil when I heard the unmistakable sounds of footsteps out in the living room.

Not again, I thought.

My heart started pounding when I realized I'd forgotten to lock the front door. I peeked my head out of my bedroom to see the huge and intimidating body belonging to Baldy stepping inside my house and looking around. I gasped. I couldn't help myself. It was just enough noise to alert the intruder. His intense gaze snapped to mine, and he started toward me, looking larger than life and oh so scary.

I slammed my bedroom door and leaned back against it, then realized I hadn't seen Prissy. I hoped she was okay. Maybe she had escaped outside.

"Ms. Ballas, is that you?" he asked from outside my bedroom, sounding breathless with excitement.

That couldn't be good, I thought. Clearing my throat, I tried to utter with bravery, "Maybe, maybe not. Who wants to know?"

"You're a hard woman to track down," he said with a voice way too deep to be safe.

"Who says I want to be found?"

"Trust me when I say I am very good at what I do. If you'll just open up, I'll—"

"Do nothing," said a rich smooth voice I'd know anywhere, followed by a whack and then a thud. "No means no, pal. Or didn't you get the memo? The lady already has a date."

"Detective Stevens?" I asked through the door, afraid to hope.

"It's Nik, the idiot who always speaks before he thinks. I'm sorry for earlier, and I'm here to answer your ad if you'll have me."

I whipped open the door and threw myself into his big, strong arms. He smelled amazing. I focused on that. It felt so good to go with my instincts instead of thinking things through first, and I barely even squirmed this time.

Progress, I smiled.

"Can I take that as a yes?" he asked, his mouth pressed against my neck and his arms holding me just as tight. *Please say yes. I don't think I can take another rejection.*

I kissed him in response, surprising him, but when he started to respond, I pulled away. "Hold that thought," I said, repeating his words breathlessly with a smile. "You have a murderer to arrest." I stepped back.

He blinked. "I do?"

I pointed to Baldy. "Contrary to popular belief, he's not my online date. Did you honestly think I would risk the germs of meeting a man through one of those websites?"

His mouth twisted into a lopsided grin. "I thought it seemed far-fetched, but the mamas were so positive."

I threw my hands up. "The mamas are crazy. We both know that."

"True. So who is this guy, then, anyway?"

"I'm not sure, but I'm thinking he was an enemy of either Scott or Bobby. He killed Scott and then tried to kill me because I was getting too close to the truth. He said he was good at what he did. You just beat him at his own game before he had a chance to do anything bad to me. I told you Maria was innocent. I think we've finally caught the real killer."

"I've gotta hand it to you. I think you might be right." Detective Stevens went to work dragging Baldy out into the living room and handcuffing the man's hands behind his back. He was a big guy. It was only a matter of time before he woke up with a whopper of a headache and royally pissed off after being knocked unconscious.

He began to stir when the doorbell rang, so the detective tended to him.

I opened it and smiled wide, no longer nervous. "Natasha, it really is good to see you this time."

She eyed me warily. "I'm glad, I guess." Her gaze landed on Baldy, and her eyes went wide. "What in the—"

"Don't worry about him. The detective's here, so we're safe. Let me just grab my book, and you can be on your way."

She looked shaken and took a step back, but she shook off her nerves at my words. "Okay, but hurry or I'll miss my train."

I jogged to my bedroom and returned quickly with my book of designs. I handed her the book, and she flipped through the pages. Her face transformed into one of pure pleasure. "Well done, Ms. Ballas. These designs are fabulous. My employer will be so pleased."

"I'm so glad you think Mr. Erickson will like them."

"Natasha?" a deep voice croaked hoarsely.

I blinked and looked to the side. Baldy knew Natasha? He was staring at her like he'd seen a ghost. "Wait," I said. "You know her?"

"I used to work with her at Interludes."

"Let me guess," Nik said to him in disgust. "You're a bitter ex-employee out to seek revenge?"

"More like the other way around," the big man said, making eye contact with me. "My name is Marcus Cantrell, and the reason I've been trying to find you is because I'm your new PR person. Natasha Newlander was fired two weeks ago."

CHAPTER 24

"Don't even think about it, Detective," Natasha growled out in the most menacing voice I'd ever heard as she grabbed me by the hair and yanked me back, pressing the sharp edge of my fabric scissors against my jugular.

I gasped. Damn, I should have been more careful in where I'd left them. I had worked in the living room last night, setting them on the end table when I'd finished, having been too tired to clean up. That was so unlike me. I lived my life by a certain set of rules, and tidiness and order were at the top of the list. But I'd been so frazzled lately, and look at what happened. Now I was paying the price.

"Natasha, what are you doing?" I was having a hard time processing the fact that she was fired two weeks ago yet had shown up anyway and had lied to me all along. Why? What could she possibly want? It wasn't my fault she got fired.

"Shut up!" she yelled at me. I stood very still when she pressed the scissors harder. *I've worked too hard not to get what I deserve. Erickson treats Marcus better because he's a man. That's not fair, dammit.* "I'm taking what belongs to me."

"Is this about my book?" This couldn't be happening to me. It dawned on me that I'd only given her my new cell, assuming she was going to pass it along to Mr. Erickson and the rest of the Interludes staff. No wonder Marcus hadn't been able to reach me. I tried to appeal to her feminist side. "You were right all along when you said it's so hard to make it in this business. I had no idea, and I can only imagine how you must feel after how hard you have obviously worked. If you let me go, we won't say a word. You haven't done anything yet. There's still time for you to do the right thing by letting us go, and then you can be on your way."

I could feel her hesitation. *Maybe I could make a run for it. They don't know everything yet. As long as they can't link me to that guy's death, then I should be—*

"You killed Scott?" I blurted, then mentally smacked myself when her arm stiffened again.

"How'd you know that?" she shrieked, sounding on the verge of a mental breakdown.

"A hunch," I said.

"You can't prove anything."

"You were looking for the book, weren't you?" Marcus said in an accusing tone. "Erickson was right to fire you after he found out you were leaking information to our biggest competitor. I just can't believe you were desperate enough to kill for it."

"Oh, my gosh," I said, feeling sick as the truth dawned on me. "This whole time the murder had nothing to do with Scott or Jaz. It had to do with me and my book of designs. First Full Disclosure, then Jaz's car, and then our house. All because of a silly little book."

"That wasn't just any book. It was going to help take Interludes to the next level. I couldn't let that happen after what they did to me. Their competitor was willing to pay me big bucks to beat Interludes to the punch. They appreciate what I can do for them. That guy just caught me by surprise and got in my way. I couldn't let him live after he'd seen my face. The fashion business is war, and there are always casualties when it comes to war, Ms. Ballas. I suggest you get used to it," she snarled. "I should have finished choking the life out of you when I had the chance. Now give me the damn gun, Detective."

"Easy," the detective said, carefully setting his gun on the floor in front of him. "No one else has to get hurt."

"Kick it to me," she hissed. After he complied, she said, "Now handcuff yourself to Marcus."

"Listen—"

"No, *you* listen. Do it now, or I'll slice her throat."

"Okay, okay," he said, doing as she asked with slow careful movements. "Just calm down."

"It won't matter," Marcus said. "She's going to kill us all anyway because we're the only ones who know she's the murderer."

"Very good, Marcus," Natasha said. "You're not as dumb as you look."

"And I'm not as helpless as you think," I said as I jabbed my elbow into her stomach, catching her off guard.

She stumbled back a step but didn't drop the scissors. I bolted to the nearest exit, which happened to be the door to our deck. Running down the stairs, I headed toward the front gate when I heard her behind me.

"Freeze, unless you want to get shot."

I jolted to a stop, holding my hands up and slowly turning around to face her. Just as I feared, she had picked up Detective Stevens' gun along the way. She continued walking down the steps, looking around to make sure we were alone, then she positioned herself between me and the gate with her back to the fence.

I had her exactly where I wanted her, and she didn't even know it.

"Did you really think you could get away from me so easily?" she asked, looking a little crazed. I hoped I never let the fashion world turn me into a monster like her.

Trying to reason with her hadn't worked, so I did the next best thing and stalled, hoping my hunch was right. Nik couldn't help because he was handcuffed to Marcus, so I had to get creative and find help from other sources. "Did *you* really think you could get away with murder?"

"I already did." She raised the gun.

I swallowed hard and prayed my instincts were right. I spoke a little louder. "One time was a fluke. You can't possibly kill three more people and think you'll just walk away."

"Don't yell at me. You're the one who chose to live at the end of a dead-end road. There's no one out here except the detective, and he's tied up at the moment while Jaz and his partner are still at her store. In fact, pretty much the entire town is at her store." She stared me down. "I know. I checked." Then she laughed harshly. "That means it will be a while before anyone finds you three, and I'll be long gone with your book by then. I'll make it look like Marcus was the killer all along. He showed up to attack you and the detective came to your rescue, only to wind up dead as well. How tragic. Case closed. End of story."

"None of us are ever truly alone," I said as much for my benefit as hers. I had to count to ten and breathe deep to maintain my composure, feeling a major panic attack coming on.

"How philosophical of you. Pity. We might have actually worked well together. Unfortunately, you're up first, darling. Any last words?"

"Yeah, I'm *sick* of people trying to control my life," I said loudly, then waited a beat.

"Okay." She frowned. "Is that all?"

"No," I said, feeling real fear set in, realizing things might not go according to plan. "I'm tired of people *attacking* me!" I yelled, then waited again.

"Sorry to say, but that's life." She aimed the gun at my head.

Oh my God, I really might die! "You're an *animal*. A *beast*. A *wolf* in sheep's clothing, dammit!"

"Honey, I think you're crazier than even I am," she said, and started to squeeze the trigger.

"There's a method to my madness, *honey*, and I think you're going down. Your reckoning is *coming*!" I slapped my hands on my thighs, and a loud howl and crashing noise sounded behind Natasha.

Her eyes sprang wide, and she whirled around all in one motion. The fence that Nik had resurrected came crashing down upon her, knocking her to the ground and the gun out of her hand. With my heart pounding, I scrambled to retrieve the gun, then pointed it at her, but she was out cold.

"Good boy," I said, as Wolfgang stood on top of the fence, keeping his hostage secure. Nik came home for lunch most days and let Wolfgang out. When he'd surprised Marcus, I'd assumed he'd stuck to his same routine, so it was a safe bet that Wolfgang had still been outside. And I knew from past experience that no fence, no matter how big, could keep him out when he set his sights on me.

He started his habitual wiggle all over from head to tail when his eyes settled on me. His muscles bunched like he was about to pounce. Panic started to seize me, but then I realized I was stronger than I thought. I was through with letting everyone and everything control my life. It was time I took charge for a change and push my fear aside.

"Don't you dare!" I pointed my finger at him. "Stay right there until I tell you that you can get up, mister."

He let out a big whine and then plopped his humongous fanny down on the fence, wearing the biggest doggie pout I had ever seen. The expression on his face was pathetic, and yet I felt my heart crack and begin to melt. But then I saw a stream of saliva ooze from the corner of his mouth, drip off his jaw, and land on Natasha's forehead.

I gagged and called 911, then snapped my phone closed.

"Listen, Wolfy, you and me... we need to have a talk." His tail whipped wildly and he still shook a bit, but he sat right there obediently, listening better than any human I'd ever met.

After all the scary things that had happened lately, the emergency crews arrived in record time. Detective Matheson was first on the scene. I gave him a quick version of my report just as Natasha was coming to.

She gasped. "Elephant...on my chest...get it off," she rasped.

Boomer went to grab Wolfgang's collar.

"That's okay," I said confidently. "I've got this," I continued, shocking him judging by the arch of his sky-high eyebrows.

"You sure?" Boomer asked, looking skeptical.

"Positive. The beast and I have come to an understanding, so to speak. I will show him a *little* affection, and he will absolutely positively refrain from licking me."

"And he agreed?" Boomer's brows lifted even higher. "How can you tell?"

"Instinct." I shrugged. "Sometimes you've just gotta have faith."

"Kill me already," Natasha wheezed.

"That would be too easy," I snarled at her. "No one takes something that belongs to me," I snapped. "Wolf, come," I said, and he immediately obeyed. I held up my hand. "Okay, okay, that's far enough." I petted the top of his head, and his eyes rolled back beneath his fur. He plopped down onto the ground and rolled over, squirming back and forth with his bare belly beckoning me. I nearly gagged again as I eyed his stomach. "You're pushing your luck, buddy," I managed to say. "That one's gonna take some time. Come on, let's go see Daddy."

Wolf rolled back over at the word Daddy and bolted up the steps of my deck, charging through the open sliding door and out of site.

"As I live and breathe..." Boomer's jaw practically hit the ground it hung so low.

"Killer...unhandcuffed...danger..." I pointed to Natasha attempting to slide out from beneath the fence.

"Right. I'm on it." He snapped to attention and did his job.

Meanwhile, I followed Wolfgang up the steps and inside my house to see him sprawled out on top of Detective Stevens, slobbering all over his face as Nik pleaded with him to get down, to no avail.

"Wolf!" I snapped. "*What* did we just talk about?"

He immediately backed off and sat down at my feet, whining pathetically, his fanny wiggling nonstop. I stroked him between the eyes and behind the ears this time, and he looked as though he were having a seizure. He rolled onto his back one more time and gave me a hopeful look.

"I told you we'll renegotiate that at a later time, depending on how well you behave, but it's not going to happen today. So you may as well go lay down."

He blew out a snort that was in a word—disgusting—and got to his feet, then walked over and eyed my couch. I would have to mop with bleach at least three times. Prissy reappeared, let out a loud hiss, and vaulted to the highest part of the couch she could reach. He turned his sights on her with *almost* as much affection as he had for me.

"Don't even think about it," I said, stabbing my finger at him, "because that, my friend, is a total deal breaker."

He plopped down onto the carpet and let out a huge sigh that said *oh, woe is me*, his tail thumping the floor steadily, but he wasn't fooling any of us.

"Okay, who are you and what have you done to my dog?" Nik asked, his face etched with a mixture of shock and total amazement.

"Let's just say we've come to an understanding." I unlocked his handcuffs.

"Good," he said as he got to his feet and rubbed his wrists. "Because there's something I've been meaning to talk to you about."

The rest of Saturday had been a whirlwind of interrogations and paperwork, so Nik and I had to put our talk on hold. Sunday he picked me up for church, and we went together for the very first time, much to the delight of the mamas. Then we went to my parents' house for our family brunch as usual. There was no getting out of that one, and we both knew it. Only nothing was same ole same ole anymore.

For one, his dog and my cat lounged under the same tree together. Granted Wolf was at the base and Prissy was high above in the branches, but still... progress was progress in my book. Then there was Jaz and Boomer. After he'd arrested Natasha, he'd shown up at the house and threw Jaz over his shoulder, not taking no for an answer. She hadn't come home all night long. Now they were together, looking like a happy set of love birds.

Marcus Cantrell, my new PR guy, sat at a table with all the mamas, getting grilled on his plans to take me to New York the next week now that my book was done. Anyone else would have needed rescuing, but the gentle giant held his own. If I wasn't mistaken, I'd swear he captivated a few of the women with his magnetism and charm.

Oh, he was good! I had high hopes my new spring line would be a huge success.

Nik wandered off to get us a drink. While the mamas were occupied, I continued to take in the scene unfolding before me. Eleni was there with her boyfriend, and even his sister Marigold who had put the voodoo curse on Jaz and had had a crush on Sully was there, but she wasn't alone. To my utter shock, she was there with Max. He shot me a wave and a wink. I was happy for him, but I had to admit, I was a little jealous and just hoped our friendship stayed the same. Ana was no doubt off somewhere still licking her wounds, and he was better off without her. Jaz had told me she'd convinced Marigold to lift the voodoo curse, and I suspected she used her connections and hooked them up.

Just then Sully walked in with Maria of all people, but I wasn't surprised. I'd heard he went to see her after she was arrested. They'd always been friends, but she'd been with Jonny and he'd been hooked on Jaz. With other options taken away, they must have realized what had been before them all along. Each other. Maria had been cleared of all charges and released early this morning.

Needless to say, the mamas were thrilled with all the matches they had made this spring, and I wouldn't be surprised if a slew of summer pregnancies popped up. Spring fever had a way of doing that to people. The only match they were still unsure about was between me and Nik. They stopped talking to Marcus and focused on us, then put their heads together.

That couldn't be good, I thought.

Nik came back and saved me by handing me my drink.

"Thanks," I said. "What is it?"

Instead of saying the name out loud, he leaned over and whispered a name in my ear that made me blush. God, he smelled amazing and looked amazing and, let's face it, he *was* amazing!

"What are you doing?" I asked, trying not to sound breathless.

"Just following orders, kind of like Wolfgang." He shrugged, wearing a lopsided grin. "He's not the only one who adores you, you know."

"What do you mean following orders?" I asked, trying not to sound desperate this time.

"Oh, just doing what you told me to do in the future." His blue eyes darkened. "Remember what that was?"

I swallowed hard. "Yes," I said weakly, feeling my knees start to get wobbly. "How could I forget?"

"Good." He stared hard at me, his eyes so intense I felt them clear to my soul. "Guess what time it is?"

"The future?" I squeaked.

"You're one smart cookie, Ballas." He winked. "The case is solved, and I'm in desperate need of a distraction."

"Funny, that's exactly what I was thinking." I bit my bottom lip.

"What can I say? I have a gift," he said, and for a moment, I wondered if he'd figured out my secret. But then I realized that was unlikely.

"Me too," I responded daringly. Part of me wanted to tell him everything. "Imagine that. What a coincidence."

"I don't believe in coincidences. I believe in destiny." He tweaked my nose. "Something tells me we might just be a perfect match."

"Careful, Detective. That sounds an awful lot like grounds for a relationship. With strings, no less."

"Well, we wouldn't want to disappoint the mamas." His gaze dropped to my lips. "Heaven forbid we give them something to talk about." He raised his eyes to mine. "You reading my mind?"

"I think I have a pretty good idea of what's on your mind." I giggled. If he only knew.

"If we were someplace private, I'd make it perfectly clear *exactly* what's on my mind."

"Is that a dare, Detective?"

"That's a promise, Ballas."

My smile came slow and sweet and I said with barely more than a whisper, "Prove it."

He didn't hesitate and kissed the sense right out of me as if he'd waited a lifetime to do so, then scooped me into his arms and carried me away while his thoughts started a dance of seduction throughout my every cell, and suddenly...

The future had never looked so bright.

Acknowledgements

To Terry Goodman for saying yes to this book as well. And to my fabulous editor, Alison Dasho, for having an amazing eye and fantastic ideas. Love your input. I have to say, working with you is already a blast. I can't wait to work with you on many more projects.

To my agent, Christine Witthohn, of Book Cents Literary Agency. We did it again. Thanks so much for everything you do.

To my husband, Brian, and my children, Brandon, Josh, Matt, and Emily, for putting up with a messy house and eating crappy dinners ☺. Your support means everything to me. And, as always, to my extended family: the Townsends, the Harmons, and the Russos, who are my biggest fans.

Acknowledgments

About the Author

Kari Lee Townsend lives in central New York with her very understanding husband, her three busy boys, and her oh-so-dramatic daughter. A former teacher with a master's in English education, she is a longtime lover of reading and writing. She is best known as the author of the Fortune Teller Mystery series, but also writes romantic comedies (under the name Kari Lee Harmon), as well as children's fiction about tween superheroes. These days, you'll find her at home with her children, happily writing her next novel.

Kindle Serials

This book was originally released in Episodes as a Kindle Serial. Kindle Serials launched in 2012 as a new way to experience serialized books. Kindle Serials allow readers to enjoy the story as the author creates it, purchasing once and receiving all existing Episodes immediately, followed by future Episodes as they are published. To find out more about Kindle Serials and to see the current selection of Serials titles, visit www.amazon.com/kindleserials.